PRAISE FOR CUT REALITY

"Intelligently conceived and well-executed...A mystery that thoughtfully reflects on the hazy line between suspicion and reckless mania."
  -Kirkus Reviews

"Zack Hacker may just have written the perfect genre book at the perfect time"
  -San Francisco Book Review

"When I heard the premise of Cut Reality *I almost died...And I wouldn't lie about that."*
  -Jonny Fairplay of Survivor: Pearl Islands, Survivor: Micronesia, *and* Survivor NSFW

"[A] poignant critique...From the first tension-filled scene of Jason's return to the final revelations, Cut Reality *will keep readers guessing, but also leave them with plenty to think about."*
  -SPR

"Cut Reality is the type of thoughtful, provocative work that you don't see much of among the reality TV fanbase anymore. I had a lot of fun reading it."
  -Mario Lanza, author of When It Was Worth Playing For, The Funny 115, *and host of* The Survivor Historians

"Grippingly realistic in its portrayal of reality TV show approaches to life, Cut Reality *will keep readers thinking long after its final, startling conclusion, and is highly recommended for those who like their intrigue steeped in psychological insights and dilemmas."*
  -Midwest Book Review

ABOUT THE AUTHOR

Zack Hacker was born in Cincinnati, Ohio, where he currently teaches English and Creative Writing. He is a graduate of Mount Saint Joseph University and received his M.A. in English from Case Western Reserve University. He lives in Northern Kentucky with his wife and three cats, where he watches too much reality TV and plans travel experiences. *Cut Reality* is his debut novel.

He can be reached at zackhacker.com or on social media:

facebook.com/zackhackerwrites

instagram.com/zackhackerwrites

amazon.com/author/zackhacker

goodreads.com/zackhacker

bookbub.com/authors/zack-hacker

CUT

REALITY

ZACK HACKER

First Printing, April 2019

Anywhere Press
Edgewood, Kentucky
www.anywherepress.com

Trade paperback ISBN: 978-1-7335049-0-4
E-book ISBN: 978-1-7335049-1-1
Hardcover ISBN: 978-1-7335049-2-8

Printed in the Uniter States of America.
10 9 8 7 6 5 4 3 2 1 0

CUT REALITY

For Maria, my partner in all things.

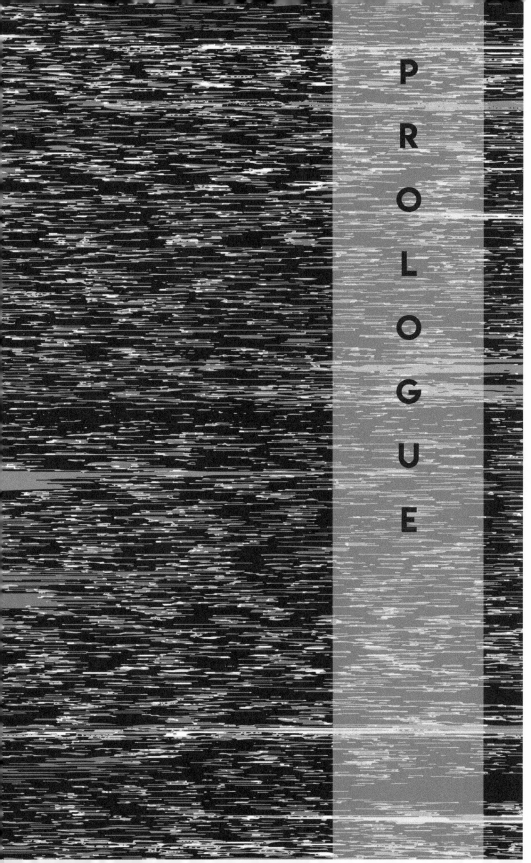

PROLOGUE

JASON CLOSED his eyes to get a break from surveilling the woman in 31E. He should have felt more comfortable than he had in months. No videocameras, no microphones. The show was over. Instead, he was aboard a twenty-five-year-old aircraft, traveling 500 miles per hour at nearly 30,000 feet, feeling irritated he couldn't turn his mind off.

He had never asked the producers how bodies were returned to their country of origin. He imagined Billy propped up next to his luggage in the cargo hold.

31E dug her index finger against the side of her cup, forcing the cheap plastic to buckle with a small crack. She was no threat to Jason and, thanks to the jet engines, he could barely hear her nervous crinkling.

Or, was Billy buried on the island? No, if there was a cobbled together ceremony the producers would have mentioned it to the cast.

After a few dragging moments, Jason sighed and opened his eyes again. Sleep would not come.

Nervousness was contagious. 31E was shaking the ice in her cup before chewing it.

Piece by piece.

Jason glanced around to see if anyone else was stirring, but the flight had been long and smooth.

He pulled his journal out of the netted seat-pocket in front of him. The book fell open from creased memory to the last lines Jason had written, and he turned to the entry's beginning:

> *I should have seen this coming instead of worrying about what food I missed the most. This experience really skews priorities. I guess that's what happened to Billy. The signs were there, but I can't wrap my head around it. He was my closest friend out here. I needed to be there for him, and so did the producers. I think I'm to blame. I can't believe he did it. And what can we do now?*

His jaw clenched. Jason had to stop. Reading the words made him want to flee, but he was belted in—the unavoidable words that he had written and could no longer face.

By the time he reached the end of the last entry from his time on the island—a mere page, front and back—tears had accumulated in the corners of his eyes, but he didn't wipe them away. He sat there, glazing over. Numb but alert.

The soft tone of the seatbelt lights illuminating cut Jason's trance short.

He tore the page out of the journal, careful to rip as close to the binding as possible so the page left no trace. His hands, however, were still too unsteady to pull this off.

He swore under his breath and folded the page, first vertically, then horizontally. Stray sand then littered the floor as he removed his sneaker. The sole was burnt from sitting too close to the fire and the shoe-string had been tied together after it snapped.

Jason considered the pairs of Vans he had worn to shreds in the past. A white pair he abandoned in London after he and Blake stayed out all night, walking in the rain. A brown pair that he had worn to run a 10k with his more fit friends while finding out in tedious detail that they were inappropriate footwear; and another brown pair he had to throw out after wearing them canoeing in Puerto Rico on a trip with friends to celebrate Blake's completion of her MD.

Here he was again, with another wrecked pair of canvas shoes. These were black, and probably in the worst state of any pair he had owned. But, these would be saved, not thrown away. These were his island shoes, subjected to weeks of sand, sea, sun, and sweat. As unique as those other memories were, these shoes were more significant. Maybe they'd go on a shelf, preserved in a box in the attic, or maybe he'd eventually sell them on eBay.

The shoe felt tacky and damp in his hand. Jason pulled back the insole, feeling more sand and grime come with it. He laid the folded paper underneath the remnants of cushion. To his relief, his writing vanished into the shoe. The paper was unnoticeable, and he was confident it would stay hidden until he could discard it later.

He slid the shoe back on with little effort. Jason returned his focus to the journal. As he opened the book, this time to the beginning, the stranger sleeping in the adjacent seat snored. Jason again glanced around. Even the ice-cup lady seemed to be asleep. To be the only person awake on a plane didn't feel eerie.

He analyzed every entry, page, and word, trying to figure out what Blake would think of it—what anyone would think of it. Through his writings he relived the most traumatizing parts of the last month of his life. Fending for himself on the island, competing against thirteen strangers, being filmed non-stop.

Now he was returning, but he needed to decide how to tell the story. The show, the network—they would have their story, but he needed to have his. If he was to share the entries he had made in his journal while on the island, then they needed reviewing. Guaranteed to be safe. Unlike the last page, now in his shoe, which no one would ever read. That story was his.

PART ONE

JASON'S ISLAND JOURNAL

DAY 23—SUNSET

PAPER. A pen. Finally, a break in the monotony. Jesus.

Well, here I am. Day 23 and I got my journal! Twenty-three days of white rice and overcooked slivers of triggerfish. Twenty-three days of an aching back. Twenty-three days of paranoia. And I've wanted to play this game since I was nine years old. It's incredible I finally got the chance twenty-five years later, which I should probably keep in mind. It's astounding the show is still on the air —I can't see how it continues to make money, but I don't regret being here, or so I tell myself. A once-in-a-lifetime experience, except for the few hundred people who have played multiple times. Hopefully, I'm entertaining enough RTN brings me back—that's mental, right, that while I suffer here I still want to come back and play again? Stranded on an island for over a month with complete strangers, sacrificing all privacy, giving up everything I care about.

Everyone here is amused that I hate the outdoors so much. Bugs. Sand. Water. Sun. Gross. Especially considering what a "super-fan" they've labeled me. I learned enough to get by in Shipwrecked School the show put us all through before the season. I learned my basic skills, what not to eat. I can't spear fish or climb trees like some of these people, but how many can? That's why Billy's here, to do that stuff.

Note to self: be careful what I write in this—no telling who will sneak in my bag and read it. Only write positive stuff about people.

Twenty-three days of experiences, and not a single thing to write. And I teach English.

I'm in a good place within the group now and I've made a few solid friends. I worried it would take me too long to fit in comfortably. We haven't voted anyone out yet, though, so it's hard to tell. The group on the other island must be miserable—they've had to vote out three of their members, leaving them with only four people. We're still at seven strong. Let's hope this continues. Things are easy now. But you can't tell what's going on just beneath the surface since we've all been so safe.

DAY 24—DINNER

WELL, a little more to report now: I get to vote someone out tonight, finally. A day of nerves, scrambling into the foliage, and painful knots in my stomach —good stuff!

We didn't lose but have to get rid of someone because our team merged with the other team. Still, we haven't lost a competition (thanks to my Herculean strength and skills in the outdoors, I'm sure). I'm basically halfway to the end. It should be a standard vote. We have more people, seven to four, so one of the enemy team should go home. They seem nice, but I have a good thing going with my people, especially Billy and Phoebe. We all agreed to go after Ronnie, from the other group, because he's such an impressive player. I can't compete with a cop who camps every weekend for fun. Keep the weak around, and we'll all go further.

Anyway, I want to keep a record of how surprised I am at my friendship with Billy. We don't have much in common, but he's so easy to get along with. As of now, he's my ally to the end. Plus, since I'm the more strategic-minded, I'll probably get an easy win. Note to self: visit Billy in Massachusetts and take him on a massive trip if I win. He's had a rough life. No real family to speak of besides his sister. He's a construction worker and aspiring photographer. (On that note, I should introduce him to Seth—he might have industry connections for Billy.) I love that there can be someone who had such a different life than me, yet we get along so well. I assumed we would once I saw his fake name on his hotel door.

Before the game started, we all got sequestered in this hotel, but weren't allowed to talk to each other or even know real names. The weirdest part is, there were other random tourists staying in the hotel. I can't imagine what they thought was going on. Anyway, we got to choose our fake names that appeared on our doors and call sheets. Billy chose Elliot. In my infinite boredom I came to the conclusion that he chose it as a mixture of T.S. Eliot and Elliott Smith. Single "t" for T.S., double "l" for Smith. He told me he just liked the name and wasn't sure how to spell it. We had a good laugh anyway.

That's why I love this game—the social experience. Even if they don't emphasize that on the television show anymore, it's still alive and kicking. I'll be the first to say so. I should try to do an episode of *Beached Bums* talking about that when I get back. Hopefully, I'm popular enough that people will want to hear from me on a podcast. I could be a regular guest.

Also, I tried to fish today and sliced my hand with a hook.

Back to fearing the outdoors.

DAY 26—AFTER LUNCH

I JUST GAVE a good interview on camera. I can't wait for people back home to see those. I'm hoping I can provide comic relief—I feel like all I do is sit and think of funny things to say and do on camera. Is anything anyone does or says real on this island? Am I acting or merely living? Where's the line between those? This entry is forced. I'm just trying to keep journaling, though I never was big on it—again, ironic considering I teach courses in writing.

Also, I forgot to take note, Ronnie's gone. It may be time to turn on Dimitri even though he's on our side.

DAY 29—BEFORE BREAKFAST

SOMEONE'S definitely been through my bag and read this journal. No way of telling if it was another contestant or production. Either way, fuck them. Ten of us left now. I may hate them all. I can't tell. Maybe I love them all? What do I know?

They're all I know.

We had fruit today. I'm exhausted, and I just woke up. I also realized that I'm using meals (well, as much meal as we can scrounge up) to keep track of time now in lieu of a clock. Fitting. I would kill for a cheeseburger. Or spaghetti. A cheese platter. I need to stop.

DAY 30—BEFORE SLEEPING

SO TONIGHT WE ELIMINATED DIMITRI. I guess the struggle of the alpha males is over. He was our team's first player to walk off the island.

It was a tricky elimination. I'm still figuring it out. My first time getting votes. I worried I was going home. It was a chaotic vote.

Bad news for me, because if Maddy or Nick and Kendall flip and they continue targeting me, I'm out of here. We should have kept Dimitri around longer, but I had to back Billy. He's the only one I trust implicitly. I never thought I'd trust someone out here, or make a real friend. I mean, we're all supposed to be enemies. Billy's too good a person, and he's a real friend outside of here. Or, I'm stupid and getting played, but I couldn't betray him at this point.

That makes nine people left and five eliminated. Here we are— immortalized forever in the halls of history—the jury and final contestants in the fiftieth season of America's (third?) favorite reality game show. At least three million people are still watching, and to them we are heroes. Selfishly, I hope this is the last season so we're burned into the game's history. The final impressions of a limping, dying, prime-time television gargantuan. A survivor of the network days, another time, when people tuned in to live television. Families watched together after dinner. America had a shared culture. Now, instead, the show appeals to a small niche of viewers. Viewers who total less than a fiftieth of the show's original audience. We talk about the show's history on the island almost every day. These other people are surprisingly interested.

None of us can believe the show is still airing. Are we shouting into a void, or can we be so entertaining we cause a resurgence? Production seems indifferent. They're going through a daily grind. Filming, eating, sleeping, building. Ever since the show bought its own private island, off the coast of Panama, it's so cheap to make that it seems likely to endure forever. But who knows?

This is all to say, life is feeling pointless. My daily activities are pointless. And I care about this show more than anything in life.

That's an overstatement. Friends, especially Blake and the cats, are more important. I hope they're okay.

Wow. I wrote that. It's been in the back of my head since I landed on the beach to make a TV show, without communication to the outside world. But I haven't allowed myself to vocalize, write, or consider nightmare scenarios. Now I'm crying. This has to stop. I'm making myself look weak. Billy's staring at me like I'm insane. He'll probably go through my shit and read this, to see what's wrong with me. If not him, someone else.

DAY 31—AFTER LUNCH

AM I IN A BETTER MOOD—MAYBE? I talked with Phoebe while we were getting water and had a good cry in front of a camera. She worries about everyone back home, too. I tried not to say anything intriguing or insightful so they don't air that footage. Crying might make me more endearing? Who cares—I want to be the deadpan comedic relief for the season. I don't want people to think I have emotion.

Anyway, she also worries continuously. But she's always crying and upset. That's her character. We all have a character we play out here. Thinking through the roles we're playing might help me break down the strategy. I don't know.

Nick is definitely the villain of the season. He's an ass to everyone. Today he ate about three times his share of food and proceeded to nap on the beach and complain that we didn't do enough work while he slept. I hope I never see him again. And he's so shady; always sneaking around and snooping. Unfailingly alone, too. And the way he slinks around it's as if he knows the island better than the producers, or like he's lived here his whole life. Reminds me of Gollum, hunching around through the forest, spying on us, concocting some evil plans. But, I need him here now, and production seems to love him like they're old friends. Don't want to piss off the show, or I might get eliminated.

DAY 32—AFTER LUNCH

SPEAKING OF BEING PISSED, production is pissing me off. I've been trying to get a talking-head confessional recorded for

like three hours. I need to outline my plans before we go to vote someone else off. I'm providing solid gold TV here, and they're fucking wasting it. They just want to chat with Nick in the forest. He has to be talking horribly about all of us, or they wouldn't focus on him so much.

I again thought I was going home, but I flipped the game, I guess. If I'm right, Desiree is out of here! No one has a read on how she's playing, so she's the most significant threat because she's flexible. She can change so easily. And she's so nice.

Now I'm being arrogant, so that will probably lead to me getting voted out. But it makes sense.

I'm just going to walk up to production. They'll be angry, but I need to shit talk everyone in front of the camera—the viewers demand it (or, maybe they will when this finally airs)! Who knows?

▭▭

WELL, it's a few hours later. They chewed me out for trying to go over there.

That must be base camp for the cameramen and producers. Weird it's right on the beach though. I assumed they'd hide in the jungle to keep us from stealing their food and supplies. Not a bad idea there, eh?

DAY 35—SUNRISE

I'M GETTING INCREASINGLY suspicious that my allies don't trust me. I know Billy does. We lay around camp and told stories about growing up. He was in foster care a lot as a kid, but loves his sister and her children. We bonded over not having many living family members, and it's rare to meet someone who shares that experience.

I'm still weirded out by production. I thought they'd have cameras jammed in my face 24/7 since I'm spearheading this next elimination vote, but they always seem so preoccupied with the beach front, and their interview questions seem canned—I'm not entirely sure they are even up on what's happening at camp. It's so damned dull here; Billy and I will check out what they're up to. Try to mess with them, make them fall over with their equipment on—anything to distract from the slow flow of time. Maybe they'll drop a Snickers or water bottle. We've all heard those stories. These are the myths and legends of the temporarily starving.

DAY 37—AFTER BREAKFAST

THINGS out here are so crazy. Remembering that this is a game is nearly impossible. It took about two full days to appease everyone who was shocked by the Maddy vote. I wanted Desiree out, but this had to happen. Turns out I was wrong.

No one thinks of life outside the game, off this island. We're all real people, and that's what makes lying and backstabbing so difficult—it reminds us that there are lives to go back to, that there are real emotions and real people at play. None of us are the invulnerable game pieces that we strategize as in the abstract. Maddy is sure to be actually, genuinely upset and mad at us. The cut Billy has on his foot is getting bad, which could easily get infected and affect his ability to work after the game. This game, this show, is simultaneously unimportant because it's just a game, and important because these are our actual lives we're playing with. Emotions, physical health, time.

Anyway, the producers and camera operators took an interest in us again. The interviews resumed, and we're back to being followed into the woods to take a piss. Riveting footage. They also cleared off from their spot down by the beach. I figured their camp was there, but Billy and I went exploring (hoping to find any discarded food or personal items) and there's no trace that there was ever anything built or set up there. Whatever they were doing, there wasn't a set structure, and they're no longer up to it.

I figure that maybe they just move around because they need a variety of camera angles and don't want a totally unfilmable stretch of beach (production can't be seen in the actual television show).

Billy's suspicious of them. I told him to stay out of it—if he pisses them off, they can make our lives even more miserable.

He continues to harass them, asking them questions about what they're up to, and why they randomly seem to disregard us for days at a time. I must say, he is right: they missed filming the strategizing and planning for the Maddy vote—no clue how they'll cut the episode with no footage. It's all Billy talks about now —"what are the camera guys up to?"; "why are all the producers blocking off this section of forest?"; "who are these new crew members who suddenly appeared?" They're definitely up to something, but my opinion on the matter is Tennyson's. Ours "not to reason why"; ours "but to do and die." Well, that might be dramatic. We're starving, sleep-deprived, suffering injuries, stressed, and living in fear of each other, but not dying. It only feels like it.

DAY 42—DAWN

WELL, I haven't written for a while. Things are tense around here. Billy couldn't let his questioning of the cameramen go, and now they can't let us go for a second without "accidentally" knocking into us with a camera, stumbling over our food and ruining it, forcing us into interviews as soon as we try to strategize. It's a full gauntlet of tortures that a camera operator can inflict upon his subject. And, since they'll probably read this, I would like to tell the entire production they can fuck right off, and I will not disclose a single detail of my strategy to them anymore because of this childish shit. I'm too closely associated with Billy, and he's in their business, so they're hating on him. And by extension me. I can't trust them at all now. I'll just keep my thoughts, plans, and all the comments that make for good television wrapped up in the confines of my mind, well off camera. They don't deserve the footage anyway.

I warned Billy. I'm worried about him. He's kind of losing it. People discussed voting him out tonight to make our daily life easier—that would get production off our ass. But, along with Phoebe, he's the only original member of our group I trust. I need him here. I hope whatever's wrong with him isn't psychological. I've heard the island can do that—with all the deprivation and deception. Plus the constant cameras in your face. I thought they'd fade into the background and we'd forget, but they don't. Not really. But, Billy has wild ideas I can't talk him out of—

things he "swears" he's seen. It's not even worth writing about, the crazy stuff he's "seeing." Just paranoia. Anyway, he sounds like he needs aluminum foil to line his fishing hat. I'm sure he's dehydrated.

Nonetheless, we've had a lot of fun out here and pulled off some impressive moves together. If I cut him loose it'll look like I have no loyalties.

Just for record-keeping, I'm making this entry. I guess I'm always writing these to share with Blake when I get home—she'll love to see them and know what's going through my head. I usually can't remember what I taught in lectures from a week ago, so this will be great to look back at, sitting on the couch, with a Guinness, eating an entire banana pepper and bacon pizza with a bowl of black-raspberry chip ice cream. Beer. Food. I digress.

Tonight we're voting out Bailey, leaving just Hunter of the other group. She's next to go. Her antics almost got everyone else in our group to turn on Billy and me. She knows we would never turn on each other. She's impossible to get along with—randomly screaming at people and going nuts if we move anything around our campsite. She might be losing it too—just like Billy.

1.

BLAKE THUMPED the sun-scorched notebook onto Jason's coffee table. It remained stiffly open.

"That's all you wrote?"

"I couldn't be sure who was reading it."

"What happened after Day 42? I thought you said you went to the end?"

She returned to thumbing through the book, waiting for Jason's response. Her index finger traced the torn fringe from where Jason had removed a page while on the plane.

Jason shifted in his chair and shrugged. It frustrated him that while he could manipulate and lie to every person on that island, he couldn't even make eye contact with Blake now. His life felt askew.

She broke the silence. "Well, your writings are a fun look behind the curtain, but you didn't write much. Why did you want me to read this so badly? Did I miss something?" It was generally forbidden to share details from the show—each cast member had signed a non-disclosure agreement that family and friends were also permitted to sign. That way they had someone to talk to, which was unavoidable. Blake's name was the only one signed on Jason's NDA.

Jason inhaled and readjusted his legs underneath the table. Blake, with a puzzled yet sympathetic look on her face, didn't break her stare. After days of sun exposure, his hair was long and much browner than its typical near-black. His beard was longer than usual. It made his face look round and distorted. On the drive to his house, Jason joked that he kept the long hair and beard after the show ended because he liked them, but Blake felt there was something more profound to it—an inability to cut off the last couple months of his life. The typically sturdy, two-hundred-pound frame of his body now looked skeletal. Every aspect of his appearance was depleted. Jason's presence itself seemed to be elsewhere.

"Nothing about those entries seems weird to you?" Jason asked her. Blake shrugged a half-smiling response.

What struck Blake most, however, were his eyes. Depleted wasn't appropriate for those. No, his eyes drooped and contained little life behind them. It was as though Jason was simultaneously approaching tears and falling asleep.

The man before her was a broken version of the person Blake had met roughly fifteen years prior.

Earlier, Blake had picked Jason up from the airport in Northern Kentucky and driven him home. In the car, she had a surprise care kit waiting—Cheese-Its, M&Ms, carrot cake cupcakes, Taco Bell, and a cooler of iced tea. At home, there was a case of pumpkin ale waiting. Tonight should have been a mixture of indulgence and celebration. Blake was eager to hear about the experience—to have Jason fill in every single behind-the-scenes detail he could, to find out how he did in the game, and to be regaled by his many adventures which she'd see unfold on television for the next few months. This experience would consume their day-to-day lives for the foreseeable future, and Blake was still as excited as Jason had been when he left to compete on Beached.

They were super-fans together—and always had been since Jason convinced her to watch season 17 with him in college. They had gone to Kenyon together, meeting during their freshman year. They both stayed in the campus dorms, and each had an awkward roommate that first year. So, once they hit it off, they were inseparable. By the following year, they gathered a solid group of four others and moved into a house together off campus.

As Jason sat at the table, Blake hugged him. She hadn't considered how much she missed physical contact while he'd been away. There was no one else she embraced like that.

"I'm sure you're tired. What can I do to help you feel back to normal?" she asked. Surely, she thought, this fatigue must be typical—difficult to get back to normal life after living on an island, in front of cameras for sixty days, with only thirteen other strangers as confidants. From her first glance at the terminal, Blake harbored the hope he may have won the game, judging by his appearance. He was so gaunt and broken-looking she hoped he had made it to the final elimination. Someone eliminated early on couldn't look so damaged. She hoped that their lives would change even more for the better. Could Jason have won the million-dollar prize? Could humility be the cause for his despondency?

"I doubt there will be a normal. Not for a long time. For me," Jason said. The corners of his eyes hinted at tears.

Jason's two cats raced by, chasing each other. Blake smiled at Tigger and London, hoping that Jason would follow suit, but her tone and laugh were cut short when she saw the look lingering on Jason's face. There was finally life showing behind his eyes.

An intensity. He cracked his knuckles and shifted his weight in the chair.

"I wish they'd told us how to explain this. You're probably never going to see my season on TV. I can't imagine how, anyway. Not because I don't want to watch it—not because anything embarrassing happened to me. And the show's not canceled. Well, I guess it might be. I don't know."

Jason exhaled and Blake looked on, trying to emphasize blind compassion through her furrowed brow-line. Mostly, she was disappointed that the evening hadn't been a celebration. She had decorated Jason's house, bought his favorite foods and drinks. She had worn an outfit that always got Jason's attention, in self-denial about her hope that it might lead to one of their infrequent hook-ups.

Most of all, she missed her best friend who had been gone for months, and she wanted to spend the night catching up with him. Talking, playing with the cats. Watching all the films and television that Jason missed. Filling him in on all the events he had yet to hear about—updating him on their friends. Maybe more. This one evening—their reunion—had built up so much in Blake's mind over the preceding weeks that she mourned her daydreams, knowing she wouldn't get them.

Soon, anger replaced her other feelings—Jason got to play their dream while she stayed home and went to work. Not that he owed her anything, but didn't he care or notice? Other contestants who returned from the island weren't described like this. No Reddit threads, post-game interviews, tweets, or podcasts suggested this callous, depleted response was reasonable or typical. Jason was still sitting, motionless, staring into a random space below his front windows.

"What's going on with you?"

"Billy died on the island. Not like the accident that stopped the Russian show. I mean, it was murder. He had to have been, but it's not what they're saying. The network, I mean. And that's probably why I won the game. Or, at least think I won the game."

Blake's disappointment shifted to shock, and her thoughts abandoned the night that could have been. Instead, Blake's brain readied a stream of questions, waiting for the right moment to unleash the torrent upon Jason.

"What? How do you know you won?"

"Well, I don't. But I made it to the finals and feel like everyone would have chosen me to win. The few other members of the cast I've spoken to think I won." Jason's tone didn't shift.

"I mean, that's incredible. But, someone died? How?"

"I don't know if it was someone from my cast, or someone from the crew or what. But I know someone from the cast or crew killed Billy, and the network's covering it up, saying it was suicide."

Blake paused. "I'm not sure what emotion I should feel."

Jason took in Blake's reaction. "Surprise," he said. His voice was still an irregular monotone.

2.

ROLLING a Guinness from hand to hand, Jason gave a closed-mouth smirk as *Beached*'s famous intro music came through the TV. The first few flashes of the show illuminated the screen. Beyond his barstool, Blake and at least fifty local fans were crowded into a bar—McWarthy's—in Jason's home neighborhood of Delhi in suburban Cincinnati. They came to support him, take pictures with him and, most of all, get a taste of the infinitesimal fame that came with reality TV. Some were genuine fans of the show, whom Jason recognized. His real attention, however, was far from the crowd. While his eyes focused on the screen, his mind was thousands of miles away, on the island. He caught fragmented glimpses of himself in the intro—running, fishing, swimming; walking, talking, shouting.

The money was his, or probably would be when the show revealed the winner in the final episode. But how would he come across on TV? Would America hate him or love him? Would he be boring or a camera hog? Jason had spent much of his life in academia analyzing how characters were edited on reality TV, and he was now so nervous to see his own representation that he had peeled the full label off his third beer and contemplated whether he was having a panic attack. Beyond that, he felt guilty for caring about such trivial self-centeredness, knowing what had happened.

Billy wouldn't be in a local bar in Massachusetts, wondering how the country would see him presented. There would be no rounds of beer purchased to celebrate Billy. Instead, mourning and sadness. The thirteen other contestants who lived would sit around the country, worried if they were likable or if the camera angles were flattering.

Billy's murderer would watch, free from justice. Along with those who had allowed it to happen. Jason's anger and suspicion distracted him as the show rolled through its first minutes.

Jason had yet to appear significantly on the show. Instead, they had seen a barrage of establishing shots from a helicopter over the island where the show filmed. People around the bar looked at him, trying to read his reaction. Jason took a long drink from his beer and gave a nervous shrug at those who glanced his way. Blake squeezed his knee and smiled. Only she knew what had happened, but even Blake was unaware of his emotions. It wasn't her fault, Jason knew, because there was no way to explain how close they had all become out there, or how much he struggled to make sense of the way Billy had died.

The only people who could were the thirteen other people Jason had gone on his *Beached* journey with for sixty days. And they were appearing on TV. Involuntarily, Jason smiled as familiar faces invaded the screen.

The first person who spoke was Anna, a person bound for elimination before she set foot on the island. She had no outdoors experience, loved to nag and would pick a fight with anyone in sight. Well, that was when she was under stress. Outside the game, Jason had found, Anna was one of the most compassionate, dependable people on the show's cast. They spoke almost daily, and he felt sorry that soon, in this episode, she would earn the embarrassing distinction of being eliminated from the show first.

The rest of her team consisted of Ronnie, a burly, Southern police officer who would be the season's first significant villain, and Joan, an elderly doctor who provided morale, stories, and healthcare for her team. There was also Will, a writer famed for his outrageous schemes; Hunter, a mountain-man who was as genuine as he was strong; Desiree, a flirty, single mother in her mid-twenties. Finally, Bailey, the group's feared wild-card, who would be as happy burning the camp down as she would be trying to win the prize money.

Each person went by quickly. Many would be developed later, but others would be mostly forgotten, lost in the wake of more compelling stories and threats to win the game, their journeys offered as sacrifices for the editing gods who told the story.

But those people started the season on the other island and team. They were not Jason's people. He never interacted with Will, Joan or Anna in the game, and only lived with Ronnie for one day before the group voted Ronnie out. He knew of them through the stories told by their tribemates who survived. Victors indeed wrote the history in *Beached*, and the producers gave them the edit.

As the episode progressed, Jason's team, Darinoi, was barely featured. They didn't have to eliminate anyone for a while—the first four people eliminated were all from the Kaukoi group, on the other island—so Jason's team was conspicuously absent for most of the evening.

After a solid hour of people staring at Jason, trying to gauge his reactions, the show ended, and the television audience had learned virtually nothing about him or his allies.

It was weird, Jason thought, that there had been no coverage of the fact that a contestant died during filming. Billy was in the background during three conversations and was later seen fishing, but he wasn't prominent. Selfishly, Jason also considered it weird that he was the presumed winner of the season and its accompanying million-dollar-prize, yet he wasn't featured more. Those two events—Billy's death and Jason's win—had to be the two most significant events of the show unless he had missed something.

Jason caught himself frowning and worried who else had noticed.

Trying to suppress the racing of his heart and shaking of his hands, Jason gave a sideways smile and nod to the fans he felt looking at him. Something to reassure them. If he seemed happy, they might go back to their drinks and leave him alone. Quit staring. Maybe.

After Jason moved to get another beer, the theme music again jerked his attention back to the screen, along with the rest of the crowd. Something unexpected happened. Luke Stock, the host of *Beached*, was back on the TV, talking.

Images of the entire season's main events floated by as the host narrated brief teasers. He exclaimed that the season would feature many "firsts" for the series despite being the fiftieth season, showing a requisite number of images of the more attractive girls in their bikinis. Then, Bailey was screaming then slamming and throwing things at camp. Hunter was celebrating victory after victory in competitions. And, a package of the contestants tearily eliminating each other.

RTN was giving away the major story lines of the season, Jason thought. The fans agreed. Murmurs of disbelief spread through the crowd at McWarthy's. A few fans looked at the ground and shielded their eyes, avoiding spoilers. But these reactions were soon forgotten in favor of what came next.

The screen went black and cut to the host walking down the beach. Camera operators and crew members were visible in the shot—something unprecedented in the show, which sought to remain clean and polished. Viewers glimpsed the unmediated reality of the show for the first time.

"This season," Luke said "will be so intense—so excruciatingly challenging, physically and mentally—that a contestant will pay the ultimate price. Life has always been taken for granted on *Beached*—we talk about being 'alive' in the game. Yet, this season, a contestant's appearance on this show will cost them both their life inside and outside the game. Tune in the rest of this fall to see the season that pushes someone past their breaking point."

The *Beached* logo appeared on the screen, accompanied by complete silence. Silence from the RTN broadcast. Silence from the patrons inside McWarthy's.

New text appeared on the screen: "In memory of Billy Gerding 1989–2025."

Jason felt his cheeks and the tops of his ears grow hot. The hair on his arms prickled, and he shuffled his feet, trying to get rid of the tingling that crept up his legs. He pulled himself out of shock until he saw the horror-stricken look on Blake's face. Weeks had passed while Jason processed Billy's death, but Blake was still experiencing this for the first time.

Jason knew he had to face this reality. But the show was using Billy's death to sell itself. When he'd discovered the show would air as usual, he guessed the media storm would be relentless. Especially now, with a real death as the selling point for the former darling of reality television, this was huge news. Their island hopes of being famous may, in fact, come true, thanks to the indiscretions of RTN, the network Jason held responsible for Billy's death.

What Jason hadn't counted on was that this fury would begin immediately.

Every head in the bar turned, waiting for him to speak. The crowd's anger at the network's decision to foreshadow and spoil most of the entire season had abated and morphed into shock and bewilderment. *Beached*, in 2025, was no longer about actual survival. Instead, it was kitsch, escapist entertainment. But death had shown up and made it real again. The crowd was unsure how to feel, and they looked to Jason, hoping for an indication, or inside guidance for them. He didn't understand what to do.

⊏⊐

"HERE WE GO," Blake said as she handed her MacBook Air to Jason. He took the computer from her, set his coffee down on a coaster and settled into his usual sofa seat.

Adjusting his glasses and taking a deep breath, Jason read the internet's outrage over how the network had handled Billy's death. Billy—the first person Jason had bonded with and trusted on the island—was now the number one trending topic on every social media site. #BILLYG. His RTN profile photo was on the front page of every major U.S. news website, and was, at some point, being discussed on most television channels Jason and Blake had flipped through. This was all to be expected. No one had ever died on a reality show in America—the death would have been news enough. But, the way it was being presented and used to sell the TV show made it a viral sensation. An outrage. But also, Jason thought, as he twirled and pulled on his scraggly beard, an incredible marketing ploy. People around the world would tune in this season, many for the first time.

Hidden deep within himself, Jason also felt slighted. Confident he had won the game, although he wouldn't officially find out until the live finale, he knew the media would only remember Billy. Jason's win, something he had been fantasizing about since his adolescence, would be a mere footnote on the season, accompanied by guilt. He'd be talked about as a profiteer, in hushed tones, if at all.

"So Real It's Unreal: RTN, *Beached* and the Death of Human Dignity," read the front page of CNN's website.

Jason glanced down the page and saw what he expected:

"How far can 'reality TV' go? At what point does our culture's voyeurism border on making psychopaths of us all?"

"Will the actual death air on TV when it happens? What right does the deceased retain when they've already agreed to be filmed?"

These were questions that Jason himself harbored.

He glanced at Blake, who sat opposite him on the sectional sofa. Sunlight streaked in on them and his two cats, London and Tigger, who perched on two middle seats. Outside, faint hints of a lawnmower firing up sounded—an older neighbor, Lawrence, hoping it might be one of the last times he needed to cut the grass until the following year. Children shrieked while chasing each other through the adjacent backyard. Everything suggested an average, leisurely, late-Sunday afternoon in the early fall. But the soon-to-be televised death of Billy Gerding had crashed over them, leaving feelings of detachment from the normalcy surrounding them. They could only focus on the tragedy before them, and Jason's inability to make sense of it yet.

"What do you think?" Jason's voice was faint, but he forced a half-smile, for encouragement.

"It's horrible. It's appalling. When you told me, I figured, I don't know." Blake held her palms up, empty.

She looked down at the floor and shook her head, incapable of looking at the strained expression on Jason's already weathered face. She had never imagined this. The show was a dream for them both, but the experience was tainted. While Jason was busy trying to make sense of the island and come to grips with reality, she had been thinking through their present situation. Soon, they would probably be the focus of this media storm. As soon as the network, RTN, declined to comment, the media would come after the season's other players to get their take. Jason's life, and by extension Blake's life, had changed forever. Their celebration had morphed into a wordless day spent pouring over news headlines, with neither knowing what to say to the other.

"I can't imagine how they think they can do this. Do you really think they killed him?" Blake asked.

Ever since Jason first told Blake about the death, she had doubted his stance on the matter. He seemed adamant RTN's crew, or another cast member, had killed Billy, and he bristled at her protests. The network's present actions possessed a certain moral disregard that only popular culture could achieve, but she doubted any network would go so far as murdering a contestant, an asset, to produce ratings. Yet, Jason's thoughts about how the network would profit from the ratings only bolstered his resolve.

Jason nodded and shrugged with a hint of exasperation.

"I told you everything," he said.

This was a conversation that had played out frequently since the broadcast.

"I was there—I mean you can believe what you believe. I'm not sure. But the longer I was out there, the less I trusted the crew— even before he died. You read that in my journal. Billy wouldn't stop asking questions and trying to investigate what they were up to on the beach, and then he turned up dead. I don't know. That's all it is. Plus, they gave psych evals before we went out there. They asked about whether we were suicidal like ten times."

Blake nodded. "But you know that isn't infallible. If someone wants to outsmart it. And it was only a screener. Without family to cross-reference, he could have avoided being a red flag if he wanted."

"Yeah, I hear you. They just put us through so much prep. I can't imagine they missed it. And trust me, it doesn't feel right. I need to do something about it to figure it out. Someone else was involved here. I become more convinced with time."

"What will you do? You know the media will be all over us as soon as the show continues to air and the story gets bigger. Especially if or when your thoughts become public. Think about when his death actually airs."

"I don't know. I should keep my head down, collect my check, and move on. This should be the best time of my life." Screw the network and screw the press, he thought.

"Can you live with doing nothing? If you believe what you're saying? You're fluctuating between apathy and turning into a vigilante," Blake said. "I know the situation is hard, but we need to prepare what you'll do or say. And to whom. When you first got back, you were ready to fight the network and expose this.

Get on top of this before it's too late if you're serious. I only know what you tell me."

Jason, with his gaze out of the window, jerked to his feet and threw his arms up.

"You're right," he said. "But I need to teach a class tomorrow. And you have meetings you've been prepping for. Let's go to dinner tomorrow night and map out a plan. If I'm right, this is dangerous."

He had emphasized the "you" to the point of confrontation, but Blake backed away from conflict for the moment and responded, "And I'm right there next to you."

Jason wrapped his arm around Blake's shoulders. His temper had not yet subsided, but the situation was consuming him, and he was much more comfortable moving forward than standing still.

Jason knew Blake was right. She was his moral better half—the more composed of the two.

"Are you hanging out here?" Jason asked.

"No. I have work at home, and I need to get up early."

As they left the living room, Jason again hugged Blake. Though two weeks had passed since he had returned, Blake was still taken aback by Jason's frailty. When she hugged him, she felt his bones, as if she would crush him, and she pulled out of the hug early. The rest of their goodbye was a blur in Blake's mind. He kissed her on the cheek, then opened and closed the door for her; she scampered from his front door to her car and was home without remembering getting there.

After Blake departed, Jason brushed his teeth, made his bed, stripped down to his briefs and collapsed onto the mattress. He had missed the emotions that had overtaken Blake during their goodbye. Instead, Jason was passing the other contestants through his mind, deciding who he could trust expressing his beliefs to, and who he could contact. He lay in bed for half an hour, trying to read *The Name of the Wind*, his favorite novel, which he'd read too many times to remember the number. He didn't even turn a page. Instead, he thought and plotted, shifting away from anger at the situation he found himself in.

Jason decided he needed sleep. That would clear his head and emotions, helping him think and act. Sleep, Jason thought, was a luxury Billy had been without when he had confronted the crew. Something Billy would never have again.

As he closed his eyes, his thoughts went to Blake, and more of the deep-set conflict inside himself. She would help him through this; he would need her. But that also meant his plan to tell his best friend how he felt about her was again stalled.

Jason tossed and turned throughout the night.

"RTN'S LATEST PROMO A REAL SHIPWRECK"

22 SEPTEMBER 2025 BY MAURICE OVERBAY, ENTERTAINMENT NEWS NOW

OAKLAND— Whether you still watch *Beached*, used to watch *Beached*, or have never watched *Beached*, the long-running show suddenly has a new-found significance for everyone across the country.

On September 19th, the Reality Television Network (RTN) aired the first episode of the fiftieth season of *Beached*, which went by without much fanfare. Some people were stranded in a remote location, some worked together, some fought, there was a competition, and some people turned on one of their own, exiling them, crushing their dreams. Again—not much fanfare—this is approximately how every episode of the show has gone down for the last forty-nine seasons, or 589 episodes.

The real intrigue, disgust, horror, and revulsion came after the episode, during a special message to viewers from the *Beached* host, Luke Stock. In a raw, understated promo, attempting to give gravity to Stock's proclamation, he declared that, in this season, a contestant would "pay the ultimate price."

That's right. This season, a human being will die on the *Beached* island.

Stock and RTN both declined to comment.

Viewers, however, did not decline to have their voices heard. In fact, executives of RTN were greeted first-thing this morning by protesters outside their studio. Some held signs bearing slogans such as "You Can't Put A Rating On Life,"

"You're Stranding Us All On An Island," and, more pointedly, "F— Reality Television." One took to lobbing balloons filled with fake blood over the studio's gates and another smashed old television sets in the building's entryway.

While these are simply the most obvious manifestations of the country's reaction against RTN's decision to air the death of Billy Gerding on television this fall, others spoke out across the country, as #BANRTN trended on social media platforms.

These actions, based on anger, were predictable, as was RTN's decision to air this footage, according to the University of California, Irvine's Professor Jackson Carnell. "This is an obvious reaction to the society of spectacle that we live in. For years, our culture has pushed us to share more, to make things more and more public. Well, this now meets its logical conclusion. There are some things that society isn't ready to share, and death is one of those processes. RTN is not to blame; it's our society. RTN is only a symptom."

Whether you approach this from a philosophical or personal level, RTN will undoubtedly dominate the nation's attention in the weeks to come, leading up to the air-date of Mr. Gerding's untimely death: October 31st. Yes, that's right. If you hadn't heard, RTN has chosen to speed up the airing of *Beached* to have the episode in question air on Halloween.

On Friday, *Beached* earned 2.4 million viewers and came in tenth in its time slot.

BLAKE'S OFFICE

"I DON'T KNOW," Veronica said, shifting her gaze too frequently to be casual, but giving off the air that this was her intent. "Hmm," Blake responded, setting her pen and notebook on her desk. After waiting another moment for her client to say more, Blake pushed her chair away from the desk and walked around to where Veronica sat. Blake took a seat and angled to face her.

Veronica spoke again, still avoiding eye contact but forced to acknowledge Blake's changed position. "I don't know what you want me to say. I just don't."

"Confusion is totally appropriate. Dealing with the divorce of your parents is a confusing time, but that's why we're both here. To help you figure out how you feel about it. And allow you to move forward."

"I don't want to move forward," Veronica shot back. "Everything was fine the way it was!"

Veronica was a fourteen-year-old client at Blake's private practice, and this was her second session.

"It was, for you. But you can't always understand or control other people's feelings or actions. Who's making you so angry?"

"I don't know." Veronica pretended she had calmed down, embarrassed at getting emotional.

"Do you blame one of your parents?"

"I know it's not their fault or anything. It's just, like, I don't understand."

Blake grasped what Veronica was communicating with more insight than their last session.

"What don't you understand?" Blake asked.

After nearly an hour of open-ended questioning without a destination, Veronica finally let her guard inch its way down. Blake noted the change in Veronica's tone and demeanor. She was getting less intentional with how she responded and was letting truth spill out of her carefully constructed facade.

"I don't understand how long this has been going on, why this has to happen to me, and how I didn't figure it out. I don't understand who to blame, or how to feel. I don't get it at all. And no one can explain it. No one gets it."

Blake waited a moment before replying. "If you could help someone 'get it,' what would you tell them?"

Veronica shook her head and rolled her eyes away from Blake. "That's the problem: I don't know. Aren't you listening?"

"Just try," Blake replied. "Try to put it in words. If it doesn't work, no harm has been done. But maybe you can get somewhere, and I can help you."

"Fine." Veronica shifted her glance to the floor for a few moments.

"Okay. So, it's just, like, my life isn't real. Like, everything I've ever done was a lie. Every happy memory, every good thing I ever thought existed, they're lies. If my parents aren't really in love, I feel like I have no hope. And how could I not see it? I was with them every second of my life. The world just doesn't make sense anymore, and no one else can understand that. I thought my life was real, but it was all fake. Like, I'm some idiot who my parents tricked because it was easier. I don't understand what was real from my childhood and what was them lying."

Veronica stood and asked to leave.

"Sure. You made great progress today," Blake said. "We can leave off here until our next session. I'll see you on Monday." Veronica, however, didn't hear Blake finish because she had already left the room with a mixture of angst and rage.

As the door latched after coming to a slow close, Blake let out a sigh of relief and closed her eyes.

After a few moments, she heard, "Blake?"

"Hmm, yeah?" Blake looked up, leaving her consuming thoughts behind. It was Sydney, her receptionist, standing in the doorway, looking at her with a concerned expression.

"You went over a bit with Veronica. Are you ready for Farris?" Sydney glanced down at the patient schedule in her hand, affixed to a clipboard.

"Yeah, give me a couple minutes," Blake answered. "I need to be prepared to move on to Farris."

Sydney nodded.

"Thanks," Blake added, as Sydney backed out of the door.

Veronica's session had been a difficult one for Blake, despite the hundreds of teenage clients dealing with their parents' divorce she had helped over her nine years of practice. It was one of the most common traumas she helped people work through as a psychiatrist who specialized in adolescents. And Veronica was a standard case, having difficulty reconciling what she had perceived with the reality she now knew to be true.

As she struggled to regain composure, Blake returned to her usual position, behind her desk. After sinking in, she spun around, facing her office refrigerator, and took out a bottle of water. The cold liquid was an only momentary relief as she tried to drown the thoughts clouding her head.

She understood why Veronica's session had been so jarring—it occurred to her during the session, but she had been trying to save the thought for later. Blake's initial observations about Jason's appearance had been right. He had made it to the end and likely won, but he had also been incapable of moving on from the trauma of a cast mate's death. A friend's death. So he had not cared to shave, eat much, or focus on anything else since returning from the island.

Blake didn't know how to be there for him, which was particularly frustrating, given her position. This, also, presented a dilemma for Blake, because she was decidedly against bringing her work into her personal life. Or vice versa. However, as she had spent the last week emotionally compromised by Jason's situation, she kept remembering that she had entered her career for personal reasons.

Now, Blake doubted her purpose. She didn't know how to help Jason, or if it was even her place to help Jason, and her motivation to be a psychiatrist was at odds with her life as a psychiatrist.

Blake let a few chills shake her body then composed herself. She took a last sip of water, put the bottle back in the refrigerator, cleared her throat, and focused on her computer. She readied her hands at the keyboard. On the screen was her typical screen-saver. A photo of her and her brother, Jonny, from Halloween 2006, when she was sixteen, and he was eighteen. The memory made Blake smile. There was always happiness to find, Blake reminded herself.

She sent Sydney a quick email. "Send Farris in. I'm ready."

3.

"I'LL SEE YOU IN A MINUTE," Jason's phone read. He slid it back into his pocket and continued his walk across campus. Fall was unmasking itself as leaves dappled the quad. He'd missed the end of the summer, but Blake told him it had been a humid affair. Students were more abundant than usual because of the break in weather. Plus, by 3:00, most classes finished for the day and it was pushing 4:00. They sported flannels and knit sweaters that still showed signs of awkward creases and wrinkles from being boxed up through spring and summer. These were moments Jason took joy in—moments to catch an extra deep breath and feel happy to be outdoors.

Today, he noticed none of it. He walked forward, both with single-minded intent and the crippling distraction that accompanies trauma.

The school where Jason taught was a small, liberal arts institution. Most of the students came to pursue degrees in healthcare fields, with only a few rare English majors getting the bulk of his department's attention. Nevertheless, Jason taught the introductory composition classes, so whether you studied nursing, chemistry, or history at Edgewood University, you sat through at least one of his courses during your freshman year. This semester, however, Jason was only teaching one course due to his foreseen *Beached* conflicts, and the need to adjust back into his routine life.

Nonetheless, as a gatekeeper of sorts for the school, he always stayed involved, attending the various concerts, sports matches, and events around campus. Fittingly, he had many contacts throughout the university—people he bumped into and was cordial with, but not people with whom he had close relationships. This mingling experience was what he drew from while on the *Beached* island. An ability that made him appear as equal parts trustworthy and non-threatening. The man he was meeting, however, was not someone with whom he had one of these surface-level relationships.

Remembering the first time he met Seth proved difficult for Jason. It had been a few years earlier after Seth replaced an aged film production teacher on her way to retirement. Beyond that, Jason could pinpoint neither a first encounter nor first impression of any sort. It was as if Seth suddenly and spontaneously became a fixture within the Edgewood University community, and their friendship had been the gradual result of fate. Like-minded people who, within the forced social environment of the workplace, gravitated towards one another.

As Jason made his way down the hallway to Seth's office, in the bowels of the University's oldest building, he freed himself from obsessing over Billy Gerding's life and death long enough to indulge another related preoccupation, one which lasted much longer. *Beached.* The show had been the impetus for Jason's friendship with Seth. Once, it was a national phenomenon, but now it was borderline embarrassing to declare your support. Still, the fans that remained were dedicated. Rabid. Cultish, as the media often portrayed them when they paid attention. Jason always prided himself on being in that community of fans. Yet, as an academic who wrote his dissertation on visual rhetoric and reality television, he was also arrogant enough to put himself on a pedestal above the other fans. He was one who not only loved the show, but who studied the show, understood the show. That combination of egotism and knowledge made Jason only marginally involved with the deteriorating fan base. So, meeting Seth seemed fortuitous. Jason had rarely encountered another person who discussed reality television, let alone *Beached*, on the same level.

A casual comment about areas of study prompted their first conversation about the show. Seth's explicit knowledge led Jason to pry further. Through a shy admission, laced with embarrassment and casual disregard, Seth informed Jason that he had worked on the show as a cameraman. Briefly, he insisted, before he earned his doctorate. Not only was he a fellow academic, but he knew the minutiae of production. The secrets from behind the screen. Beyond the facade. Jason's obsession with the show led to many interrogations of Seth, only veiled by frequent requests that they "go out for drinks." Jason always bought.

Now, two years later, Seth sat behind his desk, looking wary, as Jason cracked open the door. Seth didn't look up, leaving Jason to half-knock on the frame to not alarm him with his presence. After his courteous tapping on the wooden frame did not suffice, Jason cleared his throat.

Seth recoiled.

"Whoa, sorry."

"No problem! I hope you haven't been here long. Welcome back to America." Seth grinned, looking at Jason. "Quite a new style. Going for the absent-minded professor with that unkempt hair and beard? Or, what, worried someone might not recognize you from TV still without it?"

"Ha. Ha. Ha," Jason said. "Seeing how it suits me. And no, I walked in now. Hard at work?"

"Not particularly. Pretty behind. I need to publish something soon or my career's doomed. But, with the controversy happening on *Beached*, I'm inundated with old friends and colleagues."

"Interesting project in the works?"

"No, but that's what I need. I have only had four conferences since I was hired and I'm screwed if I can't put together something significant. Academia's rough and I still have PhD burnout."

"Are you thinking something creative, then?"

"I think I could get by with that to at least keep my reputation afloat, but everything keeps coming back to *Beached* for me lately."

"Yeah, that's why I wanted to talk to you."

"I figured, and I am. So. Sorry." Seth focused on emoting sympathy. After a pause, he continued, "Jason, I had no clue that anything like this would ever happen. I can't believe it. This seemed impossible when I encouraged you to go out there. I can't help but feel culpable myself. I mean, fifty seasons. Nothing even close."

It had been two years ago, after a late night of drinking, when Seth convinced Jason to take advantage of his connections to get onto the show. Jason had auditioned before but never made it far. Seth knew the right people. Eighteen months later, walking onto the beach with cameras in his face, strangers by his sides, Jason realized how thankful he was to Seth. And he pondered how serendipitous their relationship was. Seth had shown up with exactly what Jason had wanted.

Jason made a pained expression and shook his head. "How could you figure this would happen? There's no need to apologize. But, what are your people saying? What have you heard from your RTN people?"

"I mean, we haven't seen the full thing yet. Only one episode. We have, what, at least six more weeks before the actual episode airs? People are still in disbelief. The crew's going through this too. They had responsibility for you guys. For Billy. They're worried about how the media will make them look. I mean, when Billy did it, someone should have noticed. A producer, a cameraman, someone."

"When he did it? So everyone's confirming it was suicide?" Jason asked in veiled disbelief. "I don't understand why RTN hasn't asked anyone to make a statement or talk to the police. Nothing. We're being avoided, and it's a bit haunting for us."

Seth paused before continuing, "I guess because the network wanted it handled immediately, and it occurred in a foreign country. Different rules, I suspect. The last thing the network wants is a huge investigation. They still had to make the show despite, well, Billy. But you need to know, again, everyone I talk to is so traumatized by it."

"Well, there you go. I assume they'd try to avoid attention, to limit coverage of the investigation, but here they are using it to get people to watch their show."

As Jason expressed his conflicted understanding, his phone vibrated. When he finished his sentence, he glanced at the screen. It was Blake: "What did he say?"

Seth grimaced, opening his palms. He was far from considering the murderous theories Jason was exploring. Seth was uncritical of the situation. This made what Jason was about to say even more difficult, but the subject needed to be broached before one of them had to leave for class.

"Seth, I'm just going to say it. You're practically the only person I can talk to about this. I was out there and knew Billy. Well, I know that he didn't do it, so I'm suspect of the people out there with us."

Jason paused before continuing, "Do you think this could be a cover-up or something? You were out there for years. Could someone have murdered him? Just logistically?"

Seth's expression changed, and he locked his gaze on the floor, appearing in deep contemplation. Once he had decided how to address Jason, Seth raised his head. He made it clear how much this response pained him.

"How long have you been back? A week? Are you even sleeping regularly yet? You still look gaunt and starved. My point is, I've seen a ton of contestants get paranoid and make crazy allegations on the island. It affects people off the island, too. This is a social and psychological experiment. It severely got to Billy; do you think it's still getting to you?"

"Seth, I've read plenty on the psychological effects of the show and I'm probably better-versed than any contestant who's played. Consider it. I know what I'm saying."

"I'm not sure you do. And I'm sort of worried." Seth took on a familiar, patronizing tone. "Look, all I can say is that I've talked to a bunch of my people who were either there or work for the studio, and I hear terror and heartache from them. People don't get into that business and make it that far if they're murderers. Think. What would their motive be?"

Jason narrowed his eyes and glanced at his cell phone again, considering the time before responding. "I don't know. I only know what happened—what had to have happened."

"Well," Seth said, "please take this advice. Let time pass before you push this any more. If this gets out, trust that people will react worse than I am, and think you've lost it. Or that you're using the situation. I know you, and you're not acting like yourself. Recover from the experience. Do some psychiatrist visits. Talk through this. It's trauma. It's in your head."

"Okay. So you're saying that there's no way someone killed him?"

"I am, absolutely. I've been there. Cameras everywhere, no alone time. I've met almost every person on that beach, except for the other contestants. They couldn't do it. No. And you know that too." Seth rose from his desk, closed his computer, and threw his satchel over his shoulder. He approached Jason and swung his arm around his shoulder, which transitioned into an embrace.

"Thanks, man. I needed someone to talk to," Jason said. He masked his irritation.

"Yeah. And I'm here for that. I'm so sorry I have to run to class right now. I'm doing a course on horror film. But, come by anytime. I'll help you talk through it. I can't imagine going through this. But give your grief space."

"Will do. Good luck with the class. Hitchcock, *Shining*, what else are you doing?"

"No. More campy stuff. *Evil Dead*. *Slither*. Drop by the class, too."

As the two exited the office, Seth locked the door. Out from behind the desk, Jason saw his colleague was still wearing shorts despite the change in season. Seth typically donned a suit and tie. Today, instead, he had on khaki shorts which wouldn't arouse a sideways glance if not for his abundance of tattoos. Most prominent of all were intricate, eight-pointed stars, centered on his knees. Jason fancied himself as the kind of person who would have a few tattoos, but he'd never pursued the interest. He envied Seth for them, and for how unabashedly he presented himself to the world.

"You heading to North campus?" Seth asked.

"No, I need to make a call. But have a good one." The two nodded and parted ways.

Jason had lied; he was heading to North campus to meet a student in his office but wanted to end his awkward encounter. He was being offered disbelief with suggestions of mental instability and pity. He hung back and texted Blake until Seth was a solid thirty paces ahead of him: "He's against the idea. I'm not sure what to do. On my way to a meeting, and then I'll see you at the restaurant."

After he had sent the message, Jason walked in the same direction as Seth, who he could see was also texting. Good, Jason thought, he'll be less likely to notice I'm avoiding him. Before they forked in opposite directions, the bass line of Pantera's "Walk" blasted into the silence. Jason grinned despite his annoyance with his friend. Seth's ringtone had always been an old-school metal song. What was peculiar, however, was that the ring came from a cell phone in Seth's pocket, rather than from the one he had been texting on moments earlier. Before Jason turned a corner, he observed Seth slide the texting phone into his right-hand pocket while answering the second cell phone from his left-hand pocket.

As Seth did so, he glanced over his shoulder. His eyes told Jason that he hadn't expected to see him. Jason's eyes told nothing in return. Then they were out of range.

4.

JASON HAD NEVER BEEN to Bistro Boreal, though it had opened over a year ago and become one of the most talked about dinner spots in Cincinnati. Given the gravity of their meeting and the stress Jason had put Blake through, he figured it was fitting. She deserved a hundred-dollar dinner. And wine.

He sat waiting for her, blinking at the plain, white menu, unsure of what half the items were, and not even willing to attempt pronunciations. No prices were listed. Despite a developed appetite, foodies annoyed Jason. He had never taken an interest. He was fine with the cheap stuff.

A server interrupted Jason's mindless stare and set a clipboard down on the table. Jason looked up.

"A drink menu for you to look over," the server said. She was a decade younger than Jason, but made him feel immature. Out of place.

"Thanks." He nodded and picked up the new menu, trying to act like he was comfortable. He was deciding which cabernet he would go with when Blake interrupted him, flinging herself down in the chair opposite with a sigh of relief.

"Am I glad work is over—how are you?"

Jason smiled at her, all feelings of discomfort forgotten. After seconds passed without a response, he said, "Yeah, fine. Just deciding on a drink. What are you up for?"

"Wine. Loads of red wine. And let's get this figured out. I'm feeling paranoia everywhere I go, like, I don't know what's going on. Which is silly—no one has any idea."

"Yeah. I told Seth, straight-up, and he thinks I'm insane, I guess." Jason's smile had transitioned to a more stoic affair.

Blake reached out and grabbed his arm. "Hey. It's a lot to take in. That's why we're going through it now. You can't expect someone to be open to something so huge without hesitation."

"Right." Jason picked his satchel up, unhitching its two clasps.

As he pulled out a moleskin notebook and pen, the server returned. She promptly deposited bread and butter, and requested their drink orders.

Jason, rushed, selected a bottle of the first wine he could pronounce—Justin 2021—and closed the menu as if the decision had been a difficult choice between two old favorite delicacies. The server smiled and walked away.

"Nice choice," Blake said, nodding.

Jason didn't ask if she was seriously familiar with his choice of wine, but his open-mouthed expression betrayed him. Blake laughed, and Jason joined in. He was pleased that she also found the restaurant a tinge bewildering. They should have stuck with the usual—a pub with loud music and fried fish.

Their eye contact and smile again lasted an uncomfortable moment too long, and forced Jason to flip open the notebook, click his pen, and ask, "So, how do you want to do this?"

His stare locked on the paper before him, picking up on the recycled flecks, printed ink lines, and anything else that kept him from engaging in another too-close-for-comfort moment of affection.

"Hmm. Should you list people who may be involved in some kind of suspicious activity contrasted with those you think are unquestionably not involved?"

"That's a good idea. And it'll be quick."

Jason drew a line down the middle of the paper. He made two headers at the top of the page. The first read "Suspected," beneath which Jason slashed an underline. In the column, he wrote the names of Nick, Kendall, and "Most of Crew" with a question mark. In the other column, "Cleared," he wrote the names Phoebe, Desiree, Luke, Omid, and Jason. He added Hunter's name, followed by a question mark, and then the phrase "All earlier eliminated cast."

"Well, I'm not sure that's helpful," Jason said after jotting down all those he considered cleared. He struggled to come up with suspects. Even Kendall and Nick on the "Suspect" side felt like a stretch.

Jason cleared his throat. "Anna, Joan, Will, Ronnie, Dimitri, Maddy, and Bailey were all eliminated and off the island before Billy was killed, so they're definitely out. Luke was preparing to host the upcoming challenge and was helicoptered in when they found Billy's body, so he couldn't have done it. I obviously didn't do it. And then I refuse to believe Hunter, Phoebe, or Desiree did it. I lived with those three for weeks and they couldn't have. If they were that manipulative and deceptive, they would have done better at playing *Beached*. Omid's the one person on the crew I can clear. We became close, and he was off that day, on the mainland. I don't know what to say about Kendall or Nick. I played with them from the moment we landed on the beach until we voted them out, but I don't have a read on either one. And the rest of the crew is my main suspect, I guess."

Blake nodded. It was as she suspected. Jason had little to go off other than his gut feeling that his friend couldn't have committed suicide. Her thoughts drifted back to her teenage client, dealing with her parents' divorce. The disbelief. The lack of acceptance. She also thought about the stages of grief. Was Jason stuck in denial?

She needed to cast aside this diagnostic spirit and instead be supportive, allowing him to work through this.

"Have you talked to anyone from the season?"

"I've only exchanged a few texts. Nothing heavy. I don't know how to bring this up."

"Well, that's where you need to start. Gather information and opinions to help inform your reasoning."

The wine arrived. The sommelier had Jason touch the bottle, taste a small pour, nod, and she poured a full glass each for Jason and Blake. These foreign, uncomfortable tasks, however, now passed out of Jason's mind.

"Yeah. And I want to call Billy's sister. I don't have her number, but I'm sure I can find it online. If I'm going to look into this, she deserves to know. Then I can contact a few people. Ronnie and Maddy, first. They'll take me seriously. And we've been texting since the season ended."

"That's a great idea."

Blake hoped that Jason's fears and suspicions would be assuaged by the other contestants, but she was there for him. She understood how important it was to deal with grief head-on. It was her life's work, personal and professional.

The server passed by and refilled Blake's glass.

"Let me catch up," Jason said. He finished his glass in one gulp and reached for the bottle.

The server pulled the bottle back from the table. "Allow me, sir."

TEXTS

26 SEPTEMBER 2025, 11:18 AM

SETH: Hey, man! Have you been talking to any of your friends about your worries from the island? With what you brought up in my office, I mean. I thought I'd check in and see how people were reacting.

JASON: No, not really. I don't know who to talk to at this point. Still figuring out how I feel myself. I guess I will bring it up though. You think I should?

SETH: Yeah. I asked around after our talk and I'm hearing some weird stuff from the crew, but no one wants their name involved.

JASON: What did you hear?

SETH: Well, it may be hard to hear, but people are wary about Nick. What do you think of him?

JASON: Wow. I don't know. I really don't.

SETH: Well, think about it anyway. If you ask around, let me know how people react. What the consensus is.

JASON: Okay, yeah. I definitely will. That's crazy. I never bonded with him much on the island, but what are they saying about him?

SETH: Like I said, no one wanted anything specific getting around, but I just keep hearing Nick's name coming up.

JASON: Right. Well, I really appreciate you getting in touch. So you don't think I'm out of my mind? Something suspicious could be possible?

SETH: I don't want to say so, I didn't think so, but yeah. Report back with what people say. I'm really interested in developments at this point.

TELEPHONE

26 SEPTEMBER 2025, 4:30 PM

EMILY: Hello?

JASON: Hi. Can I speak to Emily?

EMILY: This is she.

JASON: Um—hey. This is Jason Debord. I'm a friend of Billy's. I was on *Beached* with him.

EMILY: Oh. Okay. Yeah, I know who you are. What are you calling about?

JASON: Uh. Yeah, this phone call is way more difficult than I thought it would be. So, I was close with Billy on the island, and I wanted to see how you and your family were holding up. That, and I wanted to offer my condolences.

EMILY: I mean, how would you expect? I just don't want my kids finding out about it.

JASON: Oh. I'm surprised they don't know. There's been coverage of the show, and Billy, everywhere. It's made me feel weird, actually.

EMILY: Yeah, well, they weren't close with him, and they would have no reason to make the connection. They have my husband's last name. We didn't want him around much because of the influence he might be on the kids.

JASON: In what way? I don't know anything about his past that would warrant that.

EMILY: Look, it's honestly none of your business, but he just could be a scumbag. Was a scumbag, I guess. I have my own family now. My husband and I find all that embarrassing, and Billy would have done something. He always did something. So no. We hadn't spoken in a few years.

JASON: Okay. Well, that makes this a little awkward, but I'm trying to figure out what happened to him and piece everything together. Do you think it would be okay if I traveled to Massachusetts to meet with you and look through some of his things? As I said, we got close, and I want to make sure he gets justice. I'm trying to do the right thing.

EMILY: Yeah, yeah, enough rambling. I get it—you think there might be money, fame or some kind of lawsuit here. Well, listen to me, my husband and I will deal with all this. Billy's no concern of yours. He was my brother. You're not swooping in and getting network money that could go to my kids' college education. Clever idea. Goodbye.

JASON: Listen, I'm not trying to make any money. I can't live with myself unless I look into this. He was my friend—

EMILY: Whatever. I don't care about your little friendship. You're not coming anywhere near here, and you'll stop this harassment right now. My husband's a judge, and I'll have him see to that. Either in the court or outside it. Billy was messed up, that's why I didn't let him close to the kids. His only sister, and his only niece and nephew. Think about what might cause that. Pretty drastic. And you know nothing about it. Now the show pushed him further than he could handle, and they're taking care of it. It's not that shocking, and it's got nothing to do with you. Lose this number, forget whatever scheme you've got cooked up, and let my family be. Figures that this would be the type of friend that comes into my life thanks to Billy.

JASON: I'm sorry, maybe if—

[DIAL TONE]

5.

"YEAH, this will be the last episode until we merge and vote Ronnie out! We're about to get a little more screen time!"

Jason said with half-real, half-mocking enthusiasm.

"Ah. More scrutiny from America," Phoebe replied. "I'm still not used to hearing my stupid voice on television. I cringe every time."

"Well, Omid, my cameraman connection, told me that on one episode there is a three-minute package of you crying. So, come to terms with your voice before you're the laughingstock of the country."

"What?"

Jason opened his mouth as if to speak, raised his eyebrows, and only shrugged. He hoped that Phoebe would buy into his joke. That footage didn't exist, as far as he knew. But, that was their relationship on the island—a brother-sister annoyance that bonded them, though they looked like enemies on the outside.

Before Phoebe could try to get more out of him, Jason's doorbell rang.

"Either pizza or Blake. I'm excited to introduce you to either,"

Jason said, walking out of his dining room towards the door. He and Phoebe had been standing on opposite sides of his long, slate dining room table for over an hour, having beers and rehashing their time since the island, laughing at old memories from *Beached*. Jason was glad that Phoebe hadn't mentioned his vote against her.

Jason saw the pizza guy, not Blake, through his door's window. The grin he had unconsciously sported fell from his face. Not that he wasn't excited to have Salvatore's pizza for the first time since returning to Cincinnati, and not that the delivery driver didn't look pleasant, but Jason had been looking forward to introducing Blake to his cast mates. Especially his close friends, like Phoebe. The bond they had developed over such a short time was something he couldn't describe to Blake, so it would be easier to show her.

"Hey," Jason said as he opened the door. He pulled it closed behind him to keep his cats inside. People delivering pizza never understand pets, Jason thought, as he awkwardly backed the guy up to allow Jason out through the screen door.

"And, you already paid, so I just need you to sign this," the delivery guy said as he reached over the pizza box to hand Jason a receipt and a pen.

After tipping four dollars, totaling the amount up, and scribbling a quick "J," Jason handed the receipt back, not bothering to sign his full name.

"Thanks so much."

"Yeah, man. Have a good night."

As soon as Jason had cleared the threshold of his house, the driver spoke again through the screen. "Um, hey, are you on *Beached*? You look like Jason on that show."

Jason about-faced. "Yeah, that's me."

"Supercool. I hope you win, man." The delivery guy gave a mock salute, and jogged down the entryway, leaving Jason to reenter his house.

The delivery driver, if he was a big fan, would be disappointed with the half-assed signature Jason had left on the receipt. He was incapable of not being a little smug. Yes, he would win, and that guy would tell all his family and friends he had met him.

"Aren't we famous?" Phoebe teased as Jason brought the pizza back into the dining room. He rolled his eyes and passed into his kitchen to gather plates and forks. Napkins were already on the table. He glanced at the microwave's clock. Already 8:30. *Beached* aired at 9:00. Blake needed to hurry. And then, filled with momentary paranoia, he wondered if she was okay.

"Smells good," Phoebe said.

"This will be the exact pizza we fantasized about on the island."

"Mm. Well, I'm diving in. I haven't eaten, and it was a long flight."

"Go for it. Blake will be here soon, and she may have already eaten. It's late, too, so we can't wait." The two tore into the pizza. Despite being back for weeks, some aspects of life were still adjusting: food was one of them. Jason had no end to his appetite, and could readily consume an entire large pizza in one sitting. Granted, he'd still feel horrible later, but that was no deterrent. He had already gained back fifteen of the thirty-five pounds he lost on the island.

As the two finished their meal in focused silence, there was finally a knock at the door and they watched, bites of pizza in their mouths, as Blake let herself in. Instead of hellos, they managed waves and grins. She made her way to the dining room table, hung her purse on the back of the nearest chair, and followed it with her khaki peacoat.

"So sorry I'm running late! I barely made it in time."

Jason glanced at the television, saw Blake was right, and hugged her while unmuting the sound. "You're right," he said. "But I'm so glad you're here. This is Phoebe as you already know."

Jason half-bowed and extended an arm towards Phoebe. Phoebe waved from the table while covering her chewing mouth with her spare hand.

"And sorry I missed dinner," Blake began, but Jason interrupted.

"No problem. But the episode's starting. Let's do real introductions at the commercial break."

Blake was used to his dedication to the show. It happened weekly. Phoebe, however, laughed at Jason. "Yeah," she remarked, "we might not find out what happens." Jason waved her off, in complete silence.

They continued to sit in silence as the show cold-opened to the Darinoi beach, where Jason and Phoebe had started. Phoebe, Maddy, Kendall, and Nick gathered around the fire. Jason, Billy, and Dimitri were not on screen. The four around the fire were discussing their families while Phoebe tended to the flames. Judging by the sky, it was morning, and she was rekindling it from the night before. Kendall was primarily the one speaking, describing how much she missed her kids and husband after only being away for a couple of weeks.

Nick interrupted. He informed the others that what he found frustrating was sitting around and waiting to play the game. He wanted to play aggressively, and he proposed intentionally losing the next competition so they could vote someone out from their own team. The others avoided eye contact or made noncommittal shrugs.

"Let me guess," Kendall said, "you want to vote Billy out."

"He's so fake. I can't trust him at all. And if any of you had a brain, you wouldn't either," Nick responded. "He'll be our ruin. He'll turn on us. We need to stick together and get rid of the cancer he is to our team. I seriously hate that guy."

Kendall, Nick's closest ally, was the only one still giving him much attention. The others had heard it before.

Kendall spoke, after considering her response. "Okay. We'll just have to be patient. He's an asset around the island and camp. There'll be time to get rid of him later."

"That's what they say every season," Nick said, "about the person who eventually cuts everyone else's throats and wins the money." He rolled his eyes.

At that moment, the camera pulled back to reveal Jason and Billy running into the camp with giant grins on their faces. Billy led the way, and he carried with him a net of four large fish. "Dinner is served, my friends," Billy said.

The camera panned to show Nick shaking his head with a grimace. The *Beached* logo flashed on the screen, and the network cut to commercial.

Jason felt out of body. Stuck in stasis, immovable, as if his arms and legs weighed tons. Phoebe wiped her eyes in his peripheral vision. He wanted to offer impossible comfort to someone— either Phoebe before him or Billy through the television—but he froze.

"I didn't think it would be so hard," Phoebe said after moments of silence.

So far, through the first couple of episodes, Billy had hardly been featured. Now, he was front and center, not only on the screen but also in conversation.

"I'm so sorry, you guys," Blake said.

"It's hard," Phoebe said, "because of how Nick was talking about him. It's like… He didn't know. What would happen. But it's so bad. And he didn't stop after what happened. I can't imagine Nick's family seeing him talk bad about Billy, and what they'll see him say even after Billy dies."

She took a breath.

"And I was right there," Phoebe continued. "Was it stuff like that, the paranoia and talking behind people's backs, that could have pushed him to do it?"

Before anyone responded, *Beached* returned to the screen. Jason, with the remote still next to him, finally moved to turn off the television.

"Will gets voted out," Jason said, "and it's recorded. This is more important right now. I can't watch any more."

Blake nodded in support, and Phoebe stared straight ahead. "Can I get you guys anything? Coffee? Tea?" Blake asked. "Coffee would be great," Jason said. "Thanks."

Blake flashed a sympathetic smile and headed towards the kitchen, placing her hand on Jason's shoulder as she passed him.

"Phoebe, you have nothing to feel guilty about," Jason said.

Still not making eye contact, Phoebe said, "I wish I could have done something."

Jason hesitated, and the only sound filling the room was distant. Off in the kitchen. Water was being brought to a boil, the coffee press being pulled out of the pantry. He wasn't sure if he wanted to confront Phoebe with the topic at the forefront of his mind. He thought of her already overwhelming sense of guilt, and the emotions she was still dealing with.

"I hate to bring this up, but maybe you can still do something," Jason said. His voice trailed off as though trying to rewind the words into his mouth.

"I thought you said his family wanted us to leave them alone," Phoebe said.

"Well, that's not what I mean." Jason took a deep breath. "Do you trust RTN? The network's opinion that Billy killed himself? Can you reconcile that with everything else we experienced?"

Phoebe sighed. "I've thought about that so much." "And where do your thoughts lead you?"

"Jason, you can't honestly believe there's some conspiracy.

Jesus. Blake, your best friend, is a psychologist." "Psychiatrist, actually. She can—"

Phoebe cut him off. "Psychiatrist. Whatever. You still know you're blaming, bargaining, or whatever."

"I definitely am. And I'm keeping that front and center in my mind when I consider everything. I want your advice and your help. You were the only person who I could trust in the game, other than Billy, and you're the only one from the cast I can trust now."

"And that's why you voted me out of the game? Because you trust me so much?"

"Phoebe, you know I had to or I was going home. I thought we were past that."

Phoebe stood, eyes narrowing.

From the kitchen, Blake could tell how the conversation was turning, and she tried to hurry with the coffee, turning the heat as high as it would go.

"Well, don't use our alliance in the show to manipulate me if you didn't even stick to it. What do you want me to say? Huh? That there was some international conspiracy? That Billy was a secret agent and had to be taken out? Does that make you feel better? What? Or that Nick snapped out there and killed him?"

They both froze. Phoebe's expression blanked, and her arms fell to her sides.

With her attitude and tone transformed, Phoebe took her seat back on the couch and spoke. "I can't believe I said that out loud."

She paused, looking at her hands. "Is that what you think? I mean, I hadn't let myself go there."

TELEPHONE

5 OCTOBER 2025, 12:30 PM

RONNIE: My man Jason, what's up?

JASON: Hey, Ronnie. Uh, you know, wrapped up in the show and trying to get life back to normal.

RONNIE: Ain't that the truth! How are you doin' with that?

JASON: Fine. Phoebe was over to visit and we watched the last episode together. I'm back to work. It's great to get to hang out with Blake again. And my cats.

RONNIE: Man, you with that girl yet?

JASON: [laughter] No. It's not like that.

RONNIE: Pssh. If I was you, it would be like that. You're straight obsessed with her, and she's a looker. I'm telling you, don't wait on it.

JASON: Wow. You're right. I should be taking advice from the forty-year-old, single sensation of New Orleans.

RONNIE: Hey, hey, I'm just sayin'.

JASON: Yeah, duly noted.

RONNIE: [laughter] Well, what else can old Ronnie the Rattlesnake do for ya?

JASON: Jesus. You are a walking stereotype.

RONNIE: Hey, I didn't give myself that nickname.

JASON: Well, cops up here don't all have nicknames. At least I don't think.

RONNIE: It's them that's missin' out. But for real, what's up?

JASON: I'm calling to see how you're taking things. I've been doing so much thinking.

RONNIE: [Laughter] About winning a million dollars?

JASON: I haven't won anything yet. And you know what I mean.

RONNIE: Billy? Man, that's your problem. You college people do too much thinking. It'll get you down. Just go on now, what good is dwelling on it doin' ya?

JASON: Yeah.

RONNIE: Well, you called, so what can I help you with about it?

JASON: You haven't given it much thought? I know you were barely with him on the island, but you guys were close for a period of time. And it's been all over the news.

RONNIE: Ha, yeah. I'm loving the publicity we're getting.

JASON: Mm.

RONNIE: Look, I'm sorry, man. I'm kidding. I can tell it's hittin' you harder. But, yeah, you were with him for much longer than me.

JASON: True. I don't know. Is anything about it off to you?

RONNIE: Hell yeah it is, like I said. The damned publicity. You know who's making money off this? RTN. Bull-fucking-shit. We're the ones that's gotta deal with all this, that put ourselves out there, and then they get that extra goddamn profit? Where's our cut of the extra publicity and scrutiny? Where's Billy's cut? It's a big load of corporate manipulation.

JASON: So you think RTN killed Billy?

RONNIE: What? Hell no! But they're being downright scoundrels about how it's handled. What happened to lettin' a man have his dignity in death? They shoulda' buried the season, never let it see the light of day, cut us an extra check for our pain and suffering, take care of Billy's kin, and move the hell on.

JASON: Yeah. It feels wrong.

RONNIE: Damn straight. It's all I've been sayin' since the damn thing started airin'. You know.

JASON: So you don't think there's any chance there's a conspiracy here? That RTN knew how much they'd profit? Or that someone else did it and they're covering it up?

RONNIE: Hell, man, ain't this enough? That they'd go this far? I mean, now you think they're murderers? No way. Who would have done it? Plus, you remember what it was like out there. You said yourself you're still trying to get back to normal. I'm sure it got to Billy. Hell, my head wasn't on straight and he lasted a couple weeks longer than me.

JASON: Yeah, I don't know. I can't make sense of it.

RONNIE: When someone takes their life, how can you? Google it; everybody does this when someone they care about commits suicide. I see it enough. People coming to the station with allegations. Sayin' things at crime scenes.

JASON: I know, I know. But, you're a cop; there was an awful lot of motive out there, right? From us and the network too. Everyone stood to profit from his death. And there was plenty of opportunity. So much time alone, taking walks, getting food, firewood.

RONNIE: Pssh, well I see you been watchin' those procedurals. Look, there's always some motive and opportunity for murder. Them's the facts. You got no evidence though. This is all in your head.

JASON: What about the way Nick was talking about Billy on the last episode?

RONNIE: Look, don't do this, man.

JASON: Seriously, think about it. Just give me a shot.

RONNIE: I absolutely will not. You sound insane, and I'm not helpin' with some witch hunt of people we got as TV family. Everyone said crazy shit at some point or another. Nothin's gonna convince me Billy didn't do it himself. I know it's hard, but them's the facts, man.

JASON: Okay, just what makes you so convinced? What about—

RONNIE: Look! I don't need to defend common sense, and I certainly don't need to hear you turn on any more of our friends. But it's like this, see. You know what Billy's life was like outside the game. No close family relationships. Most of his friends scattered around the country. Shit job. His photography career never panned out. Then he comes on the island, thinkin' this will be the answer to all his problems. And what happens? He realizes he ain't gonna win. He gets paranoid. Thinks he has these tight bonds, and starts to figure they gonna turn on him, too. Starts to see this game on the island ain't his salvation. Plus he's starvin', plus he's dehydrated, plus he ain't slept good for weeks. All of a sudden, things get to him. It's not that surprising. I can't believe it never happened before. Still, it's tough. We all wish we could have been there. But you go diggin' too far into this, and you're messin' with his memory.

JASON: Yeah, I see where you're coming from, but—

RONNIE: No but. That's what it is. If you wanna turn your anger somewhere appropriate and get these emotions to be positive, instead of flinging accusations, you turn your thoughts against the network. They's the ones fuckin' with Billy's memory. Fuckin' all of us. Not getting you help, to not feel this way.

JASON: Mm. But look, I heard some of the crew is suspicious of Nick. You know I'm friends with that guy, Seth, and he passed along some rumors. I think it's worth considering. I feel like I owe it to Billy. Plus it lines up with what I was thinking. Other people from our show don't disagree.

RONNIE: I think I laid out my thoughts on the matter. Don't think I won't take your words to heart, but there's no way Nick did anything. I don't care what some supposed rumors say. Anyway, brother, I gotta get back to work, lunch break's over. Paperwork calls. But seriously, if you need help, get it. Don't let this take over ya.

JASON: Thanks, Ronnie.

RONNIE: [laughter] And Jason. I swear, make a move on that girl. You're an idiot.

JASON: Yeah, yeah, yeah. It's not like that. But I'll be in touch.

RONNIE: Take care.

JASON: You too.

TELEPHONE

6 OCTOBER 2025, 5:15 PM

MADDY: This is Maddy.

JASON: Hey—it's Jason.

MADDY: Hey! What's up?

JASON: Oh, I just wanted to be in touch, see how you're doing. Pick your brain.

MADDY: Hmm. Yeah, I actually know why you're calling. I was texting Ronnie last night. He's worried about you.

JASON: He texted you about me?

MADDY: Mm-hmm. He cares.

JASON: Did he text everyone?

MADDY: Uh. How should I know?

JASON: Was it a group message with everyone from the season except me on it?

MADDY: No!

JASON: Who else wasn't on it?

MADDY: Well that's good evidence on why you got so far in the game. Can't keep anything from you. Yeah, it was everyone except for you, Nick, and Phoebe.

JASON: Hmm. Why weren't they on it?

MADDY: I didn't start the message. But probably because you told Ronnie that Phoebe was, like, on board with your conspiracy theories, and because you were blaming Nick.

JASON: Well that feels good. Anyway, where are your thoughts?

MADDY: About Billy?

JASON: Yeah. Or Nick.

MADDY: I literally don't want to talk about this. This is the first time we've talked since the episodes began airing. Tell me about you. What's up?

JASON: Well, you know, just getting back to life. Seeing friends, getting to work.

MADDY: That sounds vague. Nothing major going on in Cincinnati?

JASON: Well, we had a viewing party for the first two episodes at local bars. Phoebe came in town to watch episode three. So that was all great.

MADDY: Okay, cool, and how's teaching?

JASON: It's good. You know, I have my friend Seth that I teach with, so it's great talking to him and getting perspective on the production side and all that.

MADDY: Have you done, like, literally anything that doesn't revolve around *Beached*?

JASON: Yeah, some stuff. Blake and I went to a fancy dinner. I read a couple books that I missed.

MADDY: Nice. Yeah, I've been doing so much catching up. Missing that much TV is hard work. Then the people, too. I've mostly just been out with friends, like, every night.

JASON: Not surprising. How did the L.A. club scene handle your time away?

MADDY: Oh, it stayed mostly the same. How was Phoebe? I haven't seen anyone since leaving the island.

JASON: She was. Not bad. Pretty emotional about Billy.

MADDY: Yeah.

JASON: How have you been holding up about that? We were all together from day one.

MADDY: Until you bitches voted me out!

JASON: Yeah, yeah, yeah. As if you didn't try to flip on me first.

MADDY: Hey, I knew you were going to win. Can't help I'm brilliant.

JASON: True, true. But, how are you? You really don't have any thoughts on how Billy died?

MADDY: Like I said, I'm good. I don't want to talk about Billy. I've dealt with my emotions. And everyone is saying you're losing it. You need to move on.

JASON: Geez. I'm trying to move on and you bring it back to that? And I'm losing it?

MADDY: Yeah, you're just, like, uber-paranoid and creating all these conspiracies. It's not healthy. You're supposed to be the one with a PhD, mister professor.

JASON: Ha. Ha. Ha. Right. Well, anyway, you should come in town and visit. I'll be in your neck of the woods for the finale and reunion, but you might like the Midwest.

MADDY: We shall see. It was good talking to you, but I gotta peace out. Remember. Don't go crazy.

JASON: Thanks for the advice. I'll keep that in mind. See ya, Maddy. It was good hearing from you.

MADDY: You too, love.

BLAKE'S OFFICE

"SYDNEY, THANKS," Blake said. She lifted the coffee mug her assistant had placed on her desk. A small break before her next client came in. An especially welcome one, given that this was a difficult client, coming in for her third session. Maggie was a twelve-year-old who suffered from an anxiety disorder that prevented her from going to school. There had been a bomb threat about a month ago, and she hadn't set foot in the school again. This posed a problem for her parents, who were both attorneys, and incapable of dedicating the time necessary to home-school Maggie.

Sydney, pausing opposite Blake's desk, smiled at her. "How are you holding up?" she asked.

"I'm not bad. Just a tough day. Maggie gets to me, and I wish there were more I could do. It's such a slow process."

"Yeah, but how about personally? You were pretty bummed on Saturday night."

Blake smiled. "I'm fine, seriously. I may have had too much to drink." She feigned self-deprecating laughter.

"Okay. You were worried about Jason. And I know how much he means to you. I still thought there might be something there."

"Well, I'll have to figure all that out," Blake said. "He hasn't been communicating with me. He's completely obsessed with what happened on that island. He's contacting everyone he can, spending countless hours researching online, and I haven't had a genuine interaction with him in about a week. I was supportive at first, but it's been a long time."

"You would think," Blake added, "that as a psychiatrist, this would be easier."

"Oh, stop," Sydney replied. She'd witnessed the toll Blake's relationship with Jason had been taking on her since he returned from the *Beached* island. She had observed it in the office and heard about it when they'd met up for drinks over the weekend. "Look, if you want to talk about it, I'm always here."

"Thanks, Syd. I appreciate it. But there's not much to talk about. If he doesn't want me more involved in his life, there's nothing I can do. I can't force it anymore. For a moment things were perfect, but I can't enable him while I'm left ignored and unimportant."

Sydney nodded.

"So," Blake continued, "for the time being, I'm letting him go down this rabbit-hole and have his space. If it gets too serious, I'll jump in and try to help him, but it seems like he needs to work this out and he doesn't want help. Especially mine, because I don't particularly buy into his theories and mania."

Blake felt weary of the discussion. There was little else she could say, no matter how resolute she sounded now. Jason's situation saddened her. She wasn't sure whether to believe in his suspicions, and had no proof in either direction. All she wanted was to help him, but he wouldn't let her. At first, she had been the encouragement he needed to explore his emotions. She had given him the keys, and he had locked her out. Blake was letting it affect her work and other relationships, and she'd have to confront him soon.

"Okay. Just making sure you're alright," Sydney said. After a moment of silence, she asked, "Shall I send Maggie in?"

Sipping her coffee, Blake nodded.

Moments later, a girl walked through the door tentatively, despite familiarity, and smiled at Blake. Maggie had straight-cut bangs with long brown hair, wore a romper, and had clear braces. Her shirt was from Disney World and had the words "Barnes Family Reunion" printed across the chest.

"How have you been?" Blake asked.

Maggie shrugged but smiled back. "How about you?"

"I'm doing well. Happy to see you and hear about your week." Blake maintained a distinct cheeriness in her voice.

Maggie smiled. Blake continued, "So, my day's been okay. I got to have a cup of coffee and breakfast this morning and had some nice conversations with my coworkers. How about you?"

"It was okay. Just brushed my teeth and watched some TV and then my mom brought me here."

"Good. Have you seen any of your friends lately?" "Yeah. Alex came over the other day."

"Awesome. What did you two do?" "Played some video games."

"Did you talk about school at all?" Blake asked, approaching the topic. Maggie's eyes shot to the ground.

"Yeah."

"What did you talk about?"

"He told me about what they were learning. And that kind of stuff."

"How did you feel, hearing about that?"

Maggie hesitated. "I don't know. It sounded boring. And I didn't know what he was talking about."

"Did you want to understand his stories?"

"I guess. He's my friend. But it's not worth it."

Blake took careful stock of the situation, ready to push Maggie to discuss her actual issues, but not wanting to get her worked up. "What's not worth it?" Blake finally asked.

"Going to school." "Why not?"

Maggie looked up, hurt. "You know why."

"Because of the threat? I understand. But we've also talked about the likelihood, and the measures in place to protect you. Do those change the way you feel at all?"

"No. Try telling that to the kids who die at schools every week," Maggie said. She rolled her eyes.

"Okay. Why don't we make a chart? A chart that looks like a thermometer." Blake stood and drew a large thermometer on the wall-mounted whiteboard next to her desk.

"Now," Blake continued, "let's list things that scare you about school, and put them on the thermometer. The colder temperatures are things that are a little scary, and the higher temperatures are really, really scary. Let's start with five things. What about school scares you a little?"

"Taking a test," Maggie said.

"Okay, good. What's a little scarier?" "Talking to people I don't know." "Okay, next?"

Maggie thought for a moment. "Someone bringing a gun to school and shooting everyone," she said.

Blake merely nodded at the escalation.

Maggie continued, "Then, uh, someone blowing up the school and killing everyone."

Blake continued to write Maggie's responses.

"Then, last, uh, I guess they blow up the school, but I live and I'm trapped inside to die slowly, trying to escape."

"Okay." Blake handed Maggie the marker. "Would you like to add in other fears into the different levels?"

Maggie grasped the pen. She listed instances rapidly, and once the categories were filled she kept writing next to the lines Blake had drawn: knives, recess, answering questions, eating lunch, going to the bathroom, kidnappers, tornados, fire, needing a tissue, going to the nurse, art class, talking to a teacher. After filling the medium-sized whiteboard, Maggie stood back, consumed in her thoughts. Blake's mind drifted to Jason.

"There's a bunch of other stuff, too," Maggie said.

"Great, thank you, Maggie," she said. "This is a great place to stop today. Next time we can work through a few worries that are lower on the scale. That way we can work ourselves up to the bigger concerns."

Maggie returned her glance to the floor and nodded. "Okay," she said and headed toward the door.

"Is there anything else you wanted to talk about?" Blake said. "No. Thanks," Maggie said. "See you soon." She smiled back at Blake.

As soon as Maggie had closed the door behind her, Blake allowed the smile to evaporate from her face.

6.

"DAMN IT," Jason swore as he picked up his garbage can. He was rolling it to the back of his house after returning from work. The sun was baking overhead, and he had been struggling through the uneven grass for a few minutes. He'd put the bins out too late that morning and missed the garbage truck, so the full weight of the trash was challenging to pull uphill. Returning the bin to its wheels, and giving a last burst of energy, he ascended the entire yard and rolled the can into place on the concrete patio behind his house.

With energy returned, he set about getting the mail. Jason was eager to get inside and dive back into his research, looking into the personal life of every member of the crew who had access to Billy on the island.

While jogging back around the side of his house, however, something caught Jason's eye. A glint of light. Something out of place. He swore again.

Something had shattered the window beside his back door. Jason stood on tiptoes and peered over his wooden privacy fence, seeing if the two neighbor kids were back there, playing baseball. Upon not seeing them, he remembered they would still be in school. Impossible.

He ran to the front of the house, punched in the keypad code to his front door, and made his way to the back window. Broken shards littered the hardwood.

Flustered, Jason continued to swear under his breath, desperate for an explanation. He glanced around. There were no baseballs or rocks, and no objects out of place.

Jason only noticed one peculiarity. The screen.

Normally, he opened the bottom half of the window to let his cats look out, catching the smells and sounds of the outdoors. He had special pet screens that were strong enough to hold the cats inside. It was a busy neighborhood. Plus, they were declawed and had only ever been indoor cats.

Now, however, the screen was pushed to the top of the window. Jason couldn't remember a time he had ever opened the top half of his windows. Someone had moved his screen and broken the window. With this realization, Jason tried the handle. It turned and swung open. Unlocked.

Someone had broken into his house.

He backed himself against the exterior wall and scanned every direction. In contrast to the noise he had made coming into the house, he now moved in near silence. He entered the kitchen and grabbed a bread knife, unsure of where any other weapon may be in his home.

Jason proceeded to search every room systematically, throwing open closets, checking under beds, always with the knife at the ready. As he entered the final room, doubt entered his mind. Was he crazy? No, he couldn't come up with an alternative explanation.

As he finished his search, he concluded no one was in his house besides himself. No one, including his two cats, London and Tigger.

This worried him more than the threat of an intruder had, and the adrenaline gave way to panic.

He dashed to the kitchen, pulled out the cat treats and shook the bag. No cats came running.

He ran outside, continuing to shake the treats. Again, there was not a cat in sight. Jason sat on his stairs, fighting tears. Tigger and London had lived with him since college. With Blake, he had rescued them both from the local shelter, and when he bought his house, the two cats had moved with him. They meant more to him now than he had ever stopped to realize.

Jason pulled his cell phone out of his pocket and called Blake. "Hey, um, someone broke into my house, and the cats are gone. Can you come help me?" He was incapable of disguising the panic and pain in his voice.

After she responded that she'd be over right away, Jason said, "Okay. Thank you so much."

He put the phone away and stood looking helplessly and hopelessly around his yard, searching for any signs of movement. Only a few birds. And a squirrel perched fifteen feet off the ground.

Jason feared he may never see his cats again, and also recognized that he'd been robbed. Only, when he had searched the house, he'd noticed nothing missing, and he had no valuables other than his television, computer, and some rare books. He had unconsciously accounted for those items during his search.

Aware that it was not the time or place for it, Jason's mind spun and narrowed in on the conspiracy around Billy's murder. Had he brought this upon himself, London, and Tigger?

He retreated inside and returned to his computer to figure out if it had been touched. All the while he contemplated who would have done this. He regretted not being more careful, not having a home security system, and forever looking into Billy's death. He was getting too close; he was convinced.

⸺

JASON WATCHED Blake's silver Prius speed into his driveway. Without locking the doors or putting the windows up, she bounded towards his front door. Jason waited, ready to open it for her, which he did as she approached.

With a worried expression, she entered his house, looked around, and gave him a half-hearted hug before jumping into a series of questions.

"What exactly happened? Have you called the police? And are you sure you've looked everywhere?"

"Yeah. The cats are gone—I looked all over, and outside. I didn't call the police. That should have been my first move, but it doesn't seem like anything was taken. But, someone's clearly been in here."

"How do you know someone broke in? Couldn't the cats be hiding?"

"No, the back window is shattered. I'm not making this up.

And it wasn't a baseball or something." Blake nodded.

"Come with me," Jason said.

He led Blake through to his back door where the broken window was, and they continued outside to the patio.

"Okay," Jason said, glancing around his backyard. "Well, I think someone broke in to plant surveillance. A microphone or something to monitor my computer."

Blake ran her left hand through her hair and hesitated.

"So we're talking out here so they can't spy on us?" she asked. Jason nodded. "Yeah."

Blake swallowed hard. "And why would they do that?" "Because I'm figuring out what happened to Billy. On the island."

"Okay, but what are you figuring out? I didn't think you had any answers," Blake said.

"Well, I have to be right if this is happening. Maybe Nick did it because he heard I was throwing his name out. Or there's some kind of network conspiracy like I thought. Either could have pulled this off."

"Huh. If that was true, wouldn't they have stolen something to make you think it was a robbery? Or left a rock by the window?"

Jason's eyes narrowed. "How should I know? I probably got back just in time, and they rushed to leave."

"But there was enough time for the cats to run away and get so far you can't call them with food? Shouldn't they be the priority?"

Seconds of silence passed, and Jason didn't make eye contact. He couldn't produce a simple answer for any of this, yet he still felt betrayed that Blake doubted him.

"I'm just saying," Blake continued, breaking the silence, "it seems like you might be jumping to conclusions. No one could know what you were looking into. Plus, everyone else seems to be dismissive of what you're suggesting. And both RTN and Nick are states away. You're scaring me."

"Ah. Well. I guess so much for supporting me," Jason said.

Venom coated his words.

"Look, you're getting frustrated with the other cast members not believing you, but have you considered that maybe they're right all along? It's been weeks, and you're no closer to discovering anything. Don't you think you might be struggling to process what happened?"

"Yeah, I made everything up. Definitely. Please, come over with all your psychological expertise and tell me what's going on with my brain. Doesn't that get tedious, always knowing what everyone else is thinking all the time?"

"Don't."

Jason threw his hands up and turned away from her, shaking his head.

"I know what it's like," Blake said. "Not because of psychology, but because of what I've been through. And you know that."

She waited a moment before continuing, "When my brother died. When he killed himself." She again paused. "When that happened, I searched for a solution everywhere. For an explanation everyone else had missed. Trying to answer the question of why he would do it. And what did I find? Absolutely nothing. You can't understand what was in someone else's mind."

Jason faced Blake again. His anger had not subsided, yet he had the awareness to ease up. Blake only rarely spoke about her brother, which added nearly tangible weight to their conversation. A slight quaver in her voice betrayed her emotions.

"Anyway," Blake said, "I never found some neat, clean solution. No matter how much I searched for it. Because it doesn't always, or doesn't usually, exist. You're searching for that solution and you're going too far. It's consuming you. We've barely been communicating, and we're supposed to be best friends."

"Yeah," Jason said. "So you want me to give up on all this? You were the one encouraging me before."

"I was, but I was trying to help you cope with the loss so you could work towards some clarity on your own. And I still am. I think you should turn your attention to accepting and coming to terms with what happened during the show. Get over the loss. Then, if you still believe in this conspiracy—murder, whatever — you can look at it without all this other complication."

"And how do I do that?"

"I know there's no easy solution. No snake oil cure or quick remedy. It'll be personal for you. After Jonny died, I studied psychiatry so I could help other kids. To help them accept challenges and not hurt the way I did. Even though it doesn't go away. Ever. And it felt like I was turning the loss into a positive, but there was a lot of mourning before that. I had to stop blaming myself and those around me. That's where you need to start. And turn this emotion into something positive."

"Any ideas?" Jason asked, with his head tilted towards the floor.

Blake forced a smile, fighting back emotion, and put an arm around Jason.

"Let's go inside," Blake said, "and leave food out for the cats, in case they come back. Then we can come up with some plans. And maybe trim back the unkempt jungle look."

Jason gave a perfunctory laugh, and walked back into his violated, empty home, wishing he was ready to attempt moving on.

TEXTS

8 OCTOBER 2025, 11:14 AM

JASON: Hey, how's life been since the season? Long time without talking!

DIMITRI: Hey, man! Good! Such a whirlwind. What about you? Enjoying the show? Lol.

JASON: Haha. It's not bad. Been busy. My house was broken into, actually.

DIMITRI: Damn! I hadn't heard. While we were away?

JASON: No, since we've been back.

DIMITRI: I'm so sorry to hear that! How bad is it? I can't even imagine.

JASON: Well, they didn't steal anything. Which is so weird. Maybe I scared the person off. But my cats are gone.

DIMITRI: Holy shit. That's horrible and weird. Did they take them, or what?

JASON: I don't know. They probably jumped through the window the robber broke.

DIMITRI: Oh, right. Shit. I am so sorry. Anything I can do to help?

JASON: No. There's nothing. I don't know. Hopefully, they come back—it's only been a day.

DIMITRI: Wow. Yeah, best of luck. Hopefully, they ran off and are safe. I'm sure they are. Sending you lots of positive thoughts and vibes.

JASON: Thanks. But, yeah, how have you been enjoying the show?

DIMITRI: Good. It's hard seeing Billy, and my boot is coming up. People have been in town to watch the episodes. Met a bunch of former players.

JASON: Yeah—that's got to be killer in NYC!

DIMITRI: Hells yeah! You should come! Stay with me!

JASON: Sounds pretty good—I could use a distraction.

DIMITRI: Great. Don't leave me hanging!

JASON: Haha, no, I'll definitely come. How about in like 3 weeks? And then I think Blake can come with me.

DIMITRI: Sure, anytime :)

JASON: Great. I'll let you know.

TEXTS

HUNTER: Heard about your cats. So sorry!

JASON: Thanks—yeah, all I can do is hope they come back.

HUNTER: What do you think happened?

JASON: Someone was breaking in and I got home. I guess?

HUNTER: That's crazy. And you think it has something to do with your asking questions about Billy?

JASON: How do you know about that?

HUNTER: Ronnie.

JASON: Ha. Well, I don't know. It's been on my mind. I'm going to get past it though.

HUNTER: I heard. I've been really paranoid since I got back, too.

JASON: It's a tough adjustment. How are you doing now?

HUNTER: Meh. I found a dead bird in my driveway a couple days ago. Then I convinced myself my neighbors were sending me a message, so I plotted my revenge. Probably just a dead bird.

JASON: Whoa. Haha. What were you gonna do?

HUNTER: BUY GOATS' heads from the market, along with loads of pigs' blood, and make a little fake sacrifice in their backyard.

JASON: Jesus! Haha. What the hell?

HUNTER: I don't know, man. I'm telling you, the mind works differently after the game. Be careful.

JASON: You think the Billy stuff is crazy too?

HUNTER: I don't know. Maybe, maybe not. But I've been talking to RTN a lot, and I trust them. But I see where you're coming from.

JASON: You've been talking to RTN?

HUNTER: Yeah, they get in touch and check on me. See how things are going. Casual stuff. But we also have a good working relationship. I have some stuff coming up.

JASON: What stuff?

HUNTER: I probably shouldn't say.

JASON: Okay. Well, you think I'm less insane than most people. Thanks!

HUNTER: Well, you are coming to stay with me and my family in a couple weeks. Lol. Don't want to poke the bear.

JASON: Yeah, I'm looking forward to it. I've never been to Gatlinburg.

HUNTER: Can't wait!

JASON: I'll be in touch about when I'll arrive and everything.

HUNTER: Sounds good! Off to check my social media accounts for the rest of the day!

JASON: Haha. Take care.

TEXTS

VINCENT: Hey Jason—this is Vincent Salah from season 32. Dimitri told me about what was happening. I wanted to be in touch, and see if I could offer any help, advice, or just commiserate.

JASON: Wow—it's an honor to hear from you. I'm a big fan. Thanks so much!

VINCENT: Of course. How are you holding up?

JASON: I'm trying to stay positive. Not worry, or let my mind drive me crazy.

VINCENT: Yeah, Dimitri told me you were struggling over Billy. More than others.

JASON: Honestly, everyone keeps saying that. But I'm not sure. I just have some suspicions. Questions, really.

VINCENT: And do you suspect that this break-in is related?

JASON: Do you feel that it might be?

VINCENT: Anything's possible. When I got home, I sometimes felt like I was being trailed, watched. I'd take long ways home to throw off the cars behind me. Wake up in the middle of the night and scan my room for a camera. It's hard to go from constant surveillance to none. That's why I wanted to talk to you, once I heard.

JASON: Sounds like you think I'm imagining it.

VINCENT: I'm just saying, our minds take some adjusting. And you had more trauma than anyone ever on the show. Give it some time.

JASON: How did you get along with your cast, after the season?

VINCENT: There were some people I talked to more than others. But we stayed close and then gradually grew apart over three years. Why do you ask?

JASON: I feel like I can't trust them. Like, Dimitri was talking about me to you. Most of them think I'm losing my mind.

VINCENT: Dimitri is concerned about his friend and thought I could help because I had a similar experience. He didn't say anything bad about you. Trust me. Look, this will all pass.

JASON: Hopefully.

VINCENT: Have you been sleeping in your bed?

JASON: Uh, yeah... Haha. Why?

VINCENT: That's a good sign! When I got back, it took me weeks to sleep comfortably on a mattress again.

JASON: Hmm. Well, I never had too much trouble.

VINCENT: That's great. I know on our season, and from what most other people who have gone on the show have told me, there are always one or two people who really struggle. Kind of lose it.

JASON: Yeah. I can see it being a hard transition for some. What do you mean by losing it? Ha. I've been a big fan and can't recall seeing much on the topic.

VINCENT: Right, well, the cast and RTN don't want to highlight the struggle some fan favorites go through. It takes the fun away. But there's usually someone who needs a lot of therapy if you know what I mean. Hard time getting back to reality. Accepting things. My season had two. It took a while, but they're back to normal and we all see them regularly.

JASON: That's good. Ha. I'm not sure who that is on our season— maybe we need a little more time to tell. Maybe it's everyone, given the situation.

VINCENT: Maybe! I hope not. Anyway, I'm sure I'll see you soon. Dimitri said you're coming in town.

JASON: Yeah, in a few weeks.

VINCENT: Excellent. If you want to talk about anything, you have my number.

JASON: Thanks so much!

VINCENT: Well, I hear you may join the winners' club. You know, we're a pretty elite bunch.

JASON: I don't know what you're talking about!

VINCENT: Haha.

TEXTS

9 OCTOBER 2025, 11:49 AM

NICK: Hey, sorry about your cats.

JASON: Thanks. I appreciate it. How did you hear about that?

NICK: What, I'm supposed to be so out of the loop?

JASON: No, sorry—I've just heard from a few people, and I only told Dimitri.

NICK: Yeah, well, I heard.

JASON: Okay, and thanks. How are you?

NICK: Staying busy. You?

JASON: Yeah, really consumed with *Beached* still.

NICK: Ha. Figures.

JASON: What do you mean? Ha. What are you thinking of the show?

NICK: Not watching.

JASON: Okay—why not?

NICK: It's not really fun when you know that you don't win.

JASON: I guess that would make it a bit different. I might lose to Hunter though.

NICK: Right. Ha.

JASON: Sorry. You're in the show a lot though. I think it's been a good season. Still mostly focused on the other group right now.

NICK: Cool. So we're close to the great moment where you betray us all.

JASON: I guess so. Anyway, we should get together and catch up.

NICK: I probably can't any time soon. Busy with work.

JASON: Okay, bummer. And again, I'm really sorry about how things went down. Just know that it wasn't personal. I only look at it as a game.

NICK: Sure. Look, I know what you've been saying about me. Wasn't screwing me over in the show enough? Fuck you, man.

JASON: What do you mean?

NICK: I was going to be nice, but fuck you. You're still such a smug asshole. Stop talking about me. We'd all be better if it was you that died on that island instead.

JASON: What? Geez, man. I thought we were just kidding around. I'm sorry. I didn't start the conversation.

NICK: No, I am kidding. Sorry, too dark.

JASON: Okay. Wow.

NICK: Good. See you at the finale, so you can collect your check!

TEXTS

10 OCTOBER 2025, 1:21 AM

WILL: Jason, can you talk? Sorry, it's late. It's Will.

JASON: Sure, what's up? Did you get a new phone?

WILL: You're not wrong.

JASON: About?

WILL: Billy. The break-in.

JASON: How does everyone know about that?

WILL: Everyone talks all the time.

JASON: Yeah, true. But why do you say I'm right?

WILL: I've been looking into it, too. And I was being monitored.

JASON: How do you mean?

WILL: Internet. Phone calls. That's why I'm using this burner phone.

JASON: How do you know?

WILL: I'm on computers all day. I know what I found. And it was done by someone good.

JASON: Why were you being watched?

WILL: Because of Billy. I think he was murdered and know you do, too.

JASON: Oh. Really? I can't decide what I think. I'm probably better off trying to stop thinking about this for a while.

WILL: You need to cancel your internet and phone and everything.

JASON: Well, I have nothing to hide.

WILL: You want some murderer being able to track you? Who knows how well connected he is. Think about that break-in you had. Why do you think that was done, and nothing taken?

JASON: Okay, trust me. I am. So who do you think is doing this?

WILL: Someone on the crew. I don't know who yet.

JASON: Okay. But why?

WILL: Still working on it. What do you have?

JASON: Nothing really. I've thought of Nick, the network, I don't know. I guess it could be the crew.

WILL: So you know the truth. You just have to work it all out still. I'll be in touch if I find anything. You do the same. There could be something much bigger than initially thought going on here.

JASON: Okay. Thanks, Will.

WILL: Yeah—remember. If anything has electric, there's someone watching. Get rid of it all. For your own safety. They've already been in your house. Consider how you could be monitored at all times.

JASON: Will do. Thanks!

WILL: Good. Good luck.

TEXTS

10 OCTOBER 2025, 11:57 AM

SOFIA: Hey, Jason, it's Sofia Irving. I got your number from Vincent.

JASON: Oh, hey! Wow, it's an honor. I didn't think I'd be getting contacted by so many *Beached* all-stars!

SOFIA: Oh yes, nobility that I am. But, I'm sorry about what happened. And I wanted to talk about Nick.

JASON: Interesting. Thanks. Sure, what about?

SOFIA: We both live in Atlanta, and all the former *Beached* players who live around here go out for drinks, so we invited him. He was intense.

JASON: Yeah. He was texting me some pretty aggressive stuff yesterday. He said it was a joke, but I feel kind of rattled. What happened?

SOFIA: He got drunk last Friday and refused to stay and watch the episode with us. And aggressive is a kind word for how he was being.

JASON: Wow. I'm sorry. But I can't say I'm surprised. He's bitter, and people don't think that highly of him.

SOFIA: Yeah, well, he was especially hateful about you. Kept talking about how much he hated you, and Phoebe and Billy. Said some offensive stuff about Billy's death. It wasn't funny.

JASON: Geez. He was a loose cannon on the island, but that's next level. Sorry that you had to deal with that.

SOFIA: Yeah, just watch out for him. He might try to make you look bad. Or maybe start something with you at the finale and reunion.

JASON: Did he say that?

SOFIA: Yes. But please don't tell him I told you any of this.

JASON: No, I don't plan on talking to him again. He's been nothing but angry and unpredictable with me.

SOFIA: Okay, that's probably good.

JASON: Thanks for the heads up.

SOFIA: Of course. You're part of the show's family now!

JASON: Yahoo!

SOFIA: Good luck on the episode tonight! (Don't tell me any details. I avoid any spoilers like the plague.)

JASON: It should be a good one! Thanks again.

SOFIA: Anytime!

7.

JASON STARED STRAIGHT AHEAD, taking in his appearance, which was still a novelty. His eyes lost focus on the mirror as he ran his fingers through his thick beard. He knew it wasn't attractive. The scraggly brown hair that grew on the island made his face appear rounder and worked its way too far up in either direction on his cheeks and neck.

He gripped the hair hanging from his chin and held his hand there. He enjoyed the pull on his skin.

The running water, which Jason had forgotten, audibly changed pressure, lessening the amount of water pouring into the basin, but increasing the steam that worked its way up to the mirror, fogging up the lower edge. The water swirled into the drain.

Jason jolted out of his daze and back to attention. He passed his hand under the water before again tensing and pulling back. He adjusted the brass knobs, waited a moment, and tested the water again. Pleased with the results, he resumed his gaze.

With a sigh, he filled his hands with water and splashed his face. The water ran down his beard and poured onto the counter from his chin. A few trickles weaved their way down his neck and stopped at the collar of his T-shirt, absorbing into the gray cotton, turning it dark.

After shaking his hands off over the sink, Jason extended one arm, gripped his old bottle of shaving gel, and froze. With the other hand, he extracted his phone from his pocket and removed his grip from the shaving gel.

On the phone, he opened his Music app, selected search, and typed b-o-w-i-e. A list of David Bowie's most popular albums filled the screen, and Jason chose *Heroes*. The fifth most popular.

The screen displayed a rotating circle as the phone prepared to buffer and stream. Jason set it away from the water, and returned to the gel, no longer hesitating. He grabbed it, pried open the lid, and squeezed. Twice as much as he needed was in his palm.

"Damn." He laughed.

He ran the mound along his left cheek, then his right, and wiped the excess onto his neck. He tried to distribute it evenly and worked the gel into a lather. There was still enough gel to fill both his palms, so Jason rinsed his hands off in the water, which continued to pour out of the faucet.

Music hadn't played, and Jason again picked up his phone. Affecting a surprised smile and wide eyes, he snapped a wonky, shaving-gel beard selfie. He sent it to Blake, along with the caption "Here it goes." He rolled his eyes at himself.

As soon as he hit send, the smile on his face changed. Not at once, but slowly. And Jason still held his mouth open, but gritted his teeth.

Jason returned to the Music app and tried to play the song once more. Again, the loading wheel spun, and he set the phone down, waiting for his ordinarily reliable internet.

Without music or a convincing expression, Jason picked up the black, metal razor he'd sat next to the faucet. He ran the blades under the faucet and felt the water on his hand as it splashed and ran down the handle. Flicking the blade twice, he pressed it to his left cheekbone. He was ready to pull off the self-inflicted disguise he had worn, and been building, since he started his *Beached* experience. It was time. He had put this off for weeks, ignoring the itching, disregarding how much he now disliked his appearance.

He felt the wet blade against his skin, and anticipated the pulling, slicing, and rinsing-repeating monotony he had to look forward to. At the last moment, he removed the blade from his cheek and held it to his neck, inches below his Adam's apple. With no more hesitation, he pulled the blade up, and removed a chunk of his beard, from his neck to his chin, but took a small piece of his skin with it.

Jason groaned. Deep crimson blood trickled down his neck. He grabbed at it, wiping off the blood with his hand. As he reached for a tissue, on the other side of the sink, he again glanced at his phone. Spinning, but not playing.

MEANWHILE

HE RAISED the top of his laptop, slowly, and pointed the cursor to the Microsoft Word icon, tapping twice. He angled his hand towards himself and admired his fingernails. Freshly cut. Clean.

After a moment, he tilted back as far as his chair would allow without falling. His expression turned grave, and his stare focused on the blank page in front of him. He clacked his teeth repeatedly, taking pleasure in the slight grinding sensation.

This persisted for an uncomfortable few moments until a smile spread from the left corner of his lips and he was silently bouncing with laughter. He pushed his fists into either side of his jaw, cracking his knuckles, and hunched forward towards his keyboard. He began typing: "Cutting Reality: Murder, Heroin and Reality Television."

He again froze for a moment of manic analysis.

"Well, it's best to be clear from the beginning. It can always be changed later. Hell, I might go down, but I'll tell the damn story."

The faint glow from his computer screen created a halo of haze around his unkempt hair. With single-minded attention, he jabbed at his keyboard well into the night.

PART TWO

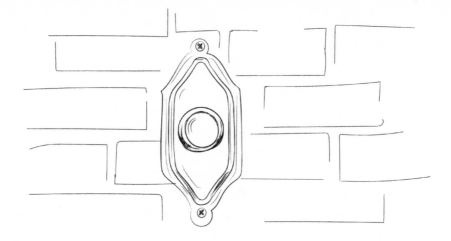

8.

JASON PRESSED the doorbell and tried to force a pleasant expression. Chimes rang, and an animal scurried somewhere beyond the door.

Without any trees to provide a blockade, he shivered as the autumn wind cut against his clean-shaven face. He'd been shaving again for nearly two weeks, but wasn't used to it yet.

Around him was a manicured front yard. Too perfect, he thought. The flowers were spaced out an even six inches, and the beds were filled with a mulch that looked fresh, although it was well into fall and only about fifty degrees outside. A basketball hoop was built into the concrete of the driveway where Jason parked his rental Volkswagen. While exiting the car, he noted a treehouse and swing set in the sprawling backyard, along with an in-ground pool. Birds chirped around him. Jason's house was suburban, but this was next-level.

Moments passed. He rang the doorbell again and added a few knocks on the wooden door. Lights were on and a car parked in front of his in the driveway. Someone was unquestionably home.

Blake had talked him into this visit, though he was nervous about the proposition. Part of him hoped that no one would answer the door. But he knew she was right; he needed to back away and have closure. He still suspected that someone was covering up something, but it didn't have to be him. Anything he found out came at too great a cost.

After again not receiving a response at the door, he threw all manners to the wind and pressed the bell repeatedly. Confidence was lost. He wouldn't be starting off on the best foot. That is, if someone let him start.

As he was giving up with the ringing, there was movement behind the tinted glass. Too tall to be a pet, even on its hind legs. Finally.

Jason straightened his shirt, stepped back, and resumed his forced smiling.

The door cracked opened and a woman of roughly Jason's age slid her head out. She was restraining a dog (it looked to be a beagle, though Jason couldn't be positive) behind the door. Billy's sister was attractive, he noted, but far too made-up to be his type. She had straight, platinum blonde hair, painted on eyebrows, blush, and pink lipstick. His smile turned genuine when he considered how well the house and neighborhood suited her, based upon the explanation Billy gave while on the island. The picture became realized.

"Emily Gerding?" Jason asked.

Her eyes widened, and she made a slight "Mm."

"Hi. We've actually spoken on the phone."

"Yeah. Look, this isn't a good time. Whatever it is, I'm sure my husband is setting it up, and we're about to have company."

"Um," Jason said, unsure how to continue. "I mean, I'm Jason Debord. From *Beached*. I'm, er, I was Billy's friend." He winced as it came out.

She frowned. "What are you doing here? What do you want?" "Well, I know you thought I was out for money or something.

I'm not. I'm having a hard time dealing with Billy's death. It's been driving me mad. And I wish that was as hyperbolic as it sounds. So I'm trying to come to terms with it, and atone for whatever role I may have played in not stopping it, or getting him help. I'm here on a pilgrimage, I guess."

"How did you even get my address? This is criminal. Get off my property. What the fuck."

"I-I got the address from a network friend. Billy gave your address and number as his emergency contact. And I have some of his stuff. Writings, things he saved on the island. So I called them and offered to deliver it to you personally if they'd tell me how to find you. And here I am. This felt like the right thing to do. I'm sorry if I upset you."

Emily's eyes darted to the manila envelope in Jason's hand and scanned to Jason's eyes. She didn't avoid eye contact.

"I thought you were convinced he was murdered?" Her tone was skeptical and, somehow, even more abrasive than it had been on the phone.

Billy's sister. But Billy had been so friendly. So informal.

"I, uh, well," Jason stammered. "So, I was having a hard time processing what happened, and the grief got to me. I believed crazy things. I thought someone was spying on me and broke into my house. It got out of hand, and I was trying to rationalize something I couldn't comprehend. I'm genuinely sorry if I alarmed you with all that."

Emily's brow furrowed. For the first time, she didn't seem on the verge of slamming the door in his face.

"Okay. Yeah. But, like I said, it has nothing to do with me or my family. We happen to share parents, and that was all a long time ago. Why are you here?"

"I know you say that, but I think one day you'll care. And you're the right person to have this." Jason held out the manila envelope.

Emily opened her mouth to speak and only exhaled. "Look," she began, but was interrupted by a shriek and the muffled, bass sound of running from inside the house. Startled back to her usual persona, she tilted her head towards the other side of the door and spoke again. "We want nothing to do with this. Whatever it is, just keep it, or throw it out. I made my decision regarding him, and nothing changes that. I can't help you, and I need to get my kids ready for dinner."

At once the door was again closed. Deadbolt thudded into place, handle lock turned. Jason took another glance around, feeling like a criminal or intruder. With his limbs tingling, unready to move, he crouched down and slid the envelope underneath Billy's only family member's doormat. Deflated, he hurried back to his car, eager to leave. He had known this would be difficult. Nevertheless, he'd seen an internal struggle within Emily that only amplified his emotions.

Flying here had been a last-minute decision after he realized that Emily had blocked his number and wouldn't accept calls from borrowed, unrecognized numbers. Jason had needed resolution, and a way to put Billy behind him. Blake had suggested visiting Emily and delivering Billy's things since he had time. She thought it could be therapeutic, and Jason had hung on to some of Billy's posses-sions with this exact intention. Inside the envelope was a piece of paper informing the castaways about an upcoming competition. Billy saved it because he had won the competition, and he was proud.

Additionally, there were three letters, written on paper Billy had ripped out of Jason's journal. Each was written to Emily and her kids. Jason hadn't read them, until recently, out of respect for Billy. Billy kept repeating similar things. He was sorry; he had done a lot to complicate their lives, but didn't know how to make it better. He needed a second chance. He loved them and wanted them all to be parts of each other's lives. Billy repeatedly referenced his and Emily's child-hood and adolescence together. It was the type of writing that was so generic and overly sentimental that it made no distinct impression on Jason, or any other outsider reading it, but it was liable to elicit tears and a change of heart from the intended recipient. If Emily found them, Jason figured, that openness he had glimpsed for a moment might take hold, and she could attain peace over Billy and his passing.

That was what Jason was after.

He backed out of the driveway, his car's shocks bouncing as he cleared the raised curb and returned to the street.

BLAKE'S OFFICE

"SEE YOU SOON," Blake texted Jason. He had just informed her that his meeting with Emily had not gone smoothly, and he would be on his way home that afternoon. Blake would be picking him up from the airport again. She returned her phone to the desk drawer and sat back up straight, staring ahead.

Carrie, a teenage client of Blake's, soon bobbed halfway through the doorway with a sullen look on her heavily foundationed face and mascaraed eyes. Her shoulders remained turned toward the doorframe. "Um, Miss, uh, Blake, do you have any more tissues or toilet paper or anything? The bathroom's out, and, like, I wasn't sure where to go."

"Sure, Carrie, I'm sorry," Blake responded. She rose from her desk and made her way to the front desk.

"Hey, Sydney," Blake said, "the bathroom needs tissues restocked. Thanks so much."

"Oh, sure thing," Sydney said with a gigantic smile. Blake noted that they needed to discuss Sydney's contrived emotions. Just because Blake's client was dealing with grief didn't mean Sydney needed to be the most jovial person on planet Earth. It seemed forced and obvious. But she meant well.

Blake returned to her office, and waited, again, for Carrie to return from the restroom. When she did, Carrie sat back in the green leather chair opposite Blake.

The whole way, she kept her gaze locked on her feet regardless of where her face pointed. Their earlier conversation had resulted in a red puffiness around Carrie's eyes and nose. But, she was no longer crying, and affected a newfound composure.

"So," Blake began, offering a moment of shared silence, "where were we before?"

"Well, we were talking about my sister. And the accident. And how it wasn't my fault."

"Right. And do you believe that?"

Carrie hesitated before nodding. "Yeah. I know it wasn't my fault. But I was driving, so the guilt I felt was a natural result of grief."

"I think you're right. But it also sounds like you're repeating what I said."

"Well, you're right. I need to move on. I can't let it ruin my life, too."

"Definitely not. But, it's something you'll always carry with you. It can't be gotten rid of immediately. Don't fake feeling better when you still harbor feelings that need to be worked through. Now, back to the guilt. Is there anyone you believe blames you?"

As with too many of her recent clients, this discussion felt all too personal for Blake, and she was struggling to force her teenage self to the back of her mind.

"No. I mean they couldn't. But they should. Or might." "Has anyone expressed this to you, Carrie?"

"Not exactly."

"Then what makes you think this way?"

After meeting with Carrie's parents a few weeks ago, Blake knew they only cared about their daughter's well-being. They were, also, having trouble dealing with the car accident that claimed their older daughter, Hellen. Blake also understood that personal responsibility was one of the most difficult elements of grief to shake. It was nearly impossible to stop feeling you needed to make it up to everyone. Or that it could have been prevented. No matter the amount of counsel, education, or reflection, it was a lifelong commitment.

"I see how upset everyone is," Carrie said, "and I need to make it better. Or say something. And I dunno what. And I could've driven a different way, or stopped to get gas or anything to, like, make us avoid that moment." At this, Carrie's eyes glistened again. "And the other driver could have been more responsible, or a cop could have pulled them over. Or they could have stopped for gas or gone a different route. Or they could have hit someone else.

There are always hundreds of alternative scenarios, but we need to focus on what actually happened."

Carrie nodded.

"Is there a way you can remember your sister, and honor her memory, for now? Something productive, instead of destructive, to you?"

"There're scholarships and stuff like that," Carrie said, "but those seem so fake. And everyone does it. It's not unique to Hellen."

"Okay, well, what would feel unique to Hellen? What makes you think of her, or what did she love?"

"I guess video games," Carrie said.

"Okay, what makes you say video games?"

"Well, video games. It was her obsession. She had every system. I'm clueless about them, but she always wanted me to game with her. She would play all day and night."

"That's a great topic to explore," Blake said. "And we're almost out of time for today, but you should brainstorm some ideas about how to best remember Hellen through video games. Maybe a charity event. I'm sure you'll come up with plenty of ideas, and we can discuss next week. Otherwise, it would also be a good idea for you to think about talking to your parents to discuss the guilt you feel."

Carrie nodded several times while avoiding eye contact. She might not be capable of handling that hurdle yet, Blake decided.

"Okay," Carrie said, standing up. "I'll think about what I want to say. What I need to, I mean."

"Great, and next time we can act out the conversation to make you more comfortable. Have a great rest of the day."

As Carrie left, Blake sank back into her chair, exhaled, and smiled.

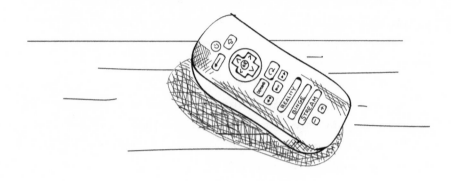

9.

"YEAH, that's great you backed off," Seth said.

"Mm-hmm. I think you were right the first time we talked. It seems impossible now that he could've been murdered, but everyone will still talk," Jason replied. "Another beer?"

Jason rose from the sofa and headed into the kitchen. Seth glanced at his phone. "Sure, thanks, man."

Jason grabbed two bottles of Guinness from the refrigerator, cracked them open, and reentered the room. Seth was still perusing his phone.

"So," Seth said without looking up, "what did the rest of your cast say? Were they in agreement with me? Or were they paranoid, too?"

Jason took a long drink. Without eye contact, he shook the dark, opaque bottle.

"Varied. Some people were ready to accept the suicide. Others weren't sure. They were more agreeable with what I was saying than you. But that was probably to appease me."

"Mm," Seth said.

Moments of silence passed, with Seth still scrolling on his phone. Jason couldn't think of anything else to say or ask.

"Well," Seth said, finally, "the episode is about to start. Shall we?" His glance turned up to Jason and the television.

"Hell yeah, this should be a huge episode. We vote out Dimitri," Jason said with a laugh. He grabbed the remote and turned on RTN.

"Damn it, dude. No spoilers." Seth pretended to cover his ears and close his eyes.

As the title sequence played, they watched a quick competition unfold. Swimming to a platform. Throwing rings at targets. Running to a finish line in the sand. Celebration. Hunter won and was safe from being eliminated. As the show went to commercial, Jason muted the audio and Seth returned to his phone.

"Man, that guy is amazing," Seth remarked. "And it doesn't stop soon."

"Anyway, what did the others think happened? Those who agreed with you at first?"

"I'm surprised you're still interested in hearing more," Jason said, "but Phoebe was on-board with suspecting Nick. Hunter was also kind of suspecting something shady. He said he had some weird interactions with his neighbors and had paranoia. But they might have been humoring me. Maddy was more hardcore. She wouldn't even talk about it with me. Will suspects a member of the crew, and he was intense about it."

"Whoa. Who does Will suspect?"

"I don't know. He freaks me out, always scheming."

"Hmm. Well, if you hear what his thoughts are, let me know."

Jason took a long look at Seth, who was still scrolling through what Jason assumed was social media on his phone.

"Like I said earlier, I'm done with that. I'm not going to talk to anyone about it again. I think I was losing my grip. Trouble adjusting. It strained my relationship with Blake, and I couldn't concentrate on work. I'm in a better place."

"Okay, Jason," Seth said. "I'm glad to hear that. But don't you think you should keep tabs on what people are saying?"

"Maybe, but it's back on." Jason unmuted the television. Between commercial breaks, Jason and Seth watched as

Phoebe expressed frustration with Dimitri during snarky confessionals, while Jason and Billy plotted to oust Dimitri to give them sole control over the team. Members of the other group, the former Kaukoi team, were made to look foolish, conspiring against Jason.

Jason grinned the entire time.

After again muting the audio, Jason said, "Well, finally looking like the edited TV show mirrors the way I saw it go down."

Seth still concentrated on his phone, typing or messaging someone, and Jason felt irritation swell. He was finally being made to look like the hero and rightful winner, but Seth didn't pay any attention.

"Yeah, nice one," Seth said.

"It's good to get screen time and see how my character is playing out on television."

"I'm sure. It'll be interesting to see how it changes in a few episodes. After Billy."

Again, they sat in awkward silence. As Seth typed away, responding to something new, Jason resolved not to be the one to start conversation again. Jason passed the moment in spite, unbeknownst to Seth.

"Anyway," Seth asked, "like we were saying, don't you think it would be good to know what everyone else thinks and what they're looking into? I mean, you started all this discussion, you said, so you'll be involved no matter what."

Jason shook his bottle, found it empty, and stood to get another beer. Awkward silences made it easier to drink more.

"Well, as I said, I'm feeling back to normal and everything. I'm better served by getting away from it. I mean, do you know something I don't?"

"Like what?" Seth asked.

"I don't know, man. You were the first person telling me I was crazy for looking into this, and how I was delusional and needed to drop it. Now, the next time we hang out, you're adamant I question people and keep pushing the issue. What changed?"

Seth frowned at Jason with a hurt expression.

"It's back," Seth said after a moment. He gestured at the television screen.

Jason sat, without a new beer.

After unmuting the television, yet again, and watching the group of contestants walk into the voting ceremony where they would eliminate one of their competitors, Jason turned the television off.

Seth started, after taking a moment too long to realize that the TV was off. He looked at Jason and slid his phone into his pocket.

"What's up, man? Are you okay?"

"It's recorded. I can watch it later. I want to know what's up with you."

"Sorry I'm on my phone so much. I have an essay due tomorrow and students keep sending emails, so I'm checking my phone regularly."

"It's cool. I didn't realize you were dealing with work. But why do you keep questioning me?"

"Yeah, I'm not trying to be rude to you. And, as for what we're talking about, I can tell it's upsetting you. I don't want you looking into this any further either, but I'm worried about you and your reputation. So I'm preoccupied, I guess, asking you about it to see how you are. And I'm a bit curious; this is all a new frontier."

"So you keep pushing it on me?"

"Because you started all this, and, no matter what, you're involved. And your mood is swinging so rapidly. First, you're super despondent, then you become paranoid and suspicious, and now you have this chill, zen vibe going on. All in a matter of two weeks. Are you down with this, or are you disengaging?"

Jason looked at the floor, waiting for Seth to continue. But he didn't.

Jason spoke instead. "I don't know. There's nothing there. I looked into everything. It could have been Nick, or the crew, or even RTN, or some government conspiracy. But I can't find anything. I need to move on. Unless you know something."

"So you aren't convinced it was suicide, then?" Seth asked. "I don't know."

"This is what I suspected, and I want you to find peace with it.

Not give up on your journey."

"How do I do that?" Jason asked. "Are you going to reach out to your friends on the island?"

Seth held up his arms. "I can. If that'll help you."

Unsure of how to proceed, Jason sighed. "Yeah, tell me what you find."

Seth stood, walked over to Jason, and put his hand on his shoulder. "Look, I'll do what I can. I'm just worried about the mood swings, and that you're faking this to mask something else."

Jason nodded.

"I'm getting out of here," Seth said. "I have this big assignment due tomorrow, and about a dozen more emails to respond to. Tightly wound freshman. I need to get that taken care of, but let me know if I can do anything else, and I'll continue keeping you posted on what I can dig up."

Jason stood and followed Seth towards the door. "Okay, man. Thanks for coming by. And thanks for caring. And helping and everything. Let's meet up after I get back from visiting Hunter."

"Yeah, have fun in Tennessee."

They hugged and Seth let himself out, closing Jason's door behind him.

Jason settled back into the same seat on his couch and pulled his own cell phone out of his pocket for the first time that evening to text Blake. He typed: "Hey. Can you come over? Or can I come over yours? I was just with Seth, and there are things I still need to consider. I think he has information, but I don't want this to take over again. You're all I have, and I don't want it getting between us. But I can't accept anything unless I ask a few more questions. There might be real leads to the truth."

Turning the television back on and finishing the episode, Jason watched Dimitri get eliminated and saw himself smiling with Billy and Phoebe behind everyone's backs. He felt guilty, seeing the deflation on Dimitri's face. And worse, thinking about Dimitri watching the episode at home in New York City with his friends. Jason would be there in a couple of weeks, visiting Dimitri, and would need to make it up to him.

When the credits rolled, fifteen minutes had passed and Blake had still not responded.

Jason's mind wandered, but after a few worried moments, his phone lit up with a notification. New text from Blake.

"Jason, I'm headed over now. I'm worried but want to hear everything. You've seemed much better, especially when I saw you at the airport yesterday, but whatever you need, I'm here for you."

MEANWHILE ON TELEVISION

NICK SAT, center screen, on a rock easily four times his size.

There were small pools of water dappling the rock, resting in indents, and reflecting the sun overhead. He shook his head and his jaw tensed, straining his angular face.

"I just can't decide."

He dragged his fingers across his left forearm. His eyes darted around as his body twitched along with them. After a few silent moments passed, his itch had turned into an aggressive scratching.

"Look. It might be time. I think I'm done with these people. Especially Jason and Billy. Like, I've never been part of those guys, and they're not looking out for me. I'm the one out here providing. I don't know why I don't get more respect. We've worked together in the game this far, but I'm done with them. For good."

He twisted at the waist and looked behind, out to the digitally enhanced turquoise of the Atlantic Ocean. Only his profile remained visible.

"I have to do it. Turn on them. We're not even friends, anyway, so I shouldn't feel bad."

━━

DIMITRI WAS SHROUDED IN DARKNESS, the fires licking his face and reflecting off his eyes. He wiped away welling tears.

He was seated on an unseen stool, without proper back-support, and his shoulders slumped forward.

An audible exhale.

"Okay. Well, I'm not sure who turned on me. [beep] Jason and Billy, I'm sure. Anyway, I wish those guys the worst of luck; I hope they don't win any money. And get eliminated soon. I'm rooting for Nick, now. He's the only one who takes this all seriously, and he's a good person. The rest of those [beep]."

He shook his repeatedly shaken head while the fire blazed as strong as ever. The screen cut to black, and Luke Stock's voice rang out from an unseen studio somewhere.

"Stay tuned and see what happens next week."

10.

JASON SWIPED his thumb upwards on his phone a few dozen times and watched his apps close.

"Fucking fuck," he muttered to himself.

He pressed the Maps app, which booted up and pinpointed his location as his home address in Cincinnati.

"Goddammit," he swore again. His phone was without signal and still unable to locate him in rural Tennessee.

He shoved the phone into his jeans and exited his car without closing the door. Glancing around, he saw he was as isolated as he had presumed from behind the windshield's containment. In each direction there was a breathtaking Smoky Mountain vista, along with a few scattered electric lines running up the mountain. A thick fog hung in the valleys, with only green pine needles piercing the gray. The sun pricked through the mist, filtered through the tree canopy, and was obscured by the mountains. The late October air was brisk, causing Jason's nose and ears to redden. He had to wipe his nose, but it wasn't cold enough for him to shiver, or feel out of place in his unbuttoned flannel shirt, T-shirt, and jeans. No, his phone was definitely wrong. Not Cincinnati.

The precariously attached road had no guardrail, but clung to the side of a mountain. He had found a small, partially paved area, where his car sat idling, door ajar.

Giving up on finding help from his surroundings, Jason took his phone back out and held it as high as possible, futilely searching for the elusive signal he knew would not come. He tried holding the phone in each direction, spun in slow circles, and walked far closer to the edge of the mountain than he felt comfortable doing. There was no enthusiasm or hope; he knew it was a lost cause. The signal was hitting the peaks and bouncing away from him. He knew this, but also felt helpless and needed something to do.

With a sigh, he took his place back inside the car. Glad he didn't need to reverse, he resumed driving up the mountain, resigning himself to reach for civilization again once he found higher ground. The mountain road crisscrossed back and forth, to prevent the gradient from becoming too treacherous, and he proceeded around the twists and turns, slopes and inclines.

Jason stayed in the center of the road, praying another car didn't come down the mountain while he went up. It all looked much the same. Pine trees, cliffs, deteriorating roads, and newly constructed log cabins. After driving, frustrated and terrified, for another ten minutes, Jason's fear was realized. And it was not merely a car.

Two bends in the road away, speeding toward him, an RV barreled down the steep incline. Jason froze. "There's no fucking way," he grumbled to himself. He tried to veer as far to the right as he felt was possible, and stopped there, cursing himself for not staying at the earlier, wider pull-off. Jason only hoped the massive RV might turn off, down some unseen road.

The approaching vehicle was painted electric orange, and had disco lights spinning in its interior with at least eight people inside. Bluegrass blared. Old Crow Medicine Show, Jason guessed.

He shook his head and sat, jaw clenched, waiting for the stressful pass. But it never came. The RV came to an abrupt halt a few meters in front of Jason's stationary Toyota. The driver exited, finished a canned beverage, crushed it, and threw it back inside. Perfect time for a beer, Jason thought. The man, with his long beard, knit hat, oversized flannel shirt and weathered jeans, approached Jason. He looked like he was from the travel brochures.

"'Ay, man," he yelled, waving an arm above his head. Jason forced a smile and exited his car.

"Hey."

"Uh, you mind gettin' outta the way? You got trouble or somethin'?"

"No, sorry. I've never been here and the roads are terrifying. I tried to move as much as I could." Jason glanced at his parking job and saw there were only a few inches between his passenger side tires and the edge of the mountain. "I don't think," he continued, "that we're both going to fit."

"Shiiit, man, sure we will. You want me to do it?" Jason studied the man's expression. "Do what?"

"Move that car over. So I can haul that big fella through."

Jason opened his mouth to say he didn't think there was any room and to mention the smell of stale beer exuding from his roadside companion, but a loud cat-call from the RV interrupted him.

Both men directed their attention towards the RV as another exited the pulsing vehicle.

"Holy fuck. That you, brother?" the third man yelled.

The other driver now directed his attention back to Jason. "Oh man. You're Hunter's friend from TV, ain't cha?" he asked.

Jason, relieved from the confusion and stress, let out a chuckle.

"Yeah, I'm Jason, from *Beached*." He held out his hand, which the other driver shook.

"AJ," the other man said as they shook hands. "I'm Hunter's brother." AJ tilted his head towards the approaching figure.

"Hey, Hunter," Jason yelled. His Midwestern voice always involuntarily took on a country twang when he spoke with Hunter, and he didn't bother trying to conceal the quirk. It was the product of living on the Mason-Dixon line.

"Welcome to the one and only Gatlinburg, Tennessee!" Hunter called back, holding his arms extended to either side.

"Thanks. Yeah, you weren't kidding about these roads. I haven't had a signal for ages and I've had no clue which direction I was headed."

"Lucky we ran into ya. You want me an' AJ to drive the cars past and clear up this roadblock?" Hunter had reached their side, and Jason noticed his island friend had gained back the weight he had lost while filming.

"Uh, sure, but you guys seem like you've been partying."

Hunter laughed and looked at AJ. "Hell, man, if you ain't had a drink or two, these roads'd scare you shitless. Everybody on this mountain's had a couple. Or some 'shine. Welcome to my world, man."

"That's reassuring," Jason said. His eyebrows narrowed, but he flashed a hesitant smile.

Hunter and AJ laughed, while Jason opened his mouth to speak again, but aborted the effort. For a moment, the three stood there and listened to the running motors of their cars: Jason's whirring efficiently, and Hunter's chugging aggressively. After being startled by a loud shriek from inside the RV, and the fit of laughter that followed, Jason shrugged out of the uncomfortable daze.

"Alright," he said, "go for it. Whatever you guys need to do.

Keys are in the ignition."

"Whoo," Hunter yelled and jogged the couple of paces to Jason's car. While he busied himself with adjusting mirrors, AJ made his way back to the RV and switched it into drive. AJ rolled forward, and Hunter shot into reverse with a tire squeal and minor dirt cloud. Jason could see him laughing through the windows.

Rather than trying to pass each other on the narrow road, Hunter backed the car down the mountain until he found a wider section. Jason walked along with the vehicles, wishing he had gotten into the passenger seat. Reaching a twenty-foot stretch that had an extra six inches of dirt and sparse grass next to the paved road, Hunter parked Jason's car, so it was now only mostly in the way. AJ pulled the RV up, and as they were parallel, AJ flicked him the finger and laughed, while some unnamed others continued to drink and party in the back.

Meanwhile, Hunter shut Jason's door and clapped him on the back.

"You comin' in the party bus, brother?"

"Uh, well, I need to get my car up to your house. I'm assuming this is the right road? I was lost until I ran into you guys."

"Oh, shit, yeah. I forgot you were coming over to visit. Good thing we bumped into each other, man. We're headed downtown to the strip."

"Okay. What do you want me to do?"

"You wanna go down with us, and we can drop you at the car on the way back up?"

Jason hesitated.

"Or," Hunter said, "if you keep headin' up the road, some of my family is home, and they can get cha set up until we get back."

"Would that be alright? It's been a long trip. I could use a moment of quiet. But then I'm all for hanging out."

"Sure thing," Hunter yelled over the RV's engine. He clapped Jason on the back again and ran to the RV without a goodbye.

Hunter growled, "I need a beer y'all, let's go," as he entered the vehicle.

Before that beer could have been opened, the RV was again speeding down the mountain.

⸺

"WANTED to let you know I made it safe," Jason said into his phone, which had, mercifully, once again found service with higher ground.

He was pacing through the bedroom Hunter's older sister had told him he could use. The entire house was a massive log cabin, and the decorations in his guest bedroom were so thematic that the kitsch bordered on creepy.

"Yeah, it was a bizarre journey. I didn't have service, and then I passed Hunter on the road in a huge RV. I'm at his house now, and I think he's getting dinner, but he'll be back soon. How was your day?"

As Blake filled him in on the details of her day at work, Jason picked up a golden bear sculpture on the dresser in his room. It was heavy and still had a price tag on the bottom. He read it with astonishment. Nine hundred dollars for the statue.

"Yeah, Hunter's house is super nice. It seems brand new. It's not what I pictured. We should have a fun time here. What do you have going on this weekend?"

Jason continued to pick up random items around the room. A mounted bass, a wood-carved clock. Each object still featured a price tag from the same store, still white and unweathered by time. The price from Smokey Suppliers on each was shockingly high. The duvet was covered in cartoon bears, but Hunter sprung for a hand-carved headboard.

"Well, that's awesome. Yeah, I'm sorry I can't be there. Definitely, text me your thoughts on the episode tonight."

As Jason set down a lamp, there was a knock on his door. He jumped. Hunter's sister, Victoria, stood in the door frame. When she had let him in, she was wearing a sweater and jeans. Now, she was wearing a black bikini with a towel draped over her left shoulder, and was holding a glass of something red and slushy.

Jason covered his phone's mouthpiece and greeted Victoria.

"I was seein' if you wanted to hop in the hot tub with a few friends and me, since you're here and all. Hunter kinda ditched ya." She transitioned to leaning on the door frame and did so clumsily. She laughed and gulped her drink.

"I'm finishing up on the phone, and I'll be down," Jason said with a smile.

"Okay. I hope you get in," Victoria said, before giving a brief wave and heading down the stairs. She held onto the rail.

Jason returned to his phone after pushing the door the rest of the way closed.

"I'm sorry, Blake. Hunter's sister came up and invited me to join everyone in the hot tub. Everyone here seems to be living it up. Fancy stuff and everyone's just drinking and partying. On a Thursday. Again, not at all what I expected from farm-boy Hunter." Jason laughed.

Jason was trying to sound dismissive of the situation, masking the confusion and concern that built with each new experience he had in Gatlinburg.

"Mm-hmm. Yeah, he should be back soon, and I'm sure we'll watch the episode. But I had better get going. I may seem rude, staying up here."

Pulling the phone away from his face, Jason finished their conversation. "Bye. Miss you."

As soon as he ended the call, he swore and put his phone on the nightstand. After a brief hesitation he headed downstairs, following Victoria's lead.

⸺⸺

HOURS LATER, A LOUD "WHOOP" came from the front door, startling Jason and Victoria from their place on the couch. It was a signature Hunter holler that Jason had grown to recognize and appreciate while they competed on *Beached*. In the background, the show had begun.

Hunter, AJ, and three girls Jason did not recognize but assumed had been within the RV, stumbled through the entryway, carrying a case of beer each.

"Sup y'all," Hunter yelled upon seeing Jason and Victoria. "Who's ready to watch some *Beached* in anticipation of your mother-fuckin' million dollar winner?"

The whole room looked at Hunter and cheered while clapping their hands a few times, but Jason felt uneasy joining in and just smiled.

"How many episodes then, bro?" AJ asked as he slapped his hands on Hunter's shoulders.

"Uh, like, five or six or somethin'. Shit, I can't remember.

Jason?" Hunter responded.

"Well, tonight is a double-feature of episodes six and seven. There are twelve total episodes before the reunion show. So, what, after tonight only six left. That's crazy how quickly we're moving along."

"Woo," Hunter yelled.

The entourage of newcomers settled onto the oversized sofas and armchairs surrounding Hunter's at least seventy-five-inch television. Jason sat between Hunter and Victoria.

"So, what are you thinkin' of the place, man?" Hunter asked Jason.

"It's not what I expected from Tennessee, the way you described it."

"Oh, yeah, we're all doin' it up while we can." Hunter laughed. "And hell, why not, with a payday comin'."

"Yeah, Hunter, who do you take to the end again?" AJ asked, interrupting their conversation. Jason tried to get used to pressing up against Hunter and Victoria, but remained tense from the contact.

Hunter laughed and gestured towards Jason. "This guy," he said.

AJ slammed his fist on the side of his armchair a little too hard. "Shit, man, I knew that. My bad." He laughed, louder than necessary.

Jason's ears grew hot. He wanted to change the subject, but with attention focused on *Beached*, he only hoped that they'd become engrossed in the show. His desires were realized. The next two hours of television went by with little conversation, other than some loud swears from AJ and Hunter during challenges, and a few comments from AJ about how much he hated Bailey, Nick creeped him out, and how much he thought Hunter was a "beast."

However, most of the silent viewing resulted from Victoria, two of Hunter's nameless friends, and Hunter himself all falling asleep.

As Jason's sofa mates both fell deeper into sleep, they became even more pressed up against him. Hunter's breathing bordered on snoring but wasn't drastic enough to warrant nudging him awake. So, he sat in entangled, overlapped displeasure and watched first Maddy and then Bailey get eliminated from the show.

The episode was nearly over, and Hunter and Jason were still not aligned in the game. Instead, Jason was working with Phoebe and Billy, his closest friends on the island. Realizing what the next episode would be about, Jason felt claustrophobic and had to stand. He headed for the restroom to compose himself. In the process of standing, the shifting weight woke Hunter and Victoria.

"Be right back," Jason called behind him.

When Jason returned, Hunter had the television paused, was turning to look at Jason, and had a much more somber expression than earlier.

"Thought you'd wanna see this bit."

Luke, the host, was in front of the camera with an expression that matched Hunter's. Jason nodded, and Hunter hit play.

What followed was a montage of Billy competing in competitions, making a fire, swimming, fishing, laughing, and interacting around their team's camp. While the footage was airing, Luke voiced commentary and reminded the audience that in the next episode, Billy's life would be lost. The promo had much more taste, Jason thought, but also knew RTN only had to alter their presentation after the fervor that the first promo had created. They had already captured the nation's attention, so now went for the sympathy and pulling of heartstrings.

As a final still image of Billy filled the screen, Luke made his closing statement. "This has always been a show that tested boundaries, relationships, and human reactions, but next week, boundaries will be crossed that we never considered. It will test contestants in new, unheard-of ways as they not only grapple with the conditions but also losing someone they grew to know and care about. As *Beached* continues, we at RTN are humbled and horrified by Billy's loss, and encourage our audience to take the time to love those around them, raise awareness of depression, and always get help."

The screen flashed to black, and the words "Dedicated to Billy Gerding 1989–2025" filled the screen. Next, the National Suicide Prevention Lifeline phone number and website appeared. 1-800-273-talk.

No one in Hunter's house spoke until Jason broke the silence. "That'll be hard to watch."

"Yeah," Hunter said, "I feel extra bad. Profitin' a bit from his death. Are people gonna hate me?"

"No way, or they'd have to hate both of us and we're two goddamned loveable guys."

Hunter stood up and leaned over the arm of the couch before talking at a whisper so only Jason could hear. Everyone else was beginning to stir anyway, cracking beers, getting snacks. "RTN's been asking me a lot of questions; have they talked to you?"

"No, what have they said?"

"This whole thing is fucked, brother. I didn't know if you saw the gifts they send." Hunter nodded at the kitchen, where a lot of packaging was scattered. Jason hadn't paid it any thought. "That's some props and stuff from the show they thought I might want. They also sent some champagne. All they've said is to remind me of my NDA. Makin' sure I wasn't gonna do any press. They seemed really interested in whether I enjoyed my experience. It made me uncomfortable. Like, I couldn't answer whatever the subtext of what they were sayin' was. They didn't do any of that to you?"

Jason shook his head.

"Well, I do not know what in the damn hell that means. But it gives me a whole helluva lotta pause. Did you see anythin' weird out there? I know you talked about suspicions in the past."

"I don't know, man. I'm trying to move past it. Plus, that all sounds like good stuff. They haven't said a word to me. I have to say, I'm a bit jealous. Have they talked about you going back on the show?"

Hunter nodded. "Yeah. I would too. But, damn. Let me know if you hear anything else. This all makes me feel so off. Guilty conscience, almost, but I have no reason to."

TEXTS

27 OCTOBER 2025, 9:46 AM

SETH: So how was the trip down south?

JASON: Oh, man. Illuminating. I got back yesterday and Hunter was nothing like he was on the island.

SETH: That happens to some people, I've heard—how so?

JASON: I'm kind of freaking out about it. He thinks he won.

SETH: Oh, bizarre. Could he have? Are you positive it was you still?

JASON: How could I be? But he didn't play a good game. He only won competitions. And everyone I talked to said they voted for me to win.

SETH: I dunno. It could've been him. Would you be ok with that?

JASON: I mean, no. I should win. I know the game, and I deserve it.

SETH: I don't doubt you. But maybe prepare for it?

JASON: Yeah. It's just now, even if I win, I'll feel terrible because Hunter is already spending the money and he needs it.

SETH: Well, you can't control him. Don't let it get to you.

JASON: Yeah. It was just rough. I haven't really been able to do anything since I got back because I'm so worried about it.

SETH: I'm sure, he's a friend.

JASON: Yeah. Hard. But I have amazing news—my cats are home!

SETH: What?! That's awesome, man!

JASON: Yeah, thank you so much. I can't believe how much I was freaking out about it and creating some crazy explanations. I think they were just around my neighborhood, maybe caught in someone's garage. They seem fine and already adjusted back to normal. Tigger was here when I got back, on the porch. The next morning I went out with food in case London was around and she came running out from behind the shed.

SETH: That's great. See, nothing to worry about.

JASON: Speaking of, have you found anything about what we talked about?

SETH: I thought you wanted nothing more to do with any of the "crazy theories"?

JASON: I don't. But you were the one who brought it up. I was just curious. And Hunter kind of weirded me out.

SETH: Hmm. Well, I've been having trouble getting any other information. People seem reluctant to talk.

JASON: I thought these were friends?

SETH: I mean, it's not like we're family. And their jobs are potentially on the line. This is pretty serious. Plus, you have to admit, murderous plots within a reality show make me sound like a fucking nutter.

JASON: Thanks for that...

SETH: Well, anyway, the only person who would give me anything was Omid.

JASON: Yeah, I thought about reaching out to him. He was great on the island, and afterward. What did he think?

SETH: He said things are a little shifty. He's nervous around other crew members. And he said there has been huge employee turnover between seasons. Much more than normal.

JASON: So RTN is investigating and clearing house?

SETH: Maybe. Or maybe it's natural for people to leave the show after someone under their care dies. It's traumatic. That's what you're dealing with. Omid's feelings are pretty natural too, right. I think it all seems like a bunch of nothing.

JASON: Hmm. Yeah. I suppose.

SETH: Anyway, I guess this is to say that there's nothing fishy going on with the staff or crew.

JASON: Nothing they told you.

SETH: True, I guess. But I thought it'd be useful for you to cross that one off. I know you're trying to get some peace out of all this. Just trying to help.

JASON: Yeah, well, I was at peace, and you brought all this back up.

SETH: Hey, I'm sorry. You didn't have to tell me to talk to them. You could have dropped it.

JASON: I know. It's not a big deal.

SETH: Cool. Then, you mentioned Hunter was weird?

JASON: Big time strange. Like I said, he was partying like he won. He's also told me twice that RTN is in regular contact with him. Like, keeping tabs. And sending him gifts, reminding him not to talk to the press, honor his NDA.

SETH: Huh. That does seem strange. So what do you make of it?

JASON: I really don't know. It's like they're trying to keep him quiet.

SETH: Does he think he saw something?

JASON: He's suspicious of the crew, asked what I'd heard. But I don't know if he was holding back.

SETH: Okay. Well, I'll keep reaching out. Let me know what else I can do. Or if you need someone to talk to with the episode coming up.

JASON: Will do.

SETH: See you at school! I need to get you a copy of a short story I'm trying to publish. I'd love your thoughts.

EMAIL

DESIREE.ZIMMERMAN@GMAIL.COM
Date: 27 October 2025 11:18 am
Subject: Checking in before Friday

JASON!

Long time, no talk. Hopefully, you're enjoying the season. We're halfway through! It's hard to be excited, though. I know the next episode will be tough for all of us, especially you. I didn't start on Billy's side like you and Phoebe, but I lived with him for three weeks, and I'm still struggling to come to terms with what happened. That's why I'm reaching out.

Phoebe came over to visit last week, and we watched episode five together. We weren't too far away—she was in Denver for work and made the long drive to Santa Fe for the weekend—so we've been hanging out. It's weird for you not to be here, especially after the three of us worked together so closely in the game. And Hunter. Have you heard from him? I can never get in touch.

Anyway, we got to talking about you and Phoebe's strategy, and why you two flipped on your original team after Billy died. And we talked about Nick. Phoebe was saying troubling things about Nick, and it got me thinking. It seems crazy to even consider, but I'm not sure I disagree with her. She also seems convinced that you're the person to get in touch with about this. When she visited you, I guess you two discussed your mutual suspicions?

I'd love to hear from you and have your input. I had tried to bury everything, but after talking to Phoebe, and hearing you are suspicious of Nick, too, I've been thinking. I just feel weird.

Thanks, Jason. It's good to know you're looking at this critically, too, especially since it seems like RTN is just ready to capitalize on it in any way possible.

Much love,

—Desiree

EMAIL

JASON,

Hey! How's my favorite conspiracy-driven lunatic holding up? Hopefully, better than my old team is on the television show. You're picking them off!

So, on to the point: stop spreading your fear-mongering! I already heard from both Phoebe and Desiree, asking me leading, prodding questions about Nick. He's got a screw or two loose, but there's nothing to him. It was one thing when you were out after big-bad RTN, but Nick's one of our own. Like him or not. It'll mess with both of your reputations, and it makes you sound a little crazy. You have nothing on him.

He'll want revenge if this gets out, and I can't protect you from getting the shit kicked out of you at the reunion. Which is coming up! Shit, just a few weeks.

I know this has got to be hard on you, but I don't want to be getting any more calls from people asking questions about some "Billy murder conspiracy." People are trying to get me to abuse my resources and look into Nick's past, pull records on camera operators, and all kinds of shit that would lose me my job.

So, just this once, I pulled a few files that might help put this to rest. Because we're friends, and because I don't want to see you ruin yourself over this one. And, hell, to get people off my damn back, too. They're attached. They're documents from when Billy was admitted to a state-run psychiatric hospital about fifteen years ago. They were easy to find online. No clue how this all got past RTN. Unquestionable negligence. But Billy had a history of depression. There's nothing else behind this.

Let me know if you need me to clear anything else up. I'm here for you, brother, but I can only go so far with you if you don't see reason and facts.

Ronn

ATTACHED: billy_records.pdf

EMAIL

DESIREE.ZIMMERMAN@ GMAIL.COM
Date: 31 October 2025 02:35 am
Subject: ???????

JASON,

I still haven't heard from you. What's going on? I wrote days ago, and I'm freaking out. Not sleeping well and everything. Phoebe seemed to think you were serious about this. Has something happened to you? Let me know what I can do to help. Phoebe says she is in to help as well, but I haven't heard from her all day either. Do you think anyone else knows we're talking about this?

Also, I spoke to Ronnie and he thinks we're crazy. He may be in on something. Best not to involve him any further.

Please get back to me. The episode airs tonight, and I don't know if I'm ready for it. Something has to be done. We're running out of time. I need answers, and I may have information you need. I did some digging.

Sorry for rambling. I haven't been sleeping. Reply as soon as you can.

—D

11.

UNSURE OF AN APPROPRIATE time to end their hug, Jason broke away from Blake. He felt off. He couldn't cry even though he felt like crying, and couldn't take comfort from the hug though he desperately wanted to. Everything was numb with anticipation and dread as though his consciousness was filtered through tunnel vision. He wasn't sure what to say or do, and his foggy mental state was crippling. Blake, likewise, didn't know how to proceed and rubbed Jason on the back.

"It's so good to see you. I missed you," Jason said.

"Mm-hmm. It sounded like you may have had a good time with the never-ending Hunter party and the girls everywhere. Asking you to get in the hot tub."

She had managed a laugh from him. "You have no idea," he said with noted sarcasm. "Or how glad I am to be back. Hunter seemed rich after presenting as a humble hillbilly on the island. He was partying hard, too. That experience was bizarre. "

"So we won't be making that a vacation stop?"

Jason shook his head, and Blake continued to beam a small, supportive smile.

They were standing in Jason's doorway, ready to spend a few minutes together before the episode began. The fateful episode that Jason had felt looming since he left the *Beached* island weeks ago. Episode eight.

"Are you hungry or anything?" Jason asked. Blake shook her head. "Something to drink?"

Jason moved past her into the kitchen. She followed but stayed behind in the adjacent dining room. After only a moment, he leaned around the corner, holding two bottles of red wine.

"I thought these might be necessary tonight," Jason said, "so I got a whole case."

"Cabernet?" Blake asked.

"You know it," Jason said. As they shared a smile, Blake grabbed two wineglasses from the bar cart behind the dining room table.

Jason poured an over-sized amount of wine into each glass and held his up to clink hers and make a toast. Blake, determined to follow Jason's lead for the evening, tentatively followed and they stood with their glasses raised, looking each other in the eye.

"Well, it's only fitting we toast Billy. He should be—"

Before Jason could finish, his phone vibrated from the living room, interrupting him. He glanced in that direction, but continued, "Billy should be here, watching, if not with us, with his family and friends. No matter what happened, and no matter who caused this. He was a great guy as far as I knew him."

Blake took a long drink while watching Jason through the distortion of her glass. He never took one.

Instead, Jason had his eyes locked on the painting that hung on his dining room wall, and he held the gaze as a crutch, preventing him from succumbing to emotions. The painting was one he'd bought from a gallery in Liverpool, visiting friends. The art had no particular value and was by an unknown artist, but it intrigued Jason. It depicted a horse, painted in realistic detail, but with skewed proportions, as if viewed through water. The head was massive, and its legs were too tall and curved. The background, however, was what fascinated Jason, and why he'd bought it. Rather than maintaining the same Dali-esque style in the background, the artist had gone with an impressionistic cityscape that looked like it belonged to a different painting entirely. The decision puzzled Jason when he bought it, and it served as a distraction now as he tried, and failed, to understand the artist's meaning.

The phone vibrated, yet again.

"Do you want me to check that?" Blake asked. To Jason's surprise, she was no longer beside him but had moved into the living room.

Breaking away from the painting, Jason shifted his gaze to his glass and shrugged. "We know what it's about."

"True." Blake picked up the phone, anyway, before walking back to the dining room table and placing it, face down, next to Jason's wine glass.

Jason put his arm around her shoulder, and she pulled closer towards him, both hugging each other intimately. Jason's shoulder dug into Blake's ear, and she pulled out of the hug but left her hands around Jason's waist.

"Thanks for being you," Jason said.

Blake removed her hands. "Oh shut up," she responded with a smile that Jason returned. Both expressions were limp and distracted.

Jason picked up his phone.

"Phoebe, Desiree, Dimitri, and an unknown number. I guess I should send responses. Desiree has been emailing me, and I haven't been able to reply yet."

Jason clicked through his phone in silence.

"What did they say?" Blake asked.

"What you'd expect. Phoebe is asking how I am, telling me she's distraught. Upset that whoever did this is probably watching the episode. Desiree is the same but also asking if I got her emails. Dimitri's checking in, making sure I'm okay and telling me to come visit."

"That's nice of them to reach out. What are you going to say back?"

Jason paused and took a long drink, finishing his first over-poured glass. "I don't know. I'm not sure I want to be a part of this anymore. Everything is jerking me around. Was this murder, was it not? Should I ask questions, or let it be? Phoebe and Desiree are running away with their theory about Nick. Half the cast thinks I'm crazy and the other half is pushing me to ask questions."

Blake nodded and waited a moment before proceeding. She took a big gulp of her wine, following Jason's lead.

"What about the unknown number?" she asked.

Jason's eyes lit up at the mention and he began a silent chuckle. "Yeah, that's the good one," he said. "See for yourself. Some dick's messing with me."

Jason dropped his phone on the wooden table with a thud. "See, people think I'm mental," he said as Blake picked it up and read a lengthy text message aloud.

"Jason. Do not reply to this message," she began, "or we will have no further contact. What you know is true. I have proof. It is time to act, or we may never stop the forces behind this. We both know what must be done. They're at large and tonight is the perfect night to expose them. Since you remain a public figure, you must be the one. Doing nothing with this knowledge is tantamount to committing the act. Do not be suppressed. I believe in you."

Blake's eyes widened as she smirked at Jason. "Wow, I think you're the chosen one," she said.

Jason nodded, but the smile fell off his face. "Yeah, and they're a massive asshole. It's in bad taste, too. Regardless of what they think of me, this is still the night we see Billy die. That's classless."

"Yeah," Blake said, "but you should respond to your friends. It's good to have a sense of community during this time. And the episode is about to start. Let's refill our drinks and get set, so we don't miss it."

Jason grabbed the two bottles of wine. "We'll just bring these with us," he said, and the two transitioned into the living room, which was decorated for Halloween. It had always been Jason's favorite holiday because there was no expectation of family bonding. Decorations were only nominally present, however. A few spell books on the mantel, cotton spider webs in the corners of the windows, horror film posters hung where there were typically modern prints, and twisted candelabras on either side of the television.

There would be no masks on the day this year. Instead, all would be laid bare.

The two sat a cushion-length closer than usual on the sofa. After a few minutes of discussion about Jason's strategy in the game, and which moments might make the episode, they noticed the opening credits rolling. Jason unmuted the television and tossed the remote to his side. Blake grasped his hand, and their attention focused on the spectacle about to unfold before them.

━━━

JASON AWOKE TO THE "DA-DOING" of his phone alerting him to a new message. He fumbled behind his head for the phone which rested on his headboard. First, he felt the charging cord, which he pulled to bring the telephone within his reach. He winced and narrowly avoided dropping the phone on his face. He located it once it bounced onto his pillow. He squinted through the early morning darkness his bedroom curtains provided, and closed one eye, straining to look at the bright screen. His other eye shot back open when he realized he had fourteen new messages and it was only 6:00 am. Panicked, he set the phone back down, resolving to respond later, and instead agonized over what messages he had drunkenly responded to the previous night. He hoped he hadn't, but the number of messages made that hope feel misplaced.

One more hour of sleep, Jason thought, as he flopped onto his side, wrapping the covers around his legs and appreciating the comfort of his newly purchased king-size mattress. It was a luxury he had allowed himself after sleeping on sand, sticks, and bamboo. As he raised his leg, however, his heart rate spiked again when his leg collided with another. Blake's.

He had pulled the covers off her enough to see she was only in her underwear, as was he. Combined with this cover shift, his leg contact caused her to stir.

Jason pushed, with pulsing pain, into the void of his mind, searching for anything. Any details. Under normal circumstances, when he would forget hazy events of an evening, he would ask Blake. They would always piece things out together, which seemed out of the question now. On his own, Jason recollected only brief, albeit significant, snapshots of memories from the previous evening. Kissing Blake against his refrigerator. Her fumbling to unbutton his shirt. Hoisting her onto his countertop. Her legs around his waist. The softness of her curled hair. Her smile as she pulled her dress off. Feeling the comfort of her shoulder as he kissed her neck. Her matching black underwear. The smoothness of her legs. Grasping her thighs as she climbed on top of him. Holding her face in his hands. Content to never move again.

Jason wasn't sure how to act. Their handful of flings had never felt serious. Something about the moment was new territory, and he wanted to act appropriately.

As Blake made her first waking movements of the day, Jason locked his eyes shut and feigned that he was just waking, too. Without relying on sight, he felt Blake's arm ease over his side, and her body press close against his, under the covers. She exuded a warmth to places he had been unaware were cold. All of his emotions were corny, but he took comfort in them instead of pushing back.

"How about breakfast?" she whispered in his ear. "We never ate last night."

Relief crept over Jason as Blake's body continued to envelop his. This was all he needed. Who cared if there was some conspiracy and the world was corrupt? Hadn't he always known that? He had what he needed here, and he was happy with Blake. Wasn't living just creating a sustainable life for yourself that made all the complete shit tolerable? The only words that would come to him were Jack London's. "Lame," he told himself.

The proper function of man is to live, not to exist. I shall not waste my days in trying to prolong them. I shall use my time.

A student had used the words, now echoing around Jason's aching head, to begin a recently submitted essay. Jason had considered the words, and essay, to be vague and generic. But now they had newfound resonance.

Jason rolled over and kissed Blake on the mouth, leaving her with a surprised grin overtaking her face.

"I'll take that as a yes." Blake slid out from under the covers, sat on the edge of the bed, and bent over to grab her orange dress from the floor. After the fabric slid over her head and fell over her body, she turned around to Jason's stare.

"Geez," she said, pulling on sections of her dress to straighten it out, and threw the cover at him.

"What can I say, you look good."

With a raised eyebrow, Blake asked, "Well, are you coming?" "In a minute," Jason replied. As she left for the kitchen, Jason was left with his thoughts, and he appreciated the distracting clanging of pans that helped prevent his mind from lingering on the fit of Blake's underwear.

After mentally preparing himself, Jason rose, threw on some sweatpants and yesterday's T-shirt, before following the sound of sizzling bacon and soon-to-be-boiling water in a kettle. He found Blake chopping an onion and put his hands around her waist.

"Hey, thanks. I can help." He kissed her once on the neck. "Sure," Blake said, continuing to chop. "What'd those texts say?"

"Oh, yeah. Shit, I don't know."

"Your phone was blowing up all night; you didn't check?"

"No, I don't want to bother with it. Whatever. It is what it is," Jason said, trying to avoid the topic.

"Well, that's quite a change. From dogged pursuit to speaking in clichés. Why don't you see who it is?" Blake's face revealed concern.

"Alright." He walked back into the bedroom, choosing to remain in the moment's bliss, and not concerning himself with what may wait for him in his Messages app. He unplugged his phone, and pressed his thumb to the fingerprint reader, awaiting it to reveal whatever "urgent" contact he had received.

It was all Dimitri. He had been messaging until 4:30 am. Jason's head shook with bewilderment at the exhaustion of New York City bars as he read through the progressively later and less coherent messages.

Dimitri was upset about Billy. He knew what Jason was going through. He wanted Jason to visit him in the city. That was the gist, anyway, once Jason weeded out the typos and made assumptions about misspellings and auto-corrects.

The display of friendship was welcome to Jason in his newfound place of acceptance. His diaphragm eased and he typed.

He got no further than a "Ha."

His gaze at the phone intensified, until he was no longer looking at the phone, but allowing his eyes to go out of focus, in rejection of reality. There was no easy way to put this. Dimitri's messages revolved around the idea that preoccupied Jason: Billy's death and his suspicions. Jason had resolved to put this behind him, but if he could pull that off, what was he prioritizing? Was it time for him and Blake to begin a traditional relationship? What would anyone think of him? Would Blake want that? Was he giving up his principles when things got challenging? How does one articulate any of this to a friend, nursing a hangover, through a short text message?

Jason had always defined himself on his words and mastery of language. From elementary school, where he relished each chance to read aloud, until his adult career, where he taught writing. He spent evenings and weekends reading and dissecting the English language. When he met people at parties, Jason said with mocking pretension that he was a teacher, and student, of the English language. How many people knew him and remembered him solely by this association? What was his identity without the English language? He was a word person.

And, now, the English language failed him. Not that this was a particular failing of English—he had no German or French, either. It was words. What had always been Jason's defining trait was abandoning him.

And, hadn't his investigation and care for Billy's murder supplanted this defining trait? Had English spurned Jason, or had Jason turned his back first? His mind was foggy.

Without the language or the investigation, who was he?

"You free next week?" Jason typed into his phone. After hesitation, he added, "Are you cool if Blake comes to visit, too?"

The middle path.

MEANWHILE ON TELEVISION

JASON SAT, legs crossed, surrounded by dense jungle. A vine hung above his head and leaves rested against his shirtless, gaunt body. It was unclear which supported the other.

"He's struggling. A lot. I mean, I think betraying Dimitri is still driving him mad. A lot of guilt there. But he's also getting paranoid. I guess he's worried who'll stab him in the back. But, he won't sit still and rest in the camp. He won't even talk about the game. You know, he still provides fish and everything, like he has, but he's always all over. Climbing, hiking, searching around. It's like he's trying to escape or something. Can someone tell him we're on an island?"

He smiled, revealing teeth that were a sharp contrast to his tanned skin and thick beard. He shook his head at the end of a silent laugh.

"It doesn't matter. He can keep acting like a caged animal, ignoring the game and the money we're playing for. But, nothing's more important right now. I'm focused enough for both of us. And I'll get us to the end, because I know he's with me."

As the camera panned back, it cut to different footage.

A jaguar stretched its front paws forward, arching its shoulders, and yawned. It perched on a flat rock. The camera continued to pan back, and revealed an impressive shot of the jaguar, sleepily stretching on a rock, comfortable on the side of a cliff, hundreds of feet above the jungle. After moments, it returned to a full lying position.

⌑

A LONG-SHOT of five people came into focus. They hunched in a circle, sitting on pieces of driftwood. Long shadows extended behind the bodies. A fire occupied the space between them, and occasional flames rolled up the log a few inches off the sand. The sun, now only a faint light source, was visible on the horizon across the beach. A dark shape pierced the glow, crossing the sun's path in the water. Two of the anonymous figures looked out to sea, in the disturbance's direction.

"Is that Luke?" Phoebe's voice was clear over the others' low mumbling.

Everyone rose and faced the boat, now within the frame, and waited as the shadow of a man stood on the bow. He wore a floppy-style cowboy hat and button-down shirt that blew in the wind.

Phoebe spoke. "I'll go get Nick. He's back in the shelter."

One figure rose from the fire circle and walked off-screen.

Moments passed and she returned with another figure.

"What's going on?" Nick asked as they approached the others. "We'll find out. Anyone know where Billy is? He'll want to hear this," Hunter said.

Jason nodded. "I think he went for a walk."

Luke had made his way off the bow of the small boat that brought him ashore and was taking the final steps of his approach.

The camera angle got closer, right over Nick's shoulder, and the remaining contestants' faces were visible: Jason, Hunter, Phoebe, Desiree, Nick, and Kendall.

Luke nodded at them. His eyes were narrowed, with arms hanging at his sides. He looked them all up and down before opening his mouth to speak.

"Well, guys, why don't we all take a seat?"

Luke nodded at the logs the contestants had sat upon moments earlier. After they had resumed their places, Luke took an open seat next to Jason.

"I'm sure you're wondering why I'm here. It's about Billy."

He paced his words. Slow. Intentional. And they hung in the air while the camera panned from face to face to face. Concerned reactions. Blank reactions.

"He went for a walk, maybe an hour ago. But we can't find him," Jason said.

Luke looked at Jason directly and nodded. "We found him. And he won't be coming back to camp. We don't have much information at this point. But, it appears he had an accident and fell from the cliff. Our crew found him, and the medics came immediately, but it seems it was too late."

He stopped and looked around the circle.

"I'm sure this is a huge shock to everyone. So, I'll give you a moment to take it all in. In a few moments, I need everyone to get in the boat with me, and our team will speak with you individually."

The camera lingered on Phoebe's face, which hung, motionless, staring into the fire.

"Wait," Nick said. "What? Are we coming back? Is the show over?"

Jason was shaking his head to Phoebe's side. The camera cut to Nick.

"We have yet to make any decisions," Luke said. "But, that will be determined, in part, by you all."

The camera rolled backward and shook. Nick's voice could be heard.

"Get this [beep] camera out of my face."

———

BILLY'S FACE filled the screen, and the camera pulled back as he bent over, laughing. Jason, face engulfed by a grin, slapped a hand on Billy back. Billy stood, and the camera lingered on his smile. Orchestral music rose and fell throughout the scene.

It cut to Billy in the water, swimming amongst a reef. He floated at the top, spear in hand. After a moment of motionless drifting, he darted through the water, and let the spear fly. The camera followed and caught the spear piercing a large fish.

It cut to Billy, again laughing, standing around the fire with Jason, Phoebe, and Dimitri. Billy danced, hopping from foot to foot, slapping his thighs, and rotating in a circle. The others tried to follow his lead. After moments they were all reduced to more consuming laughter.

Cut to Billy, dozens of feet off the ground, chopping coconuts out of a tree, with Jason and Dimitri on the ground gathering them. Billy held out his left arm and flexed his bicep, laughing. Jason and Dimitri cheered.

Cut to Billy sitting in the group shelter, surrounded by the rest of his team. He told an unheard story, with everyone's gaze locked on him. Maddy shed a tear which she quickly wiped away.

Cut to a long shot from behind Billy. He was walking along the beach at sunrise, alone.

The screen faded to black.

MEANWHILE

FINGER BY FINGER, he pulled the glove off his right hand, then his left. It was tedious, as the cheap plastic stuck to his sweaty skin. He threw them onto his desk, in a heap of blue plastic and white faux-fur, next to a yeti mask.

He leaned back in his chair, then closed and rubbed his eyes, trying in a futile effort to wipe the alcohol from his brain.

"Fucking Billy," he muttered, "America's darling. I think I need to change that a bit."

As his eyes shot back open after the momentary respite, he searched the room, resting his gaze on a waste bin to the left of his desk. The room was lit solely by the white glow of a computer monitor.

Plunging his hand into the bin, he pulled out a discarded paper Starbucks cup. Giving it a half-hearted shake to measure its contents and a raised eyebrow of resignation, he pried off the lid and shot the liquid down his throat.

After redepositing the cup, he turned again to face the desk.

"DYING FOR GOOD TV: WHAT WE CAN LEARN ABOUT OURSELVES FROM BILL GERDING'S UNTIMELY DEMISE"

PATRICK SCHMITEAU, ENTERTAINMENT NEWS NOW

OAKLAND— Billy Gerding did not kill himself, as the media and Reality Television Network have told you. In fact, you have killed Billy Gerding. I have killed Billy Gerding. We have all killed him.

Let that sink in.

This moment has been foretold by countless dystopian novels. We have finally reached the point of killing people for entertainment. While it may not have started here, and it may not yet be to the level of a nation-wide killing sport, we are here nonetheless. Watching death for fun is no longer confined to the dark realms of 4chan's anonymous message boards. It is no longer the fluke incidents of criminals posting their acts to social media. No, death for entertainment has entered our living rooms in the form of a family show. And we should all be ashamed because we asked for this.

In the 90s and 00s when networks began pumping "reality" television into our homes, we lapped it up. We neglected our real lives to watch sensationalized versions of other people's artificial, producer-developed lives. We watched, discussed, posted, read about, and allowed ourselves to be consumed by the fights, affairs, sexual exploits, failures, triumphs, betrayals, and over-the-top lifestyles of those who graced our screens. We tuned in to intimate moments of individuals and groups, and have become a twisted culture of voyeurs.

This cycle, now, has reached its logical conclusion. When cyclical decades of hook-ups, fights, and drama could no longer entertain us, reality TV responded. Like the twisted false-god it is, reality TV delivered more—as it always has. And it offered up Billy, and his family and friends, as a sacrifice for our perverse entertainment. Billy is the first offering at the altar of our cultural decay, but will he be the last?

Looking at the viewership and ratings for this season of *Beached*, I can only posit that he will not. The show has returned to the level of "cultural phenomenon," and has regained much of its depleted fan-base. These people, somewhere along the way, became immune to images of people suffering, starving and fighting. But now, they've been given more. It's been taken to the extreme, and they have returned.

When you turn on that television in your home or access those episodes on your phone or computer, you are casting a vote. A vote for what you want our society and its entertainment to look like.

Not only that, you are choosing to consume something that will alter who you are. It will desensitize you. It will shape you, your beliefs, and your actions. Don't forget this. And don't get caught up in the societal progression from innocent bickering in the 90s to death for entertainment in the 20s.

It's your choice—do you want good TV or good society? We've already sacrificed Billy Gerding—and we need to not forget him. But, think, who could be next? And when will it be someone you know? When will it be enough? After all, this has finally become too real.

12.

JASON MINDLESSLY CYCLED through his usual sites. He typed in "the-guardian.com," and scrolled for a moment before accepting that nothing globally significant had happened since he last checked, four minutes ago. The process continued with the *Atlantic*, the *New York Times*, and *Wired*. Convinced he was wasting his time, and that there was no fitting distraction, Jason returned to the browser tab that housed his email. Nothing new had come through. He was restless. Restless, despite the chaos he knew he had created out of his life, and anxious despite the growing stack of freshman literature essays he needed to finish grading in three days. And now he couldn't find anything worth reading online any more than he could slog through another interpretation of *The Handmaid's Tale*. Everything was overwhelming and unrewarding, but he was out of options.

With a glance at the stack of essays on his desk, Jason picked up a pen, removed the cap, and wrote. He made his list on the back of a handout from the previous morning's department meeting.

1- Message Blake
2- Decide about Billy course of action
3-Grade 10 essays
4-

After twice resting his wrist on the page to write, Jason scratched out the "4." He studied the list. It wasn't much. He feared wasting another day and the resulting paranoia that would prevent sleep.

He typed out a message to Blake, reviewed it momentarily, and hit send. He studied the words after he couldn't take them back.

"Hey! Are you free next week at all? Any interest in a trip to NYC? We can stay with Dimitri. I'd love for you to come!"

His quick, cavalier accomplishment shocked Jason. It looked acceptable, he imagined, though he couldn't stop himself from over-analyzing every word and punctuation decision. Was the word "love" too strong? Would she see through his exclamation points and notice an awkward hesitancy in the message? He wanted his words to be casual, but the short, choppy sentences conveyed hurry.

Now annoyed with himself for an entirely different reason, he turned the phone face-down on his desk. He picked up his pen and crossed out the first line of his list. "On to the next one," he mumbled.

With his eyes focused on his computer screen, Jason navigated his way to an article he had already read three times that morning. "Dying to Save Us: What We Can Learn About Ourselves From Watching Billy Gerding's Untimely Demise."

He scanned the article, yet again. He knew what it said, but needed to figure out what he thought about it. Was this a fitting end to the culture's voyeuristic tendencies? Was this what pop culture created? Jason didn't buy it. It was rare, but people died making art, television, films, music. And, frequently, because of sports. Billy wasn't the first. People were outraged not because of his death—they chose outrage over greater sympathy because they didn't deem the show he died on worthy.

These were the same critics that mocked reality television and decried it as the death of culture in the early 2000s. Had he died while making a biopic, or driving a race car, they would decorate him with awards and call him a hero. But now, it was a tragedy that showed humanity's ugly face—not because we will let people suffer for our entertainment. No. This was a tragedy because it was a reminder that people watched reality TV, something the media tried to ignore, and Billy had to be some ignorant rube if he went on the show. This wasn't worth it.

Jason felt himself getting worked up. This wasn't the first time the article had made his blood pressure rise.

The familiar vibration of his phone on the Formica desktop broke his trance. As he assumed, it was a response from Blake.

"Yeah!" Blake's message read. "I can take off any days from Friday through the following Thursday."

Jason smiled, glad Blake had also used an exclamation point.

Another message came through.

"But," Blake continued, "you need to figure out how you feel about Billy and make a plan for how you're going to talk about it. I don't believe you're fully past it, and you need to be. You need to tell the studio about your concerns, because all the rumors and swirling speculation aren't good for you or your persona. Any more weird text message since Wednesday?"

Jason glanced from phone to computer and back again.

Without pause, he typed, "You're right. I'm going to. I need to face it head-on, gather real info, interviews from other cast members, and get it all assembled so I don't sound crazy. As usual. I just need to understand the full picture, I think. Will you help me? You're amazing."

His message was far from perfect and contained none of the sentiment he wanted to convey, but it would do. For once, he didn't re-read it after hitting send.

Again clutching his pen, he made another list:

> Phoebe: suspicious of Nick; maybe production
> Desiree: suspicious of both production and cast
> Ronnie: believes it was a suicide
> Hunter: clueless—fame gone to his head?
> Dimitri: unknown
> Will: on drugs?
> Nick: potential suspect—unstable

Jason sent off a quick message to Dimitri, notifying him of their upcoming travel plans. Dimitri sent back a thumbs-up.

Jason exhaled. Now if I can finish some of these goddamn essays, he thought, and crossed through item number two on his list. Three times.

BLAKE'S OFFICE

SYDNEY PACED THE OFFICE HALLWAY, stopped before Blake's door, and knocked twice.

"Come in," she heard Blake call, muffled through the closed door.

Sydney turned the handle and peered in. Blake was typing on her laptop, transfixed by the screen.

"Hey, do you have a sec?" Sydney asked.

After a moment, Blake finished typing and closed the screen.

"Sorry. Yeah, sure. What's up?"

"Well, I know you mentioned you were taking personal time next week, and clients are calling to book appointments. Do you have firm travel plans, so I can get the dates?" Sydney asked.

"Yeah, you need those. I'm so sorry. I'm excited to be going, which is distracting while I'm trying to get all my work done ahead of time before we're in New York."

Sydney shrugged. "Hey, no worries. You've got a lot. It's no problem at all."

Blake pulled her planner over her laptop and flipped to the next week.

"Okay. I'm leaving Monday evening, and I'll be back on Friday afternoon. But, I'd prefer if nothing was scheduled until the following Monday. We're taking the train, so I'll be a little drained. I can't imagine I'll sleep well on a train car."

"Great. So I'll block out Tuesday through Friday. And if I need you at all while you're gone?"

"I'll have my phone on and answer during normal office hours. If it's an emergency, don't hesitate. We're visiting some of Jason's friends, hanging out, and doing a few touristy things—nothing I can't step away from."

Sydney's usual smile had extended to a grin while Blake had been speaking, which made Blake shift in her seat.

"Have fun, girl." Sydney winked at Blake before turning and exiting the room. She closed the door behind her.

Blake's cheeks flushed, unsure of how to process Sydney's behavior at the end of their conversation. After moving her planner, she reopened her laptop and reread the last few lines of what she had written in the open report before resuming her breakneck typing.

Yet, she stopped short again.

It had been a morning full of interruptions. Her phone was ringing. It was the front desk. Blake felt apprehensive about answering it but saw no other choice.

"Yes," Blake said, holding the corded phone to her ear.

"Geoff, on line three, looking for you."

Geoff was a client suffering from post-traumatic stress. An Army veteran in his early thirties. Blake's clients were typically adolescents, but she had adult clients. Working with them was different and sometimes required much more contact.

"Absolutely. I'll pick it up. Thanks, Syd."

"Sure thing." Sydney hung up.

Geoff had been the client for whom Blake was typing up a report only moments prior. He'd required a lot of attention lately and she worried about him. After collecting herself, Blake pressed the "3" on her phone.

"Hello, Geoff?"

"Hey, doc, how you doin'?"

"I'm okay, Geoff. How are you?"

"Well, that's kind of why I'm calling. Our meeting last week was great. And I slept well over the weekend. I did. But, the last few days or whatever, it isn't happening. I dunno what to do. I figured you could fix it. It worked last time."

Geoff sounded antsy. Restless.

"Well, Geoff, as we discussed, there's no easy fix. It'll take work to get through this. But you can and will. We'll keep working on tools to help and I'll talk through it with you."

"Yeah, yeah. What should I do?"

"It depends. What's been preventing you from sleeping?"

"I can't power down, you know. Like, I just think about everything. All night. And as soon as I fall asleep, I wake up and have the compulsion to do something. Right away."

"Okay. Have you tried any techniques we talked about? Reading or journaling when you wake? Doing something relaxing to get through it?"

"No. I mean, I need to do something. Like, active."

Loud construction noises beeped and slammed in the background, offset by an occasional car horn. Geoff was walking somewhere quickly, based on his heavy breathing.

"Okay, well I think that writing may be a good practice for you. But, if you feel the need for movement, have you been exercising throughout the day? Getting outside?"

"Yeah, usually. Most days. And I haven't been drinking. I've been avoiding caffeine. And I'm only sleeping in my bed and everything. It's not working."

"I'm sure that's difficult, Geoff. And that's great you're taking those steps. I'm encouraged that it was helpful for a few days. There are some further accommodations you can make, but let's go through your routine."

"Look. I've done what we said. Isn't there, like, medication or something? Hook me up. I need to sleep."

"There are prescriptions, but I'd like to try some further behavioral modifications before we rush to medicate. Those drugs have several side-effects you'll want to avoid if possible."

Geoff began a coughing fit on the other end of the connection.

"Do you want to come in and talk in person? I'm happy to meet."

"Yeah," Geoff said. He cleared his throat. "Look, I gotta go now. I'm meeting someone about work. But, thanks again for this. I'll try the writing when I wake up. And I'll try to book something soon to go over the routine. I need to find a job, too. I know the VA will cover it, but I gotta eat and all."

"Of course, Geoff. I'm here to help you however you best see fit. Let me know how the writing goes. That's been helpful for many people who've experienced what you're going through."

"Alright, thanks, Doc." Geoff hung up.

Blake returned the phone to her desk, tilted her head to either side and refocused her attention on her laptop. She sent a quick, one-line email to Sydney. "Make sure to book Geoff for an appointment soon; I'm worried about him."

13.

THE TRAIN JASON and Blake were waiting to board looked like a relic of a forgotten era. When it pulled up, Jason was surprised it still moved.

"Wow," he said. "Think they have Wi-Fi?"

The tickets he had purchased, which would take them from Cincinnati to New York City, had been cheap. They were finding out why. In their minds, the scene had been surreal and timeless, as they thought of soldiers leaving for world wars and lovers' last rendezvous before being torn apart by time and space. The current surroundings, however, destroyed any sense of illusion before it could begin. They stood on gravel, littered with crushed cans, discarded snack wrappers, and the occasional broken shards of glass. There was no glamorous train station, only a waiting area outside, amongst the filth. Filth that was only visible because of the fluorescent overhead lights surrounding the awaiting train crowd. Beyond them, the night was shrouded in 3:00 am darkness.

"Just wait until you're on board for twenty-four hours," a man standing in front of Jason said, over his shoulder.

"Whew. Well, we're getting off in New York, so it shouldn't be that long," Jason said.

The man gripped his backpack straps and faced Jason with a grimace.

"Me, too. We'll see how long it takes. The company's published estimates are a tad idealistic."

He offered a weathered half-smile and tilted his head towards the train. There was finally movement inside the doorway.

Blake made widened eye contact with Jason and smiled.

"Alright! Sorry for the wait, everyone. We'll get you aboard now. Line up, please. This way, this way."

Jason couldn't see the man calling to the crowd. They were clustered together with a few dozen people, each looking groggy given the 3:48 am departure time. Arrival in New York City was scheduled for 7:13 pm, but that was now in doubt after hearing the input from the man in front of Jason. He spoke like a seasoned train rider while this was Jason's and Blake's first time. Flying was their usual preference, but they had decided the train would be an experience. Something unique.

The cluster of people distilled into a line, and Jason lifted their duffel bag in anticipation.

"Have your tickets out," the man called from inside the train. "Here you are, watch your step."

"Wow, I am ready to go back to bed," Blake said.

"Yeah, me, too. Yesterday was long, and I feel like we didn't even sleep."

"Agreed."

Blake yawned, influenced by the conversation.

"There it is," Jason said.

"Yeah. The train should have lots of room, and we can actually get sleep."

The line was advancing and Jason could just see the conductor. He took up most of the aisle, and those whose tickets he punched had to squeeze and shimmy to get by him. He had a thick, gray mustache that dominated his face.

After each person boarded the train, he made a "hup" noise, as if it pained him to allow anyone aboard. After a few more groggy minutes, the line filtered through, and Jason was having his ticket punched and shuffling through the train's aisle. Blake was steps behind him.

The train met their expectations. The chrome exterior gave the appearance of an Airstream trailer, but it was replaced inside by white plastic paneling and bright, red carpet and seats. Everything was discolored from sun-bleaching and the wear of countless feet. It left the panels yellowed, and sections of the carpet were more pink than red.

Jason glanced at his ticket, trying to decide where he needed to head. The morning mental fog was clouding his ability to function. As he tried to fight through it, he read his ticket. Next to "Seat" it read "To be assigned."

"Do you have a seat number?" Jason asked Blake.

She checked her ticket.

"No. To be assigned."

Jason looked around. Most of the seats were empty. The few people seated were mostly sound asleep or watching a movie with headphones in. Only one seat light was illuminated. A man sat reading under the narrow beam. He looked distinctly Amish, with a scraggly chin-strap beard that hung a few inches off his jaw and a straw hat planted on his head. His clothes were worn but clearly hand-made. His ancient, country appearance was in stark contrast with the train's attempt at space-age decor.

"Keep on moving. Everyone needs to be seated."

The conductor was advancing on Jason and Blake.

"Excuse me," Blake called to him.

She employed her polite-as-possible tone.

"Our tickets don't have a seat number. It says they'll be assigned."

"Right," the man responded. "You, ma'am, will have 9B, and you, sir, have 27D."

As he spoke, the man jotted down the seat assignments on a notebook he had pulled from his shirt pocket.

"Oh, actually, man, we're together," Jason said.

The man looked up from his notebook and nodded.

"Great," he said and walked away.

Confused, Jason called after him.

"We're just going to snag two of these spare seats here, then."

The man halted and turned to face them.

"You've been given your assigned seats, and you need to sit in them. We're picking up more people in Pittsburgh, and you need to sit in the seats you've been assigned." He enunciated his syllables too hard, with focused clarity, and his eyes darted around the train without ever settling on a target.

"But you assigned them. Can't you just give us different seats?" Blake asked.

"They've already been assigned. I can't change assignments."

"Can't you change the note in your notebook? It doesn't seem hard. I don't want to sit next to a stranger for fourteen hours because you say so," Jason said.

"Sir, you need to sit where I tell you, or I will have you removed from this train. That is the final word."

Jason shot Blake a look of exasperation. He shook his head and muttered under his breath.

"Fucking hell. What an asshole."

"As you take your seat," the man said, "I will remind you this is a family train and you need to watch your language. Again, a repeated incident will have you removed from the train, and your tickets will not be refunded."

"So we seriously have to sit, like, twenty rows apart because of your ego?" Blake shook her head.

The man stood, resolute, still without eye contact.

"Fine. I guess let's take our seat. Hopefully, someone will switch with us," Jason said.

As they walked through the aisle the train moved, and they both had to shift to their back feet. They lurched forward. Row 9 came first, and Blake sat in the aisle seat. Next to her sat a middle-aged woman listening to headphones. She was dressed in such a variety of pinks it caused Jason to halt and stare. A faded pink hat sat atop her head while she also wore a hot pink T-shirt and clutched a pale pink backpack. Her shoes had pink accents around the laces and soles. Fortunately, she wore black leggings.

Returning his gaze to Blake, Jason tilted his head and made an expression of disbelief. She mirrored him. They were both too tired to laugh.

"Well, I guess let's try to get a nap and then we can have coffee in the dining car, together," Blake said.

"Sounds good."

Jason held Blake's hand, squeezing it as he walked away from her.

As she watched Jason proceed down the aisle, Blake stared after him. Holding hands had caught her by surprise. Years of close friendship and traveling together, coupled with exhaustion and the frustration of boarding the train had almost made her forget that the two were now actually, if not officially, a couple.

She was unexpectedly uneasy. This was what she had wanted, but fought, for a long time. And she was thrilled it was what Jason wanted, too. But she worried that he might be subconsciously using their relationship as a distraction from the *Beached* chaos.

In the days before their departure, they had discussed it. Jason said that wasn't the case, but Blake had her concerns. Something still felt off with him. He was detached at random times, and back to himself at others. The psychiatrist inside her wanted to fix things and help him work through it, but she knew he needed time and space to process what had happened. Any meddling on her part would be to the detriment of their relationship—not only romantically, but as friends.

This trip would help address a lot of doubts and questions. But now, she was forced to watch Jason take his seat from a distance, and that relationship building would have to wait. Tired but restless, she dwelt on both her desire to talk about their feelings and her fear of doing so. His holding back was making her hold back. Further stasis.

Unaware of the impact of his hand's grasp, Jason continued to walk the aisle and counted rows. Moments before he got there, he determined where his seat would be. Right next to the Amish guy he had observed earlier.

"Hey," Jason said.

Jason arrived at the row and had to attract the man's attention before he could slide past him and get to his window seat. The man had taken the aisle seat, but at least he was eerily wide awake at nearly four in the morning. He tapped his knuckle on the inside brim of his hat, acknowledging Jason, but keeping their interaction at a distance: he hadn't even turned his head or shifted his gaze.

The man didn't stand, but angled his legs to allow Jason to pass, and Jason figured that was the best he'd get.

With little space, he held his duffel bag out in front of him and scooted past his new seat-mate. With a thump, he fell into his assigned seat and pushed the bag under the seat in front of him. It didn't fit all the way and stuck out half a foot into the space at Jason's feet. He would manage.

Without looking, he felt the Amish man's gaze. The discomfort made Jason forget the earlier disagreement and he considered what the man next to him was thinking. Jason had never met, talked to, or in any way interacted with, an Amish person. He didn't understand what their beliefs were beyond rejecting electricity. They were, he assumed, anti-materialistic and religious. But he had no idea.

The discomfort only froze him momentarily. He met the man's gaze and nodded. The man repeated his earlier knuckle tap. Jason wished he was sitting with Blake.

He turned around in his seat and looked down the train. He saw Blake. She was closing her eyes and looked like she was trying to stick to the plan and make the best of their situation. She was always the better one. Jason knew he was more often the petty and irritable one.

Jason wanted this trip to be an example of how strong he and Blake could be together. He was finally committed to their relationship and mourned the years he'd let slip by. Years of false starts and ill-advised hook-ups lay behind them. He wanted to use this New York trip to prove how good he could be, not as a friend but as a boyfriend. More than anything, he wanted her to be happy—something Jason frequently impeded. And the trip was not starting off according to plan.

With a sigh, Jason stopped watching Blake try to sleep. She still hadn't noticed him looking at her. Instead, he faced the front, forced his head back against the seat, crossed his arms, and resigned himself to sleep.

That sleep, however, was stymied by the nauseating smell of the man sitting next to him. Did Amish people avoid deodorant, or was this the smelly guy of the clan? He found himself trying to differentiate the mix of smells. Something human. Something animal. Something sour. Something foul. All a blur.

"WELL, I don't know what else to do," Jason said. Hints of fog lingered at the end of each word. It only made him colder.

He slid his phone back into his pocket after staring at it, waiting for something to happen. He and Blake stood in front of a large Brownstone apartment building in Brooklyn Heights. Jason's phone informed him it was 11:15 pm. As forewarned, the train had been late by four hours. And, as Jason could have predicted, Dimitri wasn't reliable. Jason hadn't heard from him for over an hour and they had been standing outside the address he had given them for twenty-six minutes.

Blake put her arm around Jason's back. Their shared duffel bag was at their feet on the concrete.

"It's cool. He'll turn up," Blake said, though her voice lacked enthusiasm or certainty.

Jason transitioned her embrace into a hug, stretching to hold his arms around her backpack. They held each other. Despite the cold and frustration, feeling Blake against him made the tension in Jason's back release, and he could breathe.

"Typical Dimitri," he said as he pulled out of the hug.

He slid his hand into her hair and kissed her on the forehead.

"Whoa, your nose is freezing," Blake said.

"Yeah, well, it's like eighteen degrees out."

Jason shook his head and scanned the street. People walked by every few minutes. They stared but returned their attention to the sidewalk when Jason caught their eye. If he and Blake were in a worse neighborhood or didn't have luggage at their feet, the situation may have been more disconcerting.

A man in a well-fitted suit and a black woolen overcoat was deep in conversation on his cell phone when he shoved past them. He sneered at Jason, who stared at him out of sheer boredom. Jason overheard the word "mutually," but nothing else.

A group of three twenty-somethings, wearing a variety of Burberry-esque pea coats, shuffled into a single-file line to get past Jason, Blake, and the bulk of their bags. The first two to pass averted their gaze to the pavement and continued their conversation, which involved "tapas," "finally," and "break." Jason wasn't entirely listening because the pity the last woman gave him was too striking. As she passed, she ran her hand through her long black hair, frowned, and looked at Jason with drooping eyes.

Jason's gaze followed them as they reformed, filling the sidewalk, and he heard one say, "Yeah. That sucks so much. It's so cold."

Before he could express how annoyed he was with the not entirely misplaced compassion, Jason was distracted by what he saw beyond the girls.

"Oh, shit. Here he is," Jason said. "Thank god."

Dimitri was heading towards them, but his pace was irregular. Two steps straight, and the third off to the side. His left hand was shoved in his pocket, and his eyes stared intently at the ground in front of him. The other hand was locked at his side, carrying a case of beer.

"Unbelievable," Jason said.

Dimitri was three buildings away and had yet to notice them.

"He's drunk."

The hand in Dimitri's pocket fumbled around, searching for keys. Once he found them he looked up, grinning.

"Hey, hey There they are," he yelled from five feet away.

Dimitri dropped the beer and drew Jason into a crushing hug. They stumbled backward from the embrace. It had little in common with the hug Jason had ended moments ago.

"You made it," Jason said. He was doing a lousy job of masking the irritation in his voice.

Dimitri nodded, still smiling at them.

"This is Blake," Jason said and extended an arm.

Blake held out her hand, but Dimitri grabbed her in another enthusiastic hug.

"I'm a hugger."

"I am, too. Nice to meet you."

Jason could tell she was forcing a polite tone. She was as annoyed as he was but wise and controlled enough to not take it out on their host.

"You, too. This is so great."

Dimitri hadn't sensed anything wrong. He was blissfully drunk.

"Well, you want to get inside? We've been freezing," Jason said.

He adopted a more direct tack. Jason wanted Dimitri to know they were a bit annoyed, but he aimed to avoid confrontation. It wasn't that big an issue, and his friend was pleased to see them. Plus, he'd expected it.

"Awesome. Yeah. Winter is here." Dimitri hadn't stopped grinning since he'd caught their eyes.

He picked up what Jason could now see was a case of Brooklyn Lager and pulled keys out of his pocket.

Walking up Dimitri's steps was uneventful. He had evidently made the trip while inebriated many times and Jason and Blake had only brought a backpack and duffel bag. The inside of the building was average, which surprised Jason because he knew Dimitri to be extravagant. The steps had thinning carpet, and many of the hall's lights were burned out. The vague smell of Chinese food polluted the air. Someone was watching an action film in the building, and they could make out the reverberations of machine-gun fire.

Once Dimitri had undone both locks on his apartment's door, however, Jason and Blake were treated to a more elaborate setup.

Before them was a mounted deer head, complete with eight-point antlers, above a fireplace. He'd draped Christmas lights from the antlers. A solid-tin Christmas tree reflected the lights off its silvery surface. As Dimitri flipped more light switches, Edison bulbs dangling from the ceiling illuminated more of the apartment. It was cavernous and decorated as eclectically as Dimitri's Christmas entrance display.

The floor plan was open, and Dimitri moved into the kitchen area as if he was gliding, with no tour of the apartment. He ripped the top off the cardboard case of beer, pulled two beers out, and then a third. The bottle opener was already on the counter.

"Welcome." He thrust the drinks forward.

"Thanks, man."

"Yes, thank you," Blake added.

"Of course! I'm so glad you guys made it! I doubted it would ever happen. So many false starts with the plans, and then the train delay—who travels by train, anyway?"

"Well, hopefully not us ever again," Jason said, flashing a commiserating smile at Blake.

"Eh, you're here now." Dimitri held out his beer, and they touched the bottles together.

"To *Beached*," Dimitri said.

He was affecting a deep, formal voice, like a sports announcer.

"For bringing me together with other great people."

The three stood there in content silence.

"I'm so sorry," Dimitri finally blurted out. "Let me show you guys where the room is, and you can get your stuff put up and unpacked or whatever you need."

He set his drink down hard and walked out of the kitchen, turning to the left into a dark hallway. By the time Jason grabbed his duffel bag, and Blake put her backpack on, Dimitri was well out of sight. Jason, in disbelief, shook his head with a laugh.

"I thought," Dimitri called from the hallway, "well, I have no clue what your situation is. Are you two sharing a bed? Someone could sleep on the couch. You let me know."

Jason and Blake followed his voice.

"We'll share the bed," Blake said. "Thanks, though."

"Well, Jason talked about you on the island, but I could never tell. Sorry."

Jason maneuvered his jaw back and forth, unsure of what to say. While he pondered a response, Dimitri had turned the lights on to their bedroom and the spare bathroom.

"Here you guys go. Get your stuff together and come back to the kitchen. We must finish that beer and play some games."

"Thanks, Dimitri," Jason said.

He and Blake went into the room while Dimitri bounded back down the dark hallway, humming. Moments later, loud electronic music poured through the apartment.

"Well, he's exactly as advertised," Blake said.

"Glad you get the experience."

"Yeah, are you up for a few drinks, or are you too tired? I know you didn't sleep much next to your train buddy."

"I could go for a few drinks. You? I'm happy to go to bed if you're tired."

"No, that sounds good."

Jason threw his duffel bag onto the rhombus-shaped bed, which had no less than fifteen quilted pillows on top.

"Are you going to unpack?" Blake asked.

After a moment of consideration, Jason responded, "No, I never really unpack. I'm fine living out of the bag for a couple of days."

"Okay, me too. Off to drinks, games and, apparently, EDM and taxidermy."

THE NEXT MORNING at breakfast Jason typed into his phone under the table; "Thanks for being so great. Again, I'm genuinely sorry." He hit send and hoped the message would reach Blake before she returned to her seat. She had gone to the bathroom seconds ago, leaving Jason with Dimitri at their brunch table. They were at some trendy Brooklyn restaurant for bottomless brunch, which Dimitri swore by. Jason had forgotten the name. All three had ordered mimosas, which had arrived and been refilled twice. They still waited on omelets.

Jason was groggy, but knew it was nothing compared to the hangover Dimitri was surely nursing.

They had stayed awake until after 2:00 am the previous night, playing tabletop board games, drinking the rest of Dimitri's beer, and having a good time telling stories, laughing, and listening to Dimitri's eclectic music collection. It had been a great evening until the end, for which Jason now apologized.

He had pissed Dimitri off, but that was fine. Dimitri had started it and probably had limited recollection of the conversation. He was more worried about Blake.

"So what's the plan for tonight?" Jason asked.

"Should be great. A bunch of other people who live in the city are joining to watch the episode. Some are coming from nearby. Plus friends, other former contestants, everyone's dates. It should be a massive party. I can't wait. And the place we're going, The Abbey, is awesome. You guys will love it. And it's a good spot to watch the episode, too. Not too loud."

"Wow. That's quite a get-together," Jason said.

"Yeah. It's getting close to the end, and we're all here. It's a good time to support each other."

As Dimitri finished his sentence, he slowed the pace of his speech and trailed off. Jason could feel the tension in the words. So, he was wrong. Dimitri remembered some of their confrontation from the previous evening. He caught himself staring at the door to avoid commenting and took a sip of his mimosa. He was at the bottom of the glass, and before he could set it down a waiter was there with a refill.

"About last night—" Jason began, but Dimitri cut him off.

"It's cool. Not here."

Jason did care that he had pissed Dimitri off. More importantly, when he discussed Billy with Dimitri he had hoped they would be in agreement. Dimitri had spent as much time as anyone else with both Jason and Billy. Yet, he had such a different perspective.

"You're right. Not a brunch topic."

"Not even worth mentioning. I'm over it." Dimitri waved his hand.

Jason's phone vibrated, and he appreciated the distraction, but was nervous about Blake's reply.

He opened her text. "You don't need to be sorry. I've wanted you to talk about your feelings all along. But yelling at Dimitri at 1:30 in the morning is not dealing with anything. I'm not mad at you, but I am worried about you. I love you."

A wave of relief, then a wave of guilt.

Before he could write "I love you" in return, Blake was back at the table, pulling her chair in beside him.

"So, have you guys talked about tonight?"

"Yeah, Dimitri told me about all the people coming and how great the place is. Should be epic."

Jason tried to communicate with his eyes what he wanted to say to Blake, but it wasn't that successful.

"Awesome. So who is coming?" Blake turned her attention to Dimitri.

"Loads of people," Dimitri said. "A bunch of friends from around the city and almost half the *Beached* cast. It'll be us two"—Dimitri gestured towards himself and Jason—"Hunter's flying up. I still need to hear about his mountain cabin in Tennessee; I haven't had time to visit yet. Maddy's already in town from L.A. and staying with a friend from high school. Phoebe plans on driving down—she's just over in Jersey. And Nick will be here because he's moving from Atlanta and using the day to apartment hunt."

"Nick's coming? And, moving?" Jason asked.

Blake's eyes were on him and Dimitri studied him, each calculating how to proceed.

"Is that a problem?"

Jason composed himself.

"No, no. It's fine. I can be in the same bar as him, but he makes me nervous. I worry about him, and people say a lot of things."

Jason hadn't done enough to placate Dimitri, who stared him down. He sat with his elbows on the table and jaw clenched. Jason worried he was about to get punched across the table.

Instead, Dimitri pushed himself back from the table.

"You know what. Fuck you, man." Dimitri's voice was a little too loud. He stood and walked away before turning back. In Jason's peripheral vision, the entire restaurant stared.

"Here's the thing, for you I don't think the reality show ever ended. You need to wake up because these are real lives, not just some entertainment. For most of us, once they call 'cut' we go back to reality. Our actual lives. But not Jason, with his reality TV obsession. No, you're waiting for someone to call 'cut' on these scenes, this narrative, you're constructing out of reality. Well I have news, buddy. Your life, our lives, aren't a show anymore."

"Look, Dimitri, I was trying to be impartial. That was harsh. I'm sorry about—"

"Nah. Don't even. I've spent more time with Nick than you did and he's one of us. You don't know what you're talking about. I've heard everyone's whispers."

"Seriously, Dimitri, I don't know what I said. I was shocked he's moving here. It always sounded like he had it so good working in banking in Atlanta." Jason tried to save the situation for Blake's sake. Despite the conflict, he was most sorry this was happening to her. He'd experienced similar blow-ups with Dimitri and knew he'd calm down. This was part of why RTN cast him for television. He always went for the kill.

Dimitri's voice took on a calm tone. "Well, I'm out of here. You don't know Nick's story, so you need to keep your ignorant thoughts and suspicions to yourself. How shocking—someone in banking moving to Wall Street. I know what your reaction was about. Come back to reality, Jason."

He offered one last parting shot. "And you can get the tab, big winner." After two steps he turned his back and slid out of the restaurant.

"Should we go after him?" Blake asked.

Jason shook his head. It'd be more of the same.

"Let's have a day together, the two of us. This might work out to be a good thing. He'll sort himself, and everything will be fine. We'll see him tonight."

Blake smiled unconvincingly and held Jason's hand on top of the table.

14.

SEVEN HOURS after Dimitri stormed out of brunch, Jason and Blake found themselves in a Williamsburg gastropub for the third time that day. They awaited their respective orders of tacos, al pastor and mahi-mahi, which were being made behind an ordering window next to the bar. The decor was both industrial and timeless. It looked like both a film set used for the plotting of a revolution and a place where they had twelve uses for kale.

The floor was concrete with scattered oriental rugs; lights dangled from the building's exposed steel beams; aged brick with wrought-iron artworks covered floor to ceiling. The tables and chairs were steel pipe constructions, with reclaimed wood for tabletops and seats. Unfamiliar yet alluring music filled the space—indie rock with a full horns section—coming from a band playing in the back room. Appropriately, it was too loud. Every table was filled. Many more people were littered throughout the room or in the back watching the band. It was a place where they both felt comfortable, which was a sharp contrast to their recent dining experiences.

Blake watched over Jason's shoulder, as she waited for their order to come up. Jason stole glances at Blake, letting his eyes linger.

He sipped his beer and vowed to slow down, noting that his current drink was half-consumed while Blake had hardly touched hers.

They hadn't gone back to Dimitri's apartment to change or freshen up, despite a freezing downpour catching them on their walk through Brooklyn. Yet Blake looked beautiful. The warm light made her skin glow. From Blake's eyes radiated comfort—looking at her and sharing the moment felt safe. She was, Jason reflected, the best part of his life. No matter how horrible he was to Dimitri, or about Billy's death, and regardless of how indecisive he could be, Blake accepted him for who he was. And his actions were unfair.

Blake raised her arm and extended her middle finger into Jason's face. He smiled, flushed.

"What are you staring at?" Blake asked, smiling.

"I'm sorry, you look so pretty."

Blake rolled her eyes. "Yeah, I'm sure. With my awesome rain-enriched hair, day-old make-up, and soon-to-be mildewing clothes. I'm sure the subway has done wonders, too."

Jason leaned over the round tabletop, and Blake met him in the middle. They shared a quick, playful kiss.

"I'm sure it's the light in here," Blake said.

"What's this place called? It's great," Jason said.

"Something like Rock and Rolla. Not sure, but I'm glad we're here."

"Cheers to TripAdvisor."

The music stopped and raucous cheers filled the space.

"Damn. I liked them. I hoped they'd be playing throughout our dinner," Jason said.

"I know." Blake scanned the room. "Oh, actually, I think our food just came up. I'll go grab it."

Blake bounced from her seat, pushing the stool in with her ankle.

"Are you sure? I can grab it," Jason said, also standing. Blake only shook her head at him, and he sat back down.

As Jason watched Blake go to retrieve their meals, members of the crowd sauntered out of the back room, and Jason lost sight of her.

"Hey, man, you using this seat?"

Jason turned around. The guy asking for Blake's stool was wearing a cutoff leather jacket that exposed his scrawny arms and had a large Mischief Brew patch on the left breast. He was already holding the seat, ready to move it to another table.

"Yeah, my girlfriend's sitting there." The words hung in the air and the man's image was burned into Jason's memory.

"No worries, big dog." The guy scanned the bar for another seat. And he was out of Jason's sight, life, and mind. His own words, however, were not.

He turned around again, and resumed watching the crowd of people, now finishing their drinks and milling about. Then he saw Blake, with two baskets of food held eye level, shimmying between the conversations of strangers. Fortunately, Jason noticed, she smiled at the difficulty. He felt annoyed for her.

She arrived back at the table and set the food down with a dramatic exhale.

"Quite a journey."

Before Blake could respond, their attention, along with ninety percent of the establishment, was pulled towards the bar.

"Give me my fucking credit card," a man growled at the young, male bartender. The customer was massive, Jason noted, and had one of the deepest, bellowing yells he'd ever heard. The man looked out of place. He wore a Mets jersey, Mets hat, and appeared at least fifteen years older than the next closest in the bar.

Despite how quiet the entire room had become, the bartender's response was firm but inaudible.

"I'm not leaving without my fucking card. I'm not drunk."

Everyone seemed too shocked or entertained to move. Blake caught Jason's eye, and they exchanged a bewildered glance. What felt like minutes passed in stupefied silence.

"Mind your own fucking business!" The man turned on everyone else in the bar this time. "I'm just trying to have a good time, fuck you all. I'm not drunk. But give me back my fucking card, and I'll leave."

The man again turned to the bartender who was standing his ground. Again, Jason couldn't hear the bartender's response. Just return the card and this would be much easier, Jason thought.

The front door opened, and two men, in full NYPD uniforms, entered.

"Oh, come on," the Mets fan snarled.

"What's going on?" The cops positioned themselves on either side of the large man.

Jason and Blake ate their food as most of the crowd tried to ignore the developing situation.

In a much less abrasive tone, though still as loud, the man said, "I said I'd leave, but I need my credit card. I can't leave without it."

One of the officers, now at the bar, spoke to the bartender. The bartender handed over what looked like the man's credit card. The cop pocketed the card. He and his partner each grabbed one of the larger man's arms and walked him towards the door.

"Show's fucking over," the man shouted over his shoulder.

As the door closed behind the three men, the atmosphere in the room didn't escape with them. Rather, it seeped out through the cracks in the doors, walls, and ceiling. After a few minutes of dazed, confused silence, someone turned on a loud Modest Mouse song—a throwback that Jason couldn't remember the name of—and after a few verses, tension in the bar had dissipated.

"Well, that was something," Blake said.

Jason finished the last bite of his food. "Yeah, sorry we had to eat in silence. That was so awkward."

"I know. That was the loudest guy ever. I was sort of scared for the people near him. I wonder what he did."

Jason pushed his empty food basket to the middle of the table and grabbed his beer. His only response was to widen his eyes and shake his head.

"We can bail on the overly dramatized reality television, but overly dramatized reality still finds us," Blake said. She laughed and held her beer up. They clinked glasses and held each other's gaze.

"Hey, so, I want to talk," Jason said.

"Okay."

"Well, first off, thanks for coming here with me. I know the situation with Dimitri was awkward and I'm so sorry about how that happened. I had planned on this being a happy getaway for us. And it is now. I'm glad we went off on our own. I had so much fun walking through the Park and going to Forbidden Planet. So, I guess I'm trying to say thanks for being awesome, and for such an awesome day. I couldn't stomach going to that party tonight and seeing all those people. I don't even want to watch the show anymore. I guess I have to, but you know. Thanks."

"Of course," Blake said, "I came to New York to hang out with you. I'm not bothered about meeting other *Beached* players. No offense, but you guys aren't massive celebrities. And I've had a great day, too. Arguing with Dimitri, getting rained on, scary shouting guy and all. It's been great. And the night is young."

They shared another longing smile across the table.

"So, given everything. And, I don't know." Jason was sputtering, trying to figure out what to say.

"Basically," he continued, "I want to figure our relationship out. We've always had this on-and-off, best friend situation. And I've been thinking about it. I mean, I accidentally told some random guy you were my girlfriend."

Blake nodded to buy time.

"I've been there," she said. "Sometimes it's easier than to explain."

"What I'm trying to say, Blake, is that I've always loved you. I mean, we regularly say 'I love you' to each other. I've never known what to do with the feelings because I never wanted to risk our friendship. But we go through this coupley phase, and something gets in the way. And I've been an idiot to not tell you all this. I want to make it work. So, this is juvenile—do people our age do this? I don't know. Do you want to make this official and give a real relationship a shot? I think we're great together."

Blake held her smile but didn't respond. Jason felt weighed down to the table, and his legs frozen to the stool.

Blake leaned forward, and Jason was freed. They again kissed over the table, only this time with more behind it. Jason could sense the change in the contact their lips made, and in the way she held the back of his head, fingers in his long hair.

"God, you are cheesy. But, why not? Hell, we're already calling each other boyfriend and girlfriend."

15.

"I'M glad you're here for this," Jason said.

"Of course," Blake answered.

"Yeah, I know it'll be awkward. I hate meeting new people, but it's meaningful for fans, and the charity and everything. I have to do it."

The couple pulled into a parking spot in the Cincinnati Convention Center parking lot.

"So, who else will be here?"

Jason considered the personalities as he shut off the car.

"I know of at least Anna and Kendall. They live close enough. Cleveland and Grand Rapids. And there's a chance that Desiree and Hunter may show up. I wouldn't count on that though. Probably loads of people from past seasons. Ones who aren't getting a taste of fame every day and need a fix. It's actually an uneasy feeling. I'm nervous about interacting with fans and everything, but I'm really nervous to meet the former players. It's like meeting my childhood heroes, and I'm not sure I'm worthy of being in their company. This'll be awkward."

Blake leaned over the center console and kissed Jason.

"Oh, shut up. Let's do this."

Jason got out of the car, walked to the trunk, and opened the hatch. He hurried as the November wind whipped his neck, causing eye-widening cold shock. He still hadn't switched from his fall clothes to full winter coat, scarves, and gloves.

Sitting inside the trunk, along with a few stray fast food bags and an empty bottle of San Pellegrino, were two cardboard boxes. One was tattered and large while the other was compact and neat.

"Will you grab this box of photos? I'll get the other box with the clothes and props for the auction."

"Sure," Blake said. She lifted the box. "How much do you think someone will pay for your used shorts?"

"I'll have you know these shorts are not only screen used, but I haven't washed them since they left the *Beached* Island. Each article has been carefully preserved, in this heavy-duty cardboard box, and they should fetch loads of money and help cure cancer and everything."

"Let's hope. That's one realm of fandom I've never understood. At all."

"What are you talking about? Buying a stranger's used, sweaty clothing is easy to understand."

ONCE INSIDE THE EVENT CENTER, Jason tried his best to smile at everyone he saw. He had trouble, however, dedicating his attention.

Through the doors, Jason and Blake found themselves in a lengthy queue, waiting to pass through security searches and metal detectors. As they waited in line, Jason's skin itched as they adjusted from bitter cold to blazing heat.

"Well, this is overkill," Blake said.

"Mm-hmm. But, it's for our own benefit. You never know, and it's good they're being cautious. More people should."

The look on his face erased Blake's indignation.

"Yeah."

"It seems a bit weird, though," Jason added.

After removing their shoes and belts, they made their way through metal detectors and maneuvered their boxes of eight-by-ten photographs and memorabilia through security.

The space opened into a cavernous but bland event hall, filled with decorations and booths attempting to make it more inviting. Fake palm trees littered the doorway, and vendors polluted the atmosphere with their shouts, trying to sell mixed drinks in plastic coconuts. There was live steel drum music hitting them from the left, and cheers for some obscured event happening on the right.

A few people gawked at Jason from afar. He was relieved that no one was speaking to him. But why? Other reality TV contestants from various shows were hanging out, and they had lines or crowds surrounding them. It would be less awkward if fans were talking to him instead of staring.

He donned a broad, toothless grin, and tried to nod anytime someone noticed him.

"Wow," Jason said.

After a moment, he added, "I didn't realize this place was so big. I've never been here before."

"Me neither," Blake said.

Blake was quiet. Jason studied her for a moment. She was never one to experience the anxiety he picked up in public spaces. Then again, a fan convention and charity event where they were the center of attention was next-level.

With another awkward glance around, Jason set the box he was still carrying on the floor next to Blake.

"Sorry, we're just standing here. I figured they would have a volunteer or something waiting for us, ready to show us where to set up and to take our stuff," Jason said. "I think Jill, the organizer, said someone named Megan would meet us."

"No worries."

"Okay, well, while we're waiting, do you mind watching this stuff? I'm going to find a bathroom."

"I think there's one back there," Blake said, pointing over Jason's shoulder.

He took off in that direction, keeping his eyes on the gray carpet.

━━━

AFTER HE FINISHED PEEING, Jason pushed on the bar to flush the urinal, hurrying to get back to Blake. It sprayed back at him with force.

"Damn," he swore under his breath. "You have got to be kidding."

He stared down at his jeans, now flecked with water from the over-pressurized urinal.

Flustered, he looked around and saw no one else having similar issues. Another guy, of a comparable height, had flushed the urinal on the far right. He was casually zipping up his pants and walking to the sink.

Why, Jason thought, did I take the first urinal? He normally walked to the stall or urinal that was farthest away from the door. This was his modus operandi. When taking classes, he always sat at the most distant desk in the back; at dinner tables, he preferred the seat farthest away from the door. He liked being on the periphery, away from view. And here he was, grabbing the first urinal that made itself available to him.

"I didn't even have to go to the bathroom that bad," he muttered.

With no recourse, Jason pulled six sheets of thin paper towels from the supply and tried to dry the splatter patterns on his pants. As he futilely wiped his leg in the bathroom's corner and pondered why he had so cavalierly rushed to the stall, another thought hit him.

Jason froze as the frustration in his body gave way to a nauseous tingle. He couldn't move the weight of his jaw, and Jason swayed forward like he was drunk for the first time.

After fighting through a full-body chill, he threw out the paper towels in his hand and dashed for the exit with the same tenacity he had entered it. He no longer cared about getting his pants sorted, and he didn't bother to think about washing his hands. There was only one thing on his mind.

The torn page from his journal. Currently stuffed in the sole of a shoe, sitting in a box at Blake's feet, about to be auctioned off to a *Beached* super-fan who would not keep it to themselves.

MOVING through the crowd at a brisk pace, now able to bypass the chaos, Jason focused on Blake. As he neared her, he discovered she was deep in conversation with someone who happened to be holding the box Jason needed to get his hands on.

She looked about twenty-three years old and wore a lanyard name badge. Her curly brown hair was shaved on the right side and hung to the left in a messy wave. This had to be the aforementioned Megan. Hopefully, she was late because she was so busy, Jason thought, and he could distract her.

"Hey," Jason said.

Both Blake and Megan turned to face him. Megan stretched out her hand.

"Well, hey! I'm Megan, as you probably guessed." Her enthusiasm carried an unnatural quality.

Megan had a voice that sounded like she was laughing while she spoke.

"Yeah, nice to meet you."

"I'm super sorry I wasn't here when you arrived."

Blake fought back a smirk. She had seen his pants.

"No problem, Megan."

"And yeah," Jason added, looking to Blake. "The water pressure is a little powerful. Not embarrassing at all." He forced a laugh. Better to seem casual and carefree.

Megan smiled at him, apparently pleased that she wouldn't be working with someone who took themselves too seriously. Nice, Jason thought. That act worked.

"Actually," he said, still smiling, "would you mind if I carry that box, Megan? Hopefully, I can use it to cover my pants until they dry. I'd prefer people didn't get a photo of me like this."

"Hey, no problem."

Megan handed over the box.

The first part of the mission was accomplished. Now, he somehow needed to open the box, find the shoe, remove the page from its concealed location, discard it safely, return the shoe, and close the box without anyone noticing. Not even Blake. If anyone found out what he had written, or even that he was concealing information, it would be a disaster. After all, he was the one with the reputation for being suspicious of everyone else. Yet here he was, concealing evidence for personal gain.

"Alright, let's head this way, and I'll get us set up."

Megan led them through the event center, but Jason wasn't paying attention to anything they passed. He was busy brainstorming a distraction, or means of extracting the paper. Presumably, they would end up at a table and they would unpack everything. Hopefully, he could drop the shoe under the table, or try to palm the note when emptying the shoes from the box. He had to make sure Megan didn't help. Another complicating factor was that Jason didn't remember which shoe he had tucked the paper into. He remembered it being the left one, but he couldn't trust that memory.

If Megan noticed, it wasn't the end of the world. She might say something, but there was no guaranteed consequence. If Blake saw, it would be horrible. He had sworn that he was completely open with her. And he thought he'd been until he remembered this journal entry entirely too late. Their relationship, now official for a week, felt like it had been developing since their early twenties. This one torn scrap of paper could torch it all.

Jason's hands perspired and the box gained substance, straining his grip.

Crack. Megan threw her hands, with its many rings, onto the folding table before them.

"Alright, guys. So, here we are. Awesome. Let's set up and get this ball rolling."

Here it is, Jason thought.

He set the box down. Walked behind the table. Kept an eye on Blake and Megan. Smiled. Nothing to see here. He pulled the first flap. The box fell open, limply. He drummed his fingers on the box's sides. Playing it cool. He pushed the flaps apart. Looked into the box. Moved his filthy shirt. Pulled out his pants. Let them unravel. Remarked how wrecked they were. So casual. Folded the pants. Lined the legs up and turned them over twice. Everything to plan. Focus went back to the box. And the shoes. He grabbed the first one. He looked around. Blake and Megan were stacking photographs. He grasped the left shoe. And pulled the sole. His finger searched. They reached. They found nothing.

Blake glanced at him. Jason removed the left shoe.

He placed the shoe on the table. Next to the pants. His face was hot. Blake had noticed. He was shuddering. Like he did before public speaking.

"There's nothing to worry about," Blake called down the table.

Always supportive. Jason's smile was nervous, but for another reason entirely.

"You're right."

He was playing it off. Just nerves.

With his hands in the box and attention refocused, the worn canvas of his second sneaker felt fragile. He pulled the insole back, trying to do so smoothly. The glue clung, trying to hold on.

And then there it was, revealed. The paper. It looked matted, as if it had fused with the shoe. Maybe no one would have found this, Jason considered. After all, who would spend hundreds of dollars on shoes, for memorabilia, and then go about pulling them apart?

As he pulled the note out of the insole, sand and grime coated to the paper. It came free. The glue had not torn the paper, which had been one of his primary concerns.

He slid the paper to his palm and clung to it with his ring finger and pinky. With the document secure, Jason pulled the shoe out of the box, trying to act nonchalantly. He tossed it on the table and laughed.

"I haven't even thought about any of this stuff since I got back from the island. And it was all I had for so long. It's weird parting with it. It's kind of sentimental."

As he spoke, Jason put his hands in his pockets. Both. The right concealed the extracted paper and left it in his pocket when he pulled his hands out moments later.

Blake was staring at him, her brow furrowed. Jason resumed pulling shirts out of the box, but his mind was further down the table.

Meanwhile, Blake finished stacking eight-by-tens and broke down the box. As she folded the cardboard, she made her way towards him.

"What's up?" Blake asked.

She had drawn level with him at the table and turned her head when she spoke, obscuring their conversation from Megan. She had seen it. Or his expression. It was all the same.

Jason forced himself to look at her.

"Nothing."

There was no emotion in his voice. As her eyebrows raised and lips pursed, he felt his vision contracting. She glanced at his pocket.

"I'll tell you later," he said, "not here."

He had no idea what he would tell her later, but he had a solid understanding of what she'd have to say to him. And he'd have to confront the words and thoughts he'd secretly grappled with since he'd hidden them away on his return flight.

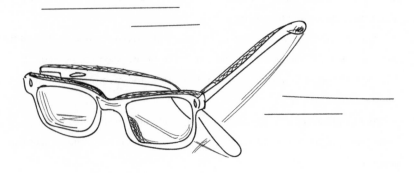

16.

JASON CLOSED his MacBook with a sigh and took his glasses off before rubbing his eyes and reclining against the back of his sofa. After the momentary respite, he returned his glasses. Before him on the coffee table, along with his laptop, sat a planner, office supplies and a stack of stapled papers. Jason picked up a binder clip, pulled back on its clasps, and secured it around the stack of essays. He flipped through and then studied the first page. It was titled "Yeats' Life/Death Paradox," and had a few comments in the margins along with a large letter "A" written on the top in green ink.

A loud chime filled the house. With one last look, Jason gave a small nod, flopped the papers on the coffee table and stood to open the door. Jason's cat, London, raced between his legs, beating him to the door. Through his curtains, three outlines: Blake, along with her passengers, Phoebe and Anna.

Jason turned the deadbolt and swung the door open. All smiles.

"Well, hey. Welcome. Come on in." Jason held the door open while gesturing his three guests inside. All the while, he kept a close eye on the cat, making sure she didn't dart for the open door.

"Wow, it's nice to see your place. Thanks for having us," Anna said.

"Thanks to Blake for picking you both up."

As they walked through the entrance hallway, Blake waited behind Phoebe and Anna, and Jason put one arm around her. He gave her a surreptitious hug, and a kiss on top of the head. They joined the others and congregated in Jason's dining room, right off the living room.

"She was a godsend. No thanks to the airline. It took my bags a damned century to come out," Phoebe said.

"You'd think they'd give you better service, considering you're about to have to watch yourself lose a million dollars on national television."

Phoebe shot Jason a smirk-filtered glare. They held the stare for a moment, but laughed.

Jason hugged Phoebe.

"Smooth drive?" Jason addressed Blake.

"Yeah, totally. I got to Anna's hotel before rush hour and dodged the bridge traffic while waiting for Phoebe at the airport."

"Good, and thanks again," Jason said.

"Yeah, we're saving a ton by flying out of CVG, and we get to have a Midwestern viewing," Phoebe said.

"Oh, the grandeur." Blake laughed.

"It sure beats hanging out at the hotel," Anna said.

"It is so good to see you guys before the madness in L.A. Can I get anyone a drink?" Jason asked.

"Beer. Duh," Phoebe said.

"Sorry. I should have known. Anyone else?"

Everyone agreed, and Jason passed behind them, into the kitchen. He opened the fridge and called back into the dining room, "Pabst or something darker?"

"Darker," Phoebe said.

It was the last night before Jason, Phoebe, and Anna flew to Los Angeles to prepare for, and film, the live finale and reunion special. It was a night for fancier drinks. Jason's bar had been understocked since he returned from the island.

While he opened four cans of Guinness, making sure the foam didn't over-flow, a few fragments of conversation from the adjacent room drifted in.

"I'm sorry we didn't catch each other at the charity event yesterday," Anna said.

"Yeah, we had to rush out at the end. There was a lot going on," Blake said. Jason couldn't detect any specific emotion in her voice. They had still not talked about the piece of paper that Blake had witnessed Jason concealing. That, Jason presumed, would happen tonight.

"Well, I'm just a few hours to the north, so we'll have plenty of opportunities," Anna said.

"My flight didn't even make it into town for the event," Phoebe said.

Jason couldn't hear what was said next, but they all laughed.

"What's going on in there?" Blake called to Jason.

"Ta-da," Jason said, as he entered the dining room with two opened beers in either hand.

Anna held her beer in the air, and the others reciprocated.

"To the greatest game on earth, making great friends, and Jason's impending victory."

They drank. Jason felt uncomfortable, but he figured he was doing what Anna wanted. She'd been the first person eliminated from the show, and she hadn't even spent any time on the island with Jason or Phoebe. Yet, somehow, Anna was like a mom to the whole season's cast. She had acceptance about being eliminated first. She never missed a chance, from what Jason could tell, to visit another contestant and meet their family. She was so earnest it made Jason uncomfortable at times, which was undoubtedly why she had been eliminated.

"Always being positive, Anna," Jason said.

"What else can you do?"

"So, two more episodes. How do you all feel about the season winding down and your adventure coming to a close?" Blake asked.

"Well, I'm hoping RTN asks me back to do the show again, so we'll see," Phoebe said.

"How quickly you want to move past tonight's embarrassment, huh?" Jason smiled.

"Something like that. But, also, I don't want it to be over. I know that so much horror has gone on—between the game itself and the lies and betrayals. And Billy. There's been so much negativity, and there's still so much we don't know or understand. May never understand. But I'd still do it again in a second. I'd quit my job and ship out at a day's notice."

"Yeah, I'm nervous about the finale and everything. I finished all my grading and lesson planning since we'll be traveling for a few days. I'm never caught up on grading, so that feels good at least."

"Nice. Do you have any other plans in Los Angeles? I was thinking we should all get together before the finale," Anna said.

Phoebe nodded. "Definitely. I have nothing planned."

"Yeah," said Jason, "me neither. I would meet up with Omid, my good friend from the *Beached* production crew, but I haven't heard from him in ages. Since the show first aired. I don't even think he works for RTN anymore. He's disappeared, from what I can tell online."

"That's odd. I'm sure he'll respond though. Probably taking a break. At least it'll be good to see the cast again. Together," Phoebe said.

"It'll be weird though. Like, I visited Hunter, and he's convinced he won. So, that's a big disappointment. Also, he's someone I thought I'd be close with after the game, but he's so different. It's weird. I don't know how to feel about certain people. It'll be bizarre to be in the same place again."

No one spoke for a moment, and everyone avoided eye contact.

"Yeah, I heard about your trip to Hunter's in Gatlinburg," Anna said. "And he came to visit me in Cleveland. He stopped by before going to a Cavs game with friends. I worry about him. I know he's in his twenties and whatnot, but he was too much for my family."

"Yeah, I heard," Phoebe said. Everyone nodded.

"Jason, do you think it'll be weird with Dimitri?" Blake asked. She had been quiet.

Jason shook his head and turned up his palms.

"It's so easy to get along with Dimitri. I'm sure it'll be fine. And wasn't that about Nick, anyway?" Phoebe said.

"Yeah."

Again, a moment of silence and downward gazes.

"So, the episode starts soon. Want to get set up in the living room? There are more snacks and drinks in the kitchen. Please, help yourself."

"Woo-hoo," Anna said.

"I can't wait to see how and why you and Hunter get rid of Phoebe and Kendall," Anna said. They sat around Jason's sectional sofa.

"Yeah, a lot of thought goes into it. I promise, Phoebe."

"Mm-hmm, it better."

Without further conversation, they oriented themselves towards the television, and Jason scrolled to RTN. They were about to watch Jason turn on the last member of his original team: Phoebe. The island would be full of paranoia, as the contestants had not yet processed Billy's death, which had occurred only a few days prior. They would see shock, mistrust, and betrayal. But, also, the game would go on. People would be eliminated. Cameras would roll.

After this episode, only Desiree would stand in the way of Jason's and Hunter's appearance at the final vote where Luke would announce the winner. The game and television show that had dominated their lives for nearly a year would end. All thirteen living contestants, scattered across the country, would converge on Los Angeles, and they would award Jason the victory, along with a million dollars. This was the lead-up to Jason's moment after he had been downplayed during the season.

Yet, Jason's focus wasn't on the show, or himself. As a full hour of television passed, Jason instead focused on Blake, her quiet demeanor, and their relationship. He focused on Billy: both what could have been, and what may have been. And, he was focused on the folded piece of torn notebook paper in his pocket, which he was ready to reveal to Blake after Anna and Phoebe left for their hotel.

MEANWHILE ON TELEVISION

JASON WAS bent at the waist, arms hanging between his legs, forcing his shoulders to point into the camera.

"I know they're coming after me. I know this game," he said. His foot tapped, silently, on the sand. His worn Vans sneakers kicked up a small puff of dust each time they landed.

"I mean, I just can't even though. It doesn't feel right."

His eyes held the gaze of the camera, bulging uncomfortably. As though noticing the audience's discomfort through time and space, Jason blinked earnestly and let his head hang limp.

Without looking up, he spoke again. "I mean, who cares about strategy or some game at this point. But, whatever, Billy would have wanted us to keep on, I think. So, I will."

⊏⊐

A SPEAR DOMINATED most of the frame, and the camera slowly pulled back and rotated forward until Hunter's flexed arm came into view. He held the spear into the ground, with a crab pinned underneath it. The crab was giving its last twitches of struggle, attempting to get away.

"Nice one," another voice said.

"Ah, yeah, son," Hunter said. "Woo." His voice's tone and their lives were in sharp contrast.

Hunter bent and picked up the dead crab after he removed his spear from its body. As he rose and stood straight, the camera followed, and Jason came into sight.

Jason smiled. "Well, at least we'll have food."

He also had a spear to accompany Hunter's, but it lay against Jason's side and he only gave it two fingers' worth of grip.

"At least we will. Hell, why don't we just make a fire and have this 'un right here? We ain't working with them, anyway. Two guys versus two girls."

Hunter laughed with his entire body and clapped his hand on Jason's back. "Hey, man. I'm only messin'."

Jason answered with a gulping smile that started in his throat.

"But we are working together. Right?" Hunter asked.

"Of course," Jason replied without letting his smile fade. "Along with Billy, you're one of the few true friends I found out here. I couldn't turn on you."

Hunter again thrust his open palm against Jason's back.

"Well then," Hunter said, "keep smilin'. Because this business trip's about over."

—

FOR THE ELEVENTH time in eleven weeks, *Beached* returned from commercial break to the stagnant image of a dejected contestant explaining what went wrong.

Phoebe wasn't crying, but only just.

"I'm not surprised. It's okay. Not a big deal. I didn't see it coming because I thought I was working with Jason and Hunter, but they thought I was working with Desiree. But it doesn't matter. We're all family. After what happened, it's all okay. Me losing isn't a big deal. Really, it's not. I'm not upset. It's all good, and we'll all be friends. I wish Jason the best of luck. We've been together since day one, the whole way. We got through the Billy thing together. I hope he isn't sad that he had to get rid of me. He definitely has my vote to win in the end. But, I wish everyone the best of luck. It's okay."

The fire flickered across her face, highlighting segments of her closed-mouth smile. She wiped her eye with a sole index finger. The camera held the frame for a few moments longer while Phoebe held, too.

"BEACHED SEASON 50 FILMING IN L.A."

ROSS KUSCHNER, TV UPDATE

SAN FRANCISCO— This week, the cast members of Reality Television Network's flagship series, *Beached*, will be descending on Los Angeles from the various corners of the United States. The thirteen people are, of course, missing their deceased cast mate Billy Gerding. Gerding's death, while filming the current season, has gained widespread media attention and criticism. His life and legacy are sure to have a front seat at the finale, and its live reunion broadcast.

This season has, however, reinvigorated attention for the nearly twenty-five-year-old series. Ratings and viewership numbers have been the best on network television for most of the eleven episodes which have aired thus far, after factoring in all recording and streaming data. What once looked like it might be the last season of the series is now serving as a launching point for a new generation. Work on season fifty-one has already begun, and those episodes are expected to begin airing sometime in the early summer.

Remaining in the game are: Desiree, a 27-year-old mother and hairdresser from Santa Fe, NM; Jason, a 34-year-old college professor from Cincinnati, OH; and Hunter, a 24-year-old postal worker from Gatlinburg, TN. Jason started out as an opponent of both Hunter and Desiree, but the three have recently begun working together to take out their opponents.

The cast is coming to film the live finale event, and the subsequent reunion, at the Redmoor Theater in Hollywood. Both will be broadcast in succession on Thursday evening beginning at 9:00 (et) on RTN.

BLAKE'S OFFICE

BLAKE LEANED FORWARD over the surface of her desk, staring inside a massive hand-bound book. She ran her hand through her hair, planted her elbow on the top of her desk, and let her head fall onto her palm. She let out a sigh.

After resting there for a moment, Blake sat up straight, flipped the book closed, and reached for her office phone. She pressed "1-3-4."

"Hey, Laura, how's it going?" Blake said, after a moment.

Then, "Yeah, thanks for picking up. Look, are you free for a moment to come down?"

And, finally, "Awesome. Yeah, thanks so much. I'll be here. I need advice."

Blake returned the phone, stood, and pulled on the ends of her shirt, running her hands along her pants.

Moments later, there was a tap on her office door, and Laura let herself in.

"Hey, what's up?"

"I need a second opinion. Thanks again for coming."

"No problem. I'm between clients for about another hour."

"Okay. So, I have a client with a prior diagnosis I'm not used to working with. I met him once, and it's someone you might normally see. So, I thought I could get some advice."

"Of course."

Laura turned one chair opposite Blake's desk to a slight angle and perched on the edge. She was roughly Blake's age—they had gone to college together. Despite these similarities, she was decidedly of a different style. While Blake dressed in dark colors and had long auburn hair, Laura's was dyed red and her outfit was bursting with color. This distinction correlated with their personalities. Regardless, they had always been close, though they never interacted much outside work. Except for the occasional after-work drink, they had primarily interacted within the confines of their career. Nevertheless, they were close, and they still went to each other with problems—whether they be work or personal.

"What's the situation?" Laura asked.

"So, I'm meeting this guy tomorrow. We did a preliminary session. He's switching psychiatrists. He has a diagnosis of schizophrenia with both delusions and hallucinations. But, he's so high functioning and has no issues with speech or disorganization. He also doesn't seem to have negativity stemming from his disorder. So, I'm not saying the diagnosis is wrong, but I'm not sure how to help him from a behavioral standpoint."

Laura took a moment, nodded, and spoke. "Yep, definitely in my wheelhouse. I have materials I can email you. I have a similar client right now, so I collected a fair bit of research. Are his meds in order?"

"Yes, for now."

"Great, yeah I'll shoot you that email with the resources. And, if it's not going well, let me know and I can help more directly. It's not as uncommon as it sounds, and I'm confident you'll be great with him. After you meet again we can walk through how it goes."

"Thank you. You're amazing."

"Aren't I? Anyway, how are things with Jason? This week's the finale, right?"

"It is, I'm so excited for him." Blake leaned against her desk, extending an arm and gripping the edge.

"Nice. Are you going to L.A. for the taping or party or whatever they do?"

"No." Blake's expression shifted. "I couldn't take any more time away from work. And he'll be busy, I'm sure."

Laura, choosing not to push the question any further, rose from her seat. "Right. That makes sense. Well, Alan, the kids, and I have been watching, and we're rooting him on. If you're not busy the night it airs, let me know. We could totally grab margaritas and then watch at my house."

Blake nodded and smiled. "Yeah. I'm not. That sounds great. I haven't seen your family in forever."

"Great," Laura said, and she headed for the door before turning one last time. "I'll text you, and we'll set it up. And I'll send that material."

"Thanks again."

Laura closed Blake's door with a slight click.

As soon as the door was closed, Blake deflated. Her shoulders sank, and she slouched back into her chair. After a moment of staring into space, she slid back a few inches and pulled open her desk's top drawer. The shallow space was meticulously organized. Two packets of sticky notes on the right, along with a box of staples, a box of paper clips, two packs of chewing gum, and an unopened box of blue pens. Three loose pens were in the drawer—all green. Blake's attention, however, was on the left side of the drawer where there was only her cell phone. After a moment, she grasped the phone, slid the drawer closed and opened her messages.

Her conversation with Jason was already open. She had re-read them with her coffee this morning. She scrolled to the beginning of their conversation from late the previous evening:

JASON: Again, I'm so sorry. I should have shared this with you earlier. I didn't know how to deal with it. I think I pushed it out of my mind.

BLAKE: I'm not mad at you. I'm not sure how to help you. And yes, you should have shared that with me instead of hiding it. I thought we were serious this time. And then you began by hiding things from me.

JASON: You're right. I'm sorry, and I love you.

BLAKE: I love you, too. But I need time and space. And I think you do, too, because our plan clearly hasn't been working.

JASON: Okay. I don't know what to do without you. You won't come to L.A. even as my friend?

BLAKE: No. It's not about friends or our relationship. Not until you own up to your feelings and quit deflecting. I can't support this anymore. I'd love to be there with you, trust me, but I can't enable your refusal to deal with what you've been through appropriately. It's messing with my life and career, too. I thought you'd talked to everyone and come to terms. You lied.

JASON: You're right. I feel scattered, on the edge of something I can't describe. Something I'm missing. I promise, though, I'll get closure in L.A. I'll prove it to you. If I can, will you give this another chance?

BLAKE: Of course I will, and you don't need one. I'm not saying we're done, only that we're not helping each other now. Always let me know if there's anything I can do for you. But I am mad you hid that page, and your feelings. If you thought Billy was suicidal while you were on the island why hide it? I know you feel guilt, but you've consumed our lives with these suspicions, and it's all a lie. Be safe in California, we'll talk about it when you get back. I'll be watching from here and supporting you in spirit.

JASON: I'm sorry. You're right. One hundred percent. And I love you, more than you know.

Blake scrolled up multiple times, repeatedly resting on Jason's last message. She hadn't answered. The entire conversation felt false. She kept trying to recreate the words, in her mind, that had populated Jason's island journal, detailing his guilt over Billy's suicide. He should have said something, he wrote, when he saw Billy getting worse. Then, at some point, he hid the page and covered his own guilt by lashing out at members of the cast and crew. And he had dragged Blake into it.

The most challenging part, however, was that Blake understood, from a psychological level. Accepting this, though, in her best friend and boyfriend, was a different story. She sighed, set the phone on her desk, and again opened her top drawer. She needed space to be mad at him. For now.

Before sliding the drawer shut, she extracted a pack of yellow sticky notes and a pen. She went to write, but the pen only indented the paper, leaving no ink. Blake shook the pen a few times before a second attempt. Again, nothing. Blake deposited the pen into her waste bin and reached for a second.

After attempting a cursory doodle, this second pen produced no ink.

"The fuck?" She shook the pen.

When try number two failed, she slammed the tip of the pen onto the corner of her planner. Again, nothing, and, again, Blake threw the pen away and reached for another.

She made another attempt at writing on her sticky notes. This time, deep green ink flowed from the pen. "Text Laura for Margs," she wrote and affixed the note to her calendar.

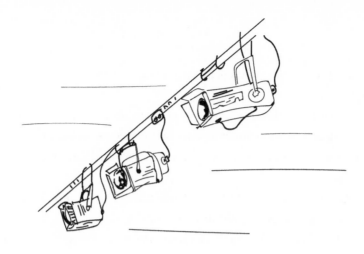

17.

JASON SHIFTED ON HIS FEET. He stood in the dim light behind the stage at the Redmoor Theater in Los Angeles, waiting for a meeting he had scheduled with Richard Brandt. Brandt was an Assistant Producer with RTN, he'd been told, though apparently not significant enough to warrant a nameplate on his door. Perhaps he was new, which explained why he was unfamiliar with Brandt. As Jason shifted from foot to foot and paced in a tight circle to the left of the cracked door, he remembered what Seth had informed him: many of the crew members who worked on *Beached* had been replaced with little discussion or justification.

Hopefully, this new guy had a fresh perspective and would be more open-minded about his concerns.

Nevertheless, the situation felt off. When Jason had called to schedule a meeting, the network tried to give him the runaround. Unreturned calls. Suggestions for a phone call the following week. They evidently didn't want to talk to him. And now he was pawned off for some brief appeasement, given out less than an hour before taping the *Beached* reunion.

He glanced at the time on his cell phone for the fifth time in a half-hour, but found out only six minutes had passed since the last. Jason cleared his throat. He needed to let Mr. Brandt know he was there, not only so he'd hurry but also so he didn't appear to be eavesdropping. Jason faced the door head-on and considered tapping on the frame.

The hallway illuminated amid Jason's contemplation and he stood in surprise as the door flew open. Reacting only on instinct, he backed up two paces and made room. Will came hurtling past him. Jason's head turned to follow his cast mate's trail.

As Jason turned, so did Will. They made momentary eye contact. Another man, presumably Richard Brandt, leaned into the hall.

"Mr. Debord," Brandt said, acknowledging Jason. The RTN exec held out his hand, which Jason took. Brandt's grip shocked Jason, who was still stealing looks in Will's direction. Perhaps Will still had similar concerns. Besides, as Jason struggled to press back against Brandt's finger-twisting display of handshake dominance, he knew how the meeting would go.

"Nice to meet you, Mr. Brandt," Jason said. He displayed none of the pain in either his voice or expression. Will had texted Jason, and Jason shouldn't have dismissed him. He may have been the ally he needed all along.

"Call me Richard. Come on in."

Jason followed him into the room, which was as stark and unadorned as its door. There was an aged metal desk with Formica countertop in the center, a waste bin at its side, and metal bookcases beyond the desk. There was only a generic laptop and a handful of books on the shelves. Jason didn't even read the titles. He was trying to reconstruct what Will had messaged. Was that really why he had seen Brandt?

Will's eyes had been wide, his hair wild, and he looked too unkempt to go on live television. Haunted was the most fitting description for his visage. The whole image turned cartoonish in Jason's short-term memory. Will had wanted to say something, but Jason had noticed a second too late.

"So, what were you meeting with Will about?" Jason asked. He tried to sound as nonchalant as possible. Richard's brow didn't soften.

"That's confidential. Tell me, though, what can I do for you? We don't have much time. Ten minutes, to be exact, and then you're needed on stage."

"I thought we had at least thirty."

"Unfortunately, we do not. Please, have a seat."

Matching the other furniture in the room, the seat opposite Richard's desk seemed a decade old and equally uncomfortable. Jason allowed himself to sit. The leather beneath him squeaked. Was this all by design, to throw his guests off ever so slightly? Will had certainly been perturbed enough.

Richard waited for Jason to sit, and only then made his way to the other side of his philistine desk to perch on his wing-back chair.

"Now," Richard began, "you have what you describe as startling information to share regarding *Beached*'s production."

Jason went to speak, but Richard continued, not pausing for the sake of being polite.

"We both know I'm new on this team, but I think you can still tell how seriously I take my job, my production, and my show. Anything that could compromise their integrity cannot be tolerated and will be dealt with. Please, enlighten me—what have you observed?"

"Well..." Jason took a moment. "I have suspicions about the circumstances of Billy's death."

Richard pursed his lips and nodded. "I see."

Continuing to nod, he swiveled to a coffeepot behind him, which his chair had obscured. He set two cups on the table and poured. After the first cup was full, he again turned to Jason.

"Coffee?"

"Uh, sure."

Richard topped off the second cup, and handed it across to Jason.

"Okay," Richard said. "So, what did you notice that our teams of legal experts and detectives missed? After all, you were out there the entire time. I'm sure you have insight."

"I don't know what you have already done to look into it. I'm not saying I'm an expert. I've been poking around, mulling over everything that happened. Asking people questions. Trying to allow processing time. I'm no expert—"

"Correct."

Jason took a long drink of his coffee and instantly regretted it as the liquid seared his tongue. He winced but swallowed. "Okay, seriously, what is your job? I'm trying to help everyone here. Someone did this. You had to find something in your investigation. There are so many potential suspects. I mean, start with the cast. I've been talking to everyone, collecting anecdotal evidence. Getting opinions. Some people think it's crazy, but just as many agree. Nick, for example, needs to be looked into. Not to mention who else could be involved. I'm concerned about a cover-up or something. No truth has come out at all. No further information. The public has questions, and the media backlash has been bad enough for this season. Don't you think we need to do something? Look into it? I might not know any specifics, but it's suspicious there hasn't been more exposure on how he died."

Jason thrust his coffee cup on the table and watched it slide towards Richard as if on a tilt.

"He died by suicide, Jason. What more do you need?"

"How do you know that for a fact?"

"Okay. I'll tell you what I see. I see privilege. A moderately successful PhD sitting before me. One who's never had hardship in his life. One who went and suffered for a month on an island, starving, not sleeping, missing home, and his friends and cats. And then, that trauma is multiplied. This guy's best friend commits suicide. Right under his nose. And he didn't see it coming. Next, this guy is thrown out of his miserable circumstances and back into the real world. He probably had trouble sleeping. Had trouble talking to and relating to his friends and family. Not only that, but he was also thrown into the national spotlight. And criticized. A lot.

"Now, furthermore, this guy has still been dealing with all that trauma from his best friend committing suicide. And he doesn't know what to do about it. He has no experience with loss, with hardship, with trauma, or with people disliking him. So, what does he do? The most natural thing a human can do. He tries to make sense out of something that doesn't make sense. He rationalizes. Fuck it, Billy didn't kill himself; there's a reason. Someone did this. There's always someone to blame. This guy I see, by the way, he's a smart guy. He's always had the answers. His whole life.

"Now Jason, I don't blame this. As I said, it's natural. We want answers. We hate the incomplete, the mystery that'll never be solved. It gets under everyone's fucking skin."

How naïve, thinking the network would listen to him. Jason tried to recall Will's text messages in greater detail. He'd said there was something bigger going on, someone was watching them, that he'd give proof later. Why hadn't he?

"I know this is getting to you, and I want to help you. So here's what we'll do," Richard said. "You will see a shrink. And not just the one you see after hours."

Jason flexed his jaw to speak, but before he came to words Richard was in control again.

"No, no. I'm talking. You've been running across the country doing enough talking. You're going to see a psychiatrist. I know you say you've had time to process. Well, I say it's only been a few months. That isn't enough time to conclude that you, yourself, are not delusional and, instead, the people around you might all be murderers. In the meantime, you will have no contact with RTN. Zero. We let you on the show today, we give you your money, we pay for your therapy, and you go away. I hear no more of this 'people are whispering that I'm a killer' garbage from any more of our cast or crew. I know that's all stemming from you."

"And if I don't do what you want?"

"Yeah, I thought you'd say that. I mean, what do you want me to say? That I know people, so watch out? Come on, you've known I exist for thirty minutes. Do you think I'm some corrupt killer, too?

"Come on," Richard said again. He stood and motioned to the doorway. "We've got to get you onto the stage. And you need to compose yourself for the cameras. Come on, Jason. You're no stupid guy. You know what's good for you. How much money have you made already? Hell, I hear you might win the million dollars."

Jason stood and trudged to the door. He planned to leave silently, but a firm hand clamped around his shoulder.

"Break a leg out there, buddy."

Jason didn't turn, but heard Richard muttering after him. "Come on. Lighten up. Jesus. Two in a row."

Heading for the front stage, and trying to compose himself for his first appearance on live television, Jason understood the look he had been trying to figure out on Will's face.

⸺

MOMENTS LATER, Jason found himself standing with a stage manager, and yet another unwanted hand on his shoulder. He was once again shifting from foot to foot, avoiding eye contact, unsettled and anxious for what was to come. The stage manager had explained that Jason would walk out on stage from the left. Hunter would be entering from the right. Once the two met in the middle, the host would give preliminary hype, and then he would announce the winner.

Jason was excited for his win but distracted by his sympathy for Hunter, who was still convinced that he, not Jason, had won. And he couldn't focus on his excitement because he was still preoccupied with the conversation that had ended only moments ago. Did Richard think he was being a nice guy and helping push Jason through a tough time, or was he trying to strong-arm him? Another sign that something wasn't right.

He wiped his nose and tried to crack his knuckles, but they wouldn't.

This was the moment Jason had dreamed of for most of his life. Had every player he'd ever seen claim victory on this exact stage felt as he did now? Was everyone else so aware of their opponents? Was this natural? How did others contend with such confrontation, only moments before appearing on live TV?

And he thought of Billy. How Billy could be standing where Hunter was, or in Jason's own place, about to receive an amount of money that would change his life. Instead, Jason would collect the victory. And Billy was a marketing ploy that Jason apparently needed to be quiet about. He didn't feel very delusional.

The manager in front of Jason removed his grip and instead held up four fingers in Jason's face. He put one down. Then two. Finally, he pointed at Jason, who tried to stretch his arms out and relieve a fragment of his nerves.

A deafening roar came from beyond the stage. His stage manager was still pointing at him with wide eyes. The man nodded enthusiastically and gestured Jason forward.

Move, Jason thought. With no poise whatsoever, he bounded out onto the stage. Somewhere en route he remembered to smile. What did people do in this situation? He waved at the crowd he was only vaguely aware of. The lights were blinding.

Alright, not so bad. He allowed himself a genuine smile.

He also began to process his surroundings—two leather sofas off to the side, some tropical island decorations, a band, and the rest of the cast standing to the right, clapping. Jason's search for composure was interrupted as the cheering intensified. This was no longer clapping; it was an ovation. And it was focused to Jason's right.

Hunter came sprinting towards him. He was screaming and throwing his hands above his head, getting the crowd going. Veins projected out of his neck as he gave what he called a "Tennessee holler." Creating atmosphere, WWE style.

As Hunter reached Jason he jumped into him, bodies colliding, and wrapped his arms around Jason, nearly lifting him into the air. Jason could only try to maintain balance, aware of how awkward he looked, not only to the crowd and his cast mates but also the millions of people watching at home. His students. His colleagues. His friends. Blake.

This entrance was apparently planned out, and Jason felt clueless. He tried to convey this in the grave look he gave Hunter.

But, what had worked on the island was no more. Hunter only laughed and clapped him on the back with a thud.

"It's the big day, man."

They stood, center stage, with their cast and a talk-show set-up to the left, a band to the right, twelve-hundred screaming fans in front, and a few dozen cameras pointed at them from every angle. Jason had been on a television show for months, and this was the first time it felt like it.

Luke Stock's voice pulled Jason out of the moment. "Welcome to *Beached*."

Seconds after they heard his voice, the host of *Beached* was on stage with them. Luke walked over to Jason and Hunter. Hunter stepped forward and shook hands with Luke so enthusiastically that Jason was left to engage in what felt like the sloppy seconds of handshakes. Hunter knew what was happening around him, but it was as though Jason had missed a meeting and no one had bothered to tell him.

"This season," Luke said into the microphone, "has been one of the most traumatic, sensational, controversial, and discussed seasons in *Beached*'s long and storied history on RTN. We are here tonight to honor, remember and celebrate everything that happened on the island."

He paused for applause and got it.

"And, of course, there is this matter of naming the season's winner."

The crowd again erupted into applause. Jason clapped along with them, politely, and Hunter continued to fist-pump. Jason felt afraid he could have lost. Hunter thought he had won; the audience was showing Hunter more support. The way they edited the show left Jason barely visible, and, based upon Jason's meeting with the network, they weren't fans of his.

No, Jason decided. I've talked to everyone, and I definitely won. They said they voted for me to win. This is just hype. And he just couldn't carry on like Hunter. He knew he would only have worse anxiety and be the subject of even harsher memes.

Once the applause died down to a minimum, Luke continued, "Okay, so I have the envelope in my hands. With the name. Of. Your. Winner. And I'm ready to read it." Luke paused dramatically, turned ninety degrees, and looked into a different camera. "Right after this commercial break."

Jason's perception of the room began dilating. People around the stage talked into headsets, the audience chatted amongst themselves, and a more relaxed feeling washed over the room.

"Damn. Do you think I have time for the restroom?" Jason said to Hunter. He gave a forced laugh.

"Are you kiddin'? Definitely not, man. Commercials are like two minutes. You too excited?"

"Well, yeah, I'm nervous. I had a cup of coffee half an hour ago. So stupid."

Jason's felt his ears get red and tapped his foot on the ground, trying to forget his predicament. Hunter again clapped him on the back.

"You'll be good, buddy."

"I'm sure I will," Jason said.

As he was speaking, one of the crew with headsets came jogging onto the middle of the stage.

"We're about to go live. Places."

Immediately the room again contracted, cameras focused, and people on stage grew quiet. Jason stood as still as possible, unable to concentrate on anything other than holding his bladder.

The music again filled the room as disorienting flares of light accentuated the percussion instruments and Luke reminded the audience he was about to declare the winner.

"I said I was ready to reveal the envelope. So, here we are. At the end of the momentous fiftieth season of *Beached*." Luke was nearly screaming at the crowd.

"And your winner is." Hunter grabbed Jason in an embrace around the shoulder. Jason felt the whole crowd focus on Hunter. He traced every line of sight. There were signs in the audience, definitely placed by the network, which read "We Love Hunter." No one would actually write that. Hunter was more composed than Jason had seen him.

The screams of excitement peaked—only not from Luke—after he announced, "Jason. Congratulations." The audience was standing, clapping, yelling either out of obligation or genuine pleasure. Either way, they cheered for him, and it was deafening. Luke, however, was on high alert. His lips were pursed, his eyes wide, and his head scanned the room before resting his gaze on Jason.

Hunter forced a drooping smile and grabbed Jason. He yelled into his ear over the roar of the crowd.

"Nice, man," was all Jason heard.

The motion of the set accelerated around him while Jason was stuck in a carnivalesque slow motion. Ringing and fog. The emotion of the moment was speeding past, delible, but for a few details. Every contestant's body language burned into his mind. Their expressions. He was still playing the game. Figuring out who was with him or against him. Whose faces told of false enthusiasm, and whose were genuine. There was a spectrum. Still, they all made an effort, except Nick, who didn't even clap.

He smiled in all their directions.

He was further reluctant to celebrate, but he forced it. A nominal fist pump and a guttural yell of excitement. The whole time he struggled to interpret the only two reactions he couldn't make sense of: Luke's manic expression of fear, and Will's bewildered look of confusion which endured from the hallway.

Luke's amplified voice cut through the relenting celebration. "Alright, we have the interviews you're dying to hear, and we'll check in with this season's fascinating cast. What they've been up to since leaving the island, what you didn't get to see. All the behind-the-scenes intrigue. Coming up next. After these quick commercials. Don't look away; you don't want to miss this."

He clapped four slow, delayed claps while staring straight into the camera. It looked menacing. And then the "Live" light dimmed.

Still focused on Luke's odd behavior, Jason didn't notice the man trying to guide him to the interview couch. This man, potentially the same stagehand from earlier, wore the same black outfit of those who toil, unseen, behind the television, but he had the force of someone with far more importance. As Jason took a seat on the overstuffed, green leather sofa, the man finally removed his hand from Jason's shoulder.

"Next time, when it's time for you to move, you need to listen. We have a show to put on, so no more delays. That's strike two."

Jason could only gape in his direction. He had won a million dollars and the season of his favorite show. Cut me a break, he thought. A little time for shock and awe. But he nodded and was briefly left alone.

Alone to feel exposed, sitting on the interview couch, the focal point of the entire set.

18.

THE NEXT MORNING Jason found himself in the same studio lot once again. He paced the sidewalk, leading from RTN's parking lot, where he'd parked the rental car, to the front of their studio offices. His mind was also engaged in repetition, repeating the same process it had been running for at least sixteen hours: reliving the events of the reunion show. He should have pushed harder for Blake to come with him to Los Angeles. Her voice would have pulled him back and torn his mind from the loop. But that only compounded his self-loathing because it reminded him that he couldn't figure out his own value. Did he ever help her?

At the front of the building, the imposing, art deco RTN sign triggered memories. Sitting on the interview couch. Cameras again rolling. Luke sitting across from him. Feeling nervous to speak on live television for the first time.

The door to the office building was more substantial than expected, and Jason slid through before it slammed shut again. The wind didn't help. Speaking on live television hadn't been as embarrassing as Jason imagined. He felt no preoccupation with his responses. But there had been so few. Three questions.

"As a big fan of the show, how does it feel to win?"

"What do you plan to do with the money?"

"What was the key to your victory?"

Cut to commercial.

Jason arrived at RTN's front desk. The only receptionist was talking into his headset. After a moment, he studied Jason with a smirk, perhaps noticing that he was wearing the same outfit he had on television last night. He hadn't slept either and felt suddenly embarrassed. His devil-may-care attitude from the car faded in the face of the crippling, stagnating bureaucracy symbolized by that reception desk. The man behind it paused his conversation. "Can I help you?"

Jason explained that he needed to speak with Luke Stock, the host and executive producer of *Beached*.

Last evening, Jason's responses had been cool and measured. Standard answers, because he anticipated more probing questions. But after he answered those surface-level, cursory questions, they again cut to commercial. The segment felt brief and peculiar. Interviews with winners were usually the principal focus of the reunion show. Yet, as soon as the "Live" light dimmed, Jason's grabby handler was again gripping his shoulders.

"Do you have an appointment?" the receptionist asked.

"No, but I'm a friend of his. I just won the show last night."

The receptionist furrowed his brow, gave an "eh" which Jason hoped was intended to demonstrate more understanding than it did, and pushed a card across the counter.

"This is the office number to schedule appointments. Unfortunately, as you can imagine, everyone here is swamped with work for the new season, and can't take walk-ins. If you call, they'll definitely be able to get you in next week."

The man in black had guided Jason from the sofa to a backstage holding area. Jason had felt only confusion as he watched Hunter, Dimitri, and Nick take his place on the green leather sofa. Perhaps it was a new segment, and he'd be back on stage in a moment, Jason had considered. Once again, he felt left out of something. "Right," the man in black had said as he forced a printout against Jason's chest. "Here's this for your records. The money will be deposited into the account you provided after we pay your taxes for you. Thanks for being part of the season."

Jason pushed the business card back. "Actually, I can't be here next week. I have to fly back to Cincinnati, so if I could see him now, that would be great. He'll understand."

Luke's behavior was inconsistent. He seemed to like Jason on the island, but was avoiding any contact now.

Today, Jason wasn't taking no for an answer. He still regretted leaving the reunion. The handler had informed Jason that he was no longer needed on set, and was free to leave. The man's demeanor and size, coupled with the shock of the situation left Jason prone to follow direction. He turned to leave, after taking a longing look at the rest of his cast mates, still illuminated under the stage lights, while he dissolved into the black abyss of backstage.

"Sir, you seriously can't see him today. I understand who you are, but it's not an emergency, and you have no appointment. There are protocols."

"I'm not going anywhere until I sit down with Luke. What would make it an emergency?"

"Is that a threat?"

"No. I can't leave without this conversation. I refuse. Just get him on the phone."

The receptionist returned his hand to his headset. Jason felt accomplished. More, potentially, than he had about winning last evening. That was more a relief.

"Security, front entrance," the man said. "This guy won't leave." After a brief pause, he added, "Yes, a former contestant. Good call."

The words collided with Jason's perception. Why was that the assumption? Everything was reminding him of his last memory from the taping.

As he was forced to exit the stage area, someone had grabbed him from behind for the last time that evening. As he spun around, he was again confronted with Will's panic-stricken face. Then, Jason had been given another question. Or delusion. It depended on how he viewed it. And his evidence, combined with his experience, pointed him in both directions at once.

At RTN, security to remove Jason was quick. They held his arms for a moment. "Is this necessary?" Jason asked. They pulled him from the receptionist's kiosk, until he twisted his arms up, causing the light grip to break.

"I'm going. Fine." Two hands on his back accelerated his pace. Without another incident, Jason was back in the sunlight, his eyes struggling to adjust.

"If you come back, we'll call the cops. No trespassing."

Squinting, Jason set off back to his car. Will's words passed through his mind.

"You're not wrong," he had said. "I know it's true. They'll never admit it. Don't give in. Call this number."

Will had held out a piece of paper to Jason. He took it, without a word. Will then tore back to his place amongst the cast, making sure he was there before the show went live again, or his absence was noted. He left Jason standing with a business card in his hand. It was a business card for someone named Charles DeStefano, who was apparently a manager at a place called "People to People." Google returned no information. The address listed was in Seattle. Jason frowned and flipped the card over, revealing a phone number jotted on the back. He didn't recognize the area code, and couldn't tell if one number was a one or a seven.

Opening his rental car and depositing himself into the driver's seat, Jason checked that his suitcase was sitting in the back seat. It was. He stretched back, unzipped the front pocket, and pulled out the business card Will had given him. He turned it over, contemplating the function of "People to People," as well as Will's mental state. Was Will a mirror to Jason? Was that how Jason looked to everyone else?

He slid the card into the inside pocket of his jacket, started the engine, and began his journey back to the airport.

19.

THE MAN SEATED next to Jason unbuckled his seatbelt and, with a grunt, removed the backpack stowed under the seat in front of him. Jason had yet to undo his seatbelt as the plane taxied to the gate. He removed his cell phone from the pocket of his jeans and took the phone out of airplane mode. It vibrated repeatedly, but he slid it back without checking the notifications.

The plane halted and the pilot's voice came over the intercom.

"Okay, local time here in Cincinnati is 8:46 pm, and it's a chilly thirty-six degrees outside. Thank you for flying with Delta, we hope you've enjoyed your flight. If there's anything we can do for you, let one of our staff know. Also, if you had to gate check a bag, we ask that you wait single file at the exit gate, and we'll bring those to you shortly. Thank you."

The fully booked flight began to eke its way down the aisle. Passengers pulled bags at awkward angles, exchanged disingenuous smiles, and, finally, emerging into the chilly November air before entering the airport to collect any other bags or arrange rides.

Jason, with his backpack on, tried to walk at as quickly as possible to make his way through the slow-walkers. After a few desolate moving sidewalks, Jason reached the baggage claim without incident, but no one was there to greet him.

He pulled out his cell phone. Two new messages from Seth. One from Blake.

Seth informed Jason first, that he was leaving his house and, second, that he was late because of traffic he hit passing the soccer stadium. Blake's message told Jason that she would love to talk, whenever he was ready, and that she missed him. I miss you so much, he thought, but only slid his phone into his jacket. He couldn't muster a response to either of them.

With nothing to do but wait, Jason took a seat on an empty bench inside the baggage claim. The passengers he'd hurried through were now making their way past him. One teenager recognized him from TV and attempted to point stealthily for his parent, then stared. Most just made their way to their ride or waited for their luggage around the carousel.

Unsure what to focus on, Jason pulled his phone out again. As he did, the business card Will had given him fell out.

After picking it up with a frown, he flipped the card over in his hand again. Why not?

He punched the ten-digit number into his phone, guessing on the confusingly twisted one, or seven.

Jason pressed the phone hard to his ear and strained to listen. The call rang five times, then a computerized message informed him the mailbox was full, and the call ended.

Jason again entered the phone number, this time replacing the one with a seven. Before actually hitting call, however, he closed the phone and shoved the card back into his front pocket. "Stupid," he muttered.

However, as he struggled to remove his hand, Jason received another text message, this time from the number he had just called. His heart rate increased, and he forgot the hundreds of people around him. Jason opened the message and saw a single name. "Joel Markani."

The name meant nothing.

"How was the flight?"

Jason looked up from his phone. Seth stood next to him with a wide grin on his face.

"Hey, man," Jason said, standing up. "It wasn't bad. I read a bit. How are you?"

"Not bad. It's good to see you again. Congratulations, too. That trip had to be amazing."

"Yeah," he lied. "Thanks."

Jason threw on his backpack and motioned to the sliding exit doors. "Shall we?"

"After you."

"Thanks again for coming to get me. I needed it. Things with Blake are a little...I don't know. Strained. My fault. And I felt bad asking."

"You don't even need to thank me. It's no problem. You live close to the airport. Plus, it's not every day one of your close friends wins *Beached*, so I'm glad I can be here for you even if I haven't seen you much on campus this semester. I'm parked over here, though. Illegally, so let's hurry or you're paying the ticket."

Seth's silver BMW was sitting in the pickup lane, along with a dozen other parked cars. Seth pulled out his keys, and the vehicle illuminated.

After they climbed in, Seth's music blasted them. It was a loud double-bass beat that Jason didn't recognize.

With a quiver in his voice, Seth apologized.

"Hey, no worries. I needed a wake-up call."

"Speaking of, did you want to grab a drink or anything?"

Jason considered the offer a moment too long.

"Or not," Seth said. "No worries either way. No pressure."

"Yeah, man, I would probably rather go home and go to bed. I'm exhausted."

They drove for a few silent minutes.

"Hey, do you know of a guy called Joel Makroni, or Markoni, or something?" Jason asked.

"I don't think so. Should I?" Seth shifted his jaw back and forth a few times.

"No. I got a random text message from an unknown number. All it said was that name. Probably just whoever's phone it is. It seemed weird, and I wasn't sure if it was someone I should know. Someone affiliated with *Beached*, or RTN or something."

"Could be. I may have heard of him, but it doesn't stick out. Someone you met at a celebration party and gave your number to? A writer or producer or something?"

"I'm sure that's what it is. I'm tired and have my mind stuck on it for some reason. No big deal. Thanks again."

After driving the rest of the way to Jason's house, the two exchanged pleasantries, a one-armed hug, and Jason said, "Goodbye," before heading through the front door. Once inside, Jason didn't unpack right away. He walked up the stairs to his computer, opened his browser, and searched for the name "Joel Markani," using his phone to make sure he got the spelling correct.

The mystery man had an IMDB page with no credits listed. There were too many random photos of the multitude of Joel Markanis on social media for any pictures to be helpful. Finally, towards the bottom of the third search results page, Jason found a link to the *Beached* Reddit page.

The thread was over two years old, but the original poster had asked if anyone knew friends who worked for *Beached* or RTN. There were a smattering of replies and links to other user accounts. The comment that had triggered Jason's search was from the username "slowsand77," who said "Yea. I know a dude from college who's going to do that. Joel Markani. He's a prop design guy, and I'll see if he wants to talk to you, but he doesn't do Reddit."

There it was. Jason clicked on slowsand77 to view his other comments. That post, despite the account being nine years old, was his sole comment.

PODCAST

JOSH: Coming to you live, from my Aunt Wanda's basement, it's Josh Riddell, bringing you a special episode of *Beached* Bums! And my guest today—your winner of *Beached*, season fifty: Jason Debord! Here for his exit interview!

JASON: Hello, hello.

JOSH: Jason—not much enthusiasm for a newly made millionaire! I'm excited to get into all this with you. Let's talk about your personal journey and celebrate your strategy before we discuss the other events that have dominated the coverage of the season. First off, what's the best part of winning?

JASON: Being home, without a doubt. Seeing my friends and students. Honestly —I haven't given a thought to the money, but it's in my account. Actually, I got home from Los Angeles, from the finale, last night. There's...
   [Beat.]
   So much going on.

JOSH: Sure, sure, totally expected that everything is so overwhelming. Let's get to it then: what do you think was your biggest move this season? You played one of the most under-the-radar games ever, and we rarely got to see a confessional with you. But, as a lifelong fan, I'm expecting that you had several key strategies going on. Were you camera shy? Were you giving them anything to work with?

JASON: Yeah. For me, it's not the cameras. It's the people. I didn't want to tell the producers and camera guys my plans. People talk.

JOSH: I can surely relate—when I played in Jordan it took a long time to open up about strategy to the camera. Probably not something we all have a talent for.

JASON: [Clears throat.] There were multiple factors that made me uncomfortable sharing my game with production—when you're out there they have all the power and you're not sure if you can trust them. The world flips on the island—traditional senses of morality, integrity, good, evil, right, wrong, they're all out the window. No one can be trusted, you think. Or maybe it's just me.

JOSH: You speak in the present tense—are you still feeling like you're on the island? Have you had enough time to adjust to normal life—this is the shortest break ever between filming and the first episode's release—one week or so, right?

JASON: Mm-hmm. I think it was just about two weeks. Yeah—a hard transition. [Laughs.] I still feel like I'm stuck in that mindset. I don't know. Maybe I'm losing it.

JOSH: [Laughs.] Yeah—this is good for the fans to hear. It took me weeks to feel normal, and it's hard to find others who can relate. Thanks for opening up. Okay —so about big moves—what do you think defined your game? What did we not get to see?

[Beat.]

JOSH: Jason, you there?

JASON: Sorry. I zoned out.

JOSH: You want to reschedule this? You seem hesitant and it's so soon. I know this has been a dark season and a rough time.

JASON: No—I'm good. My bad. Let's try again.

JOSH: Okay—we can edit this all out. With everything going on, I haven't been streaming any of my interviews live.

JASON: I appreciate that. I just don't want to come across as too celebratory, or too mournful. I'm having trouble striking the right tone. We can start again.

JOSH: Okay—so about that big move—what do you think was the defining move of your game? Maybe something that viewers at home were deprived of? Some people have been critical of your win—how do you silence those critics?

JASON: My biggest move was definitely flipping on my original allies. Once, you know, the stuff with Billy happened, I couldn't work with them anymore. It pulled us apart. Plus, the numbers were set up in such a way that I couldn't get to the end with anyone but him. Otherwise, I expected to get axed along the way because I was too big of a strategic threat. So I needed a big target to shield me, and I knew I could work with Hunter. He was desperate, on the outs. So then I dismantled my original teammates and knew they would still reward me with the money in the end. Hunter's lovable, but given this is season fifty, the people on the beach were fans and I knew they'd respect my more aggressive game. Hunter's too nice, he's a good old boy, and that's why I wanted to work with him.

JOSH: Yes, of course, the big flip. Changing dynamics. What went into that decision for you—you mentioned it—but why couldn't you continue on with Nick and Phoebe? You seemed pretty tight together.

JASON: After...
   [Beat.]

JASON: After what happened. We didn't talk anymore. It was just, too much. We lost whatever connection we had because I think Billy was the middle-man in our relationships. I'm close with Phoebe again though, and Nick's fine, I guess. We don't talk.

JOSH: Ye—

JASON: Look—sorry to cut you off—I can't do this. I want to support the fans and I love your podcast—hell, I listened to you for years before I went on the show. But this is too much right now. I highly doubt they even want to hear from me, sounding like this. I need to figure things out. I can't yet.

JOSH: I fully understand—getting anyone to talk about this season has been emotional and challenging. If you change your mind, I'd love your insight. Just text me. And don't worry about this—I won't publish the recording.

JASON: Thanks again. Good luck with the podcast. I'll definitely be in touch. Once I feel more like myself and know how I want to talk about this publicly.

JOSH: Sure thing. Talk to you soon. Take care.

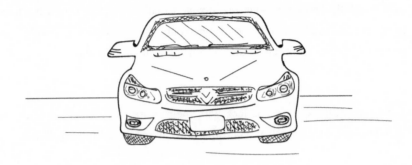

20.

JASON CLOSED HIS PODCAST APP, unwilling to contemplate his failed interview two days prior. At least no one would hear it. He scrolled through his phone, trying to find music to play but bored with his selections. Before he settled on anything, the car in front of his pulled out of line, and Jason pulled forward a car length.

As he switched gears back into park, there was a tap at his window.

A pudgy man wearing a TSA hat and bright, neon-yellow reflector jacket stood outside Jason's Camry. He rolled down the window.

"Yes?"

"You can't park here. You waiting on someone?"

"Yeah, my friend's flight landed a few minutes ago. He should be out any second."

"Alright. In the future, if you're going to be waiting here, you need to park in the lot across the street. Then, have your passenger call you when they're ready to load."

"Okay, I'm sorry. I didn't know," Jason lied.

The guard walked off to tap on the next car window and have a duplicate conversation. Jason looked out his windshield, and then in his rearview mirror.

Cars as far as he could see, and no one actively loading. The guard had his work cut out for him.

He returned to his phone and selected an older, familiar Belle and Sebastian album.

Out of the corner of his eye, he saw Will, making straight for the line of cars. Jason remembered Will had no clue what car he drove. Their conversations planning this trip had been brief, covert and lacked detail.

Jason opened his door and stuck his head over the top of his car, squinting through the harsh overheard lighting. He waved to Will, who acknowledged him with a nod.

Will brought a light backpack and a small carry-on size suitcase.

When he reached Jason's car, Will opened the door with force and slammed it shut. He didn't take his backpack off but continued to wear it as he put on his seatbelt.

"Good to see you," Jason said.

"You, too." Will looked in the back seat and tilted his head to analyze the car's carpet.

"How was the flight?"

"Average. Quick flight from D.C. I like flying at night."

"Good. Well, I'm excited to work with you on this. I knew something felt off about Billy, and I guess you're on to something."

As soon as Jason uttered Billy's name, Will grabbed the volume dial and spun it to forty. Jason forgot to read the signs as he exited the airport and had to cut off a black sedan. The driver sounded the horn, but Jason barely heard it over the music.

"We don't say specifics. We don't know who listens," Will said.

Jason nodded, trying to focus on driving, the car behind him, and Will, but suddenly regretted what he was doing. "Sorry."

"Anyway, it's good not to have to change phones every day," Will continued, not acknowledging that he had heard Jason.

"Yeah, nice. Much more secure in person."

"So, have you been able to gather anything further on Markani? I know you have contacts on the production side."

"What?" Jason had to shout over the music.

Will repeated himself.

"No. I asked my friend, Seth, but he didn't know or remember the guy. I haven't heard from my other friend, Omid, in months. He never got back. Markani seems obscure. It's weird, but why are you so focused on him? Plus, if production's up to something, should I really be asking around? I want to believe you, and it feels right, but what do you think is going on?"

Will only smiled, reached over his left shoulder and tapped his backpack.

"Okay. I'm interested to see what you have."

They were safely on the highway. Will again swiveled his head as if watching for someone following them or hiding behind the seats.

"So," said Jason, "we've been talking a lot over the last couple days. But, you've never told me what you think happened out there. Why did you approach that RTN producer, Richard, in his office?"

"Curtis David. Never trust the two-named man." Will smiled.

Jason laughed and felt a hard stare from the passenger seat.

"Okay," Jason said, "that name sounds familiar. He's a producer, right?"

Jason merged onto I-275 from I-75. They were ten minutes from his house, where he was about to let Will stay.

"People come and go from that crew. Names pop up, and they're never heard from again. But one remains. Curtis David. Billy disappears. Still Curtis David."

Jason wanted to laugh more because of the delivery and conviction, but Will's expression prevented him.

"Weird," Jason said. He wasn't convinced, but over the last week, Will had funneled him mystery after inexplicable mystery. Will might be a weird guy, but it seemed there was something beneath it all. Jason had always felt it. There was too much for it not to add up to something.

"Almost there," Jason said.

"Yeah." Will had an odd confidence.

Through the darkness of the highway, high beams pierced Jason's car. He struggled to see as the light reflected off his rearview mirror and the foggy windshield.

"Jesus," Jason said, switching lanes to get away from the headlights. "Dick."

"So do you know anything about this Curtis guy?" Jason asked.

The bright lights were almost past them and he needed something concrete from Will.

"Basically nothing, but—"

Jason lost control of the car and his consciousness spun. The force pushed him against the door. He had no control of his body. Time slowed down and then accelerated, making up for whatever had been lost. Jason's perception buffered like a video over spotty Wi-Fi. The car with the headlights had slammed into them. Jason knew there should be noise, but heard nothing. Another round of whiplash as his Camry was slammed into the median. He tried to move and only winced. When he remained motionless, he felt nothing.

There was motion he couldn't stop, though. Blinking. Bright lights filled his car from somewhere. Not another car.

He was blinded to direction and couldn't tell if he was upside-down or on his side. He tried to call Will's name, but wasn't sure if he did or not. Ringing. He couldn't keep his eyes open long enough to see if Will was okay, or gauge how badly they were bleeding. He only knew they were.

He tried to move again and failed before a coughing fit. Fumes from the gas, coolant, and everything else that was leaking penetrated the car.

Jason had to cover his eyes to avoid the lights. Some still seeped through. He focused on breathing. The silence was soothing. Blake was the last thought in Jason's head as his vision narrowed. He felt a chill he couldn't shake and faded into unconsciousness before his head fell limply to the left.

Jason's car sat on its side, littered with glass, airbag shrapnel, and leaking fluids. It was utterly alone on the highway. No one had driven by, and the other car was nowhere to be seen. It had left only a few scrapes of paint.

MEANWHILE

HE REWOUND and replayed the moment. And again. And again.

Each time he laughed. His belly heaved with the deep laughs.

He finally set the remote down and let the rest of the reunion show play. He had seen Jason cast aside enough times.

He reached into the bag at his feet, unzipped the top halfway, and extracted his laptop. He threw it open and blew on the keyboard. Dust flew back in his face.

"Pah."

He ran his shirtsleeve over his heavily stubbled face.

"Alright, back to work, back to work. What to say?"

He double-clicked a Word document, saved on his desktop as "Unnamed File." He scrolled down to the thirty-seventh page, where he had left off. He typed, slowly and methodically.

His phone went off and he swore under his breath.

Folding the computer screen forward, he again reached into his bag and fumbled for his phone. The ringing stopped. The call had dropped, likely due to the poor reception in his basement office. But he recognized the number.

"Hmm," he said to himself, pulling his computer screen back up and abandoning the phone. He again looked at the document.

"I may need you finished sooner than expected."

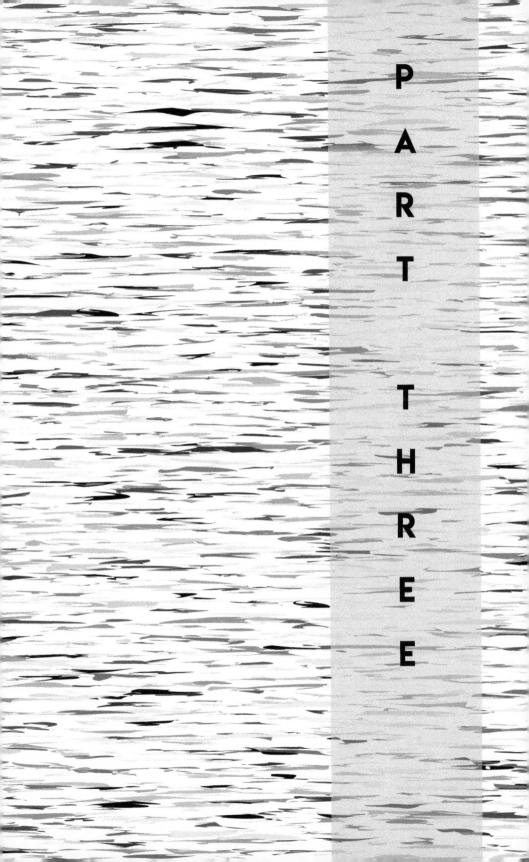

PART

THREE

21.

NEARLY THREE DAYS after first being called by the police, Blake exited through the front doors of Christ Hospital, and the glass doors slid shut behind her with a mechanical whoosh. The mid-morning sun had a disorienting effect on her eyes, which had been inside the building for most of those three days. The cold air crept up the back of her neck. She shivered but avoided putting up her woolen coat collar, realizing how much she craved a shower. She got to her car, pulled open the door and collapsed into the driver's seat. Her arms hung at her sides and she stared straight ahead. After clearing her throat, she reached out and pulled the door closed. The movements felt foreign. Of someone else's body, her mind detached from her physical surroundings. She considered whether this was all the result of a lack of sleep, food, or, somehow, still shock.

Without improved clarity, Blake started the engine and made her way through the labyrinth of lines and arrows painted on the hospital parking lot's asphalt. But another body was performing the tasks. One that was far away from Blake. A body that slept and went to work, ate full meals with friends, and enjoyed carefree evenings bingeing television and drinking wine. Not one that endured twelve hours sitting in a waiting room, ten hours sitting in another waiting room, two separate hours trying to find something edible, and nearly forty hours on an overstuffed chair in a hospital room.

As nurses and doctors swirled in and out, Blake remained. Propping up the cards that arrived, shaking the hands and hugging the shoulders of those who came to visit. Arranging the flowers that were delivered. She had spoken to many of the doctors and visitors, but that had been out of obligation. Not because she wanted to. She still didn't want to do anything. Eating, sleeping, bathing. These things felt necessary, so they were done, but they didn't tear through the foggy shroud. Blake hadn't felt like leaving, though the nurse said it was a good idea and that he'd be okay. She still moved reluctantly, her mind limiting her body from any extraneous work. No need to put on a seatbelt. Let the car beep at her. Ironic. No use in putting her usual sugar in the coffee. Black's fine. Bitter. No point in removing a stink bug from a potted orchid plant in the room. Harmless.

WHILE BLAKE LEFT, back in the hospital room, the harmless stink bug she had also left was removing its proboscis from the third of five wavy, green leaves on a potted orchid. Phoebe sent the orchid to Jason to brighten his room. It was one of the first gifts to arrive, and the one Blake situated in the window's center. Cards and flowers were arranged around the white orchid with two blooms. It was a fair collection. A few of the nurses said so. Especially for a young man with no children, and who had been in the hospital for so short a time. The word "short" had been all Blake noticed. But, the brown marmorated stink bug was unaware of all this.

It was unaware that it would have been flushed down a toilet under normal circumstances, and it was unaware that Blake's grief had spared it. Instead, the insect made its way to the next leaf, filling up, sucking sustenance from Jason's gifts.

Hours later, after Blake had showered, thrown on a robe, and fallen asleep on top of her covers, the stink bug had begun its transition away from the orchid. Full from eating, the insect moved, painstakingly, across the surface of cards from a number of Jason's *Beached* cast mates. Blake had put the *Beached* cards on the left, with all others to the right. "You're in our thoughts and prayers, always," read a card, featuring cats, from Anna and her husband. "Wishing you a speedy recovery. Love you, man," Dimitri had written on a postcard. "I hope you get better. Sorry," wrote Nick on a plain cream card. There were a variety of other niceties and hackneyed phrases, written by friends who struggled over the right thing to say. Desiree's card had stood out. "Jason, this is horrible. I am so sorry. We need to talk. Like I emailed you, I have something you need to see. Please get well and call me." Blake had noticed it but forgotten when glancing back at Jason, unconscious on the bed.

Blake had also noticed, and quickly forgotten, that there were ten *Beached* cards. Ten cards from thirteen members of the cast. Blake hadn't cared to determine, and the insect couldn't know, that while Jason obviously didn't receive a card from himself or Will, who was in a medically induced coma in a neighboring room, he also hadn't received a card from Hunter.

Without any of this knowledge, the stink bug found its final resting place for the day. It clung, defying gravity, to the side of a banner that hung on Jason's hospital room wall, just above the display of cards and flowers. Seth had delivered the banner, signed by many of Jason's students, the previous evening. But the stink bug focused on instinct. Emitting pheromones unnoticed by the nurse who came in to check on Jason and creating vibrations that were inaudible over the soccer channel that Blake left on the TV.

Nothing would result from the stink bug's quest for a mate. Not this time. But there it sat, on the banner, fighting for the survival of its species, unaware of the human surroundings, oblivious to its species' journey from Japanese soy fields to Cincinnati, Ohio, and unaware of its own signature brown bands and thorax glands that gave it a name. And Jason lay across the room, also fighting, and also unaware of the insect's existence.

Unaware, until three days later when he watched as Blake took down the banner for him, and saw the bug. She flicked it onto the wall. It remained as Jason and Blake left the room, and it didn't hear the doctor mention "See you Tuesday," or "full recovery."

22.

JASON SMILED at Blake and kissed the top of her head, taking comfort in her thick hair that was entangled in the long stubble of his rough face. The smell of lavender accompanied the affection. Blake sat further back in her seat, pressing against the couch and wrapped her arms around a throw pillow. A hand-stitched mandala covered the pillow. She didn't know where Jason had acquired it, but it had no match.

"If I'm well enough to talk to them today and drive to the doctor's, then I can get the door. It's good to do normal stuff and move," Jason said.

"Well, I'm glad. Just don't overdo it and let me know how I can help."

"Yeah. You've been amazing. Seriously."

Jason reached the door and stood beside it, waiting for his guests to make their way up to the door. Blake and Jason had been awaiting their arrival and watching out the window, but Jason felt weird opening the door before they even knocked. He let them get to the porch and ring the doorbell. Only then did he turn the deadbolt. As the screen door sprung free, the woman on the other side caught it.

"Detectives, come on in," Jason said.

"Hi there. Thanks," the first detective said as she crossed the threshold. She seemed to be a little older than Jason and was dressed in plain clothes. The second only nodded and smiled at Jason. He was much younger and wore a baggy, red sweater, which accentuated his slightness, in both age and size.

"Hello," Blake said as the detectives entered Jason's home.

"Hi," the female detective said, extending a hand to Blake. "Kate Rogers. And this is my partner, Ryan Larson."

"Blake Edel. Nice to meet you." They exchanged a firm handshake and smile.

"Blake's my girlfriend, and she's been living here to help take care of me after the accident. If we want, the dining room table's through here." Jason gestured towards the right of the living room.

"Thanks," Detective Rogers said, "and you mentioned you were doing well?"

"Yeah. Each day I'm a bit better, and I've been home for about a week. Today's been a good morning so far."

"He's mostly self-sufficient," Blake said. "Everything takes him longer still, because he needs breaks."

"Well, that's good to hear. And we're sorry for what happened to you," Rogers said. Detective Larson nodded.

The four took seats around Jason's sturdy table. Detective Rogers pulled out a notebook, and Larson followed.

"So, are you okay answering some questions?" Larson asked.

"Yeah, of course. I'm glad this is being investigated."

Rogers nodded.

"While you guys get started, can I get anyone coffee or anything? And Jason, you're about due for meds," Blake said.

"Right on, thanks. And I'll take a coffee if you don't mind," Jason said. Rogers and Larson both agreed on coffee, and Blake made her way towards the Keurig in the kitchen.

She opened Jason's clay pot, next to the machine, and extracted four coffee pods. Jason and Blake were both particular about their coffee and she smiled, thinking of when they had found the brand years ago. Such a small thing. Setting the pods on the counter, she heard the discussion in the other room. "And how would you describe your relationship with Mr. Bradford?" and "Where were you two headed?"

Before the accident, Jason and Blake had been murky. She needed a break to figure it out. Every few days Jason had been going through personality swings. He vacillated between accepting Billy's death and seeking closure with his family, only then to raise allegations of murder at RTN's headquarters. Yet, she loved him, so there was never an end in sight. There never had been.

As the first coffee finished, Blake set the mug on a tray and got the next brewing.

It had all been complicated and frustrating only weeks ago, which made her feel self-conscious and uncomfortable that the accident—near death—had brought them back together. Blake exchanged the coffee mug for the next.

In the time since she answered the call from the police, detailing that Jason was in critical condition, her thoughts had crystallized. And since the accident, Jason's mind had not been preoccupied with seeking conspiracy in Billy's death. This wouldn't be the end, but it felt like the threat clarified priorities. She hoped, at least.

As the third mug had finished brewing, Blake removed it, set the fourth in its place, reloaded the machine, and discarded the spent pod. She heard Jason saying "Wow. That's crazy. It felt intentional. Like the guy was pissed at me. But I assumed they were drunk."

Blake froze and listened further.

"Yeah. We have traffic cam footage, so we got the plates, but the car was stolen," Larson said.

Blake could hear Jason laugh in disbelief.

"So. Do you know where the driver went if you have footage?"

Blake didn't catch the detectives' response because the Keurig emitted its last trails of steam, and the coffees were finished. She placed the last mug on the tray and balanced it into the dining room. Blake could hear Detective Rogers talking, but she stopped as soon as Blake entered with the coffees.

"Thanks so much," Jason said.

"Yes, thank you," Rogers said.

"Cream or sugar?" Everyone at the table collectively shook their heads, so Blake smiled and sat on the chair next to Jason.

"So," Rogers continued, "I don't want to make any promises about catching anyone, but want to take down your statement. A lot of times, in these cases, the car turns up abandoned somewhere. We don't have it yet, but I expect it'll turn up."

"Wow," Jason said and paused. "Do you think, maybe, they were targeting me or Will? I don't know."

Blake put her hand on Jason's arm, which hung at his side. "So," she said, "this appears intentional?"

"At this point, no. It looks like a pretty standard case of impaired driving," Rogers said. "We have no reason to suspect anything otherwise, but we'll still need to talk to Mr. Bradford once he is capable. He may have seen something, though it seems unlikely given the collision."

"Is there anything about Will that raises an alarm?"

Larson shook his head. "No, no. It's just policy. Nothing suspicious. But, again, we need to take statements."

Jason and Larson sipped their coffee. Blake joined out of discomfort and appreciated having something to do with her hands. Rogers observed.

"Is there anything we can do?" Blake asked.

"You have my number. We'll be in touch if there's information you need to know, or if we can track down the driver. Otherwise, your insurance company will have to handle the expenses."

Rogers tilted her mug back and finished her coffee.

"For now, we'll look into the car theft."

Both detectives stood.

"Thanks again," Jason said before also standing.

"We can show ourselves out, sir," Larson said, glancing at the pills Blake had placed in front of Jason. "And thanks for the coffee."

———

MINUTES LATER, the police had left and driven away, but Jason and Blake still sat at the table. Blake's face gave a scrunched sense of concern and fear. After a moment, Jason spoke.

"We should let the cats out of the bedroom. Now that the cops are gone."

Blake nodded.

Jason rose and walked down the hall. He tapped the bedroom door handle, and London and Tigger barreled out. They had waited at the door, pawing the inside of it. The food and water Jason set up had been consumed in the first fifteen minutes of captivity. The empty bowls made him smile.

"So, what do you think?" Blake asked when Jason re-entered the room.

"It seems suspicious is what I kept thinking. Someone steals a tank of a car and happens to have a near-fatal car crash with us? Right when we're going to whistle-blow about Billy's murder. We must be getting close to something big. I always thought it had to be murder, but this is feeling bigger."

The words hung in the air and refused to either sink in or dissipate.

"We just don't know," Jason continued. "It could have still been an accident. Or mistake, or drunk driving. Hopefully, we can trust the police to do a comprehensive investigation and look at every angle."

Blake's gaze homed in on a knot in the table's woodgrain. "So you see this as evidence for your opinion?" she asked. There was no emotion in her voice, no tremor. She saw to that.

"My opinion?" Jason raised an eyebrow.

"RTN? Billy?"

"I guess. They asked me about everything. But I don't know. There's no proof it relates at all. I hope it doesn't, actually. I don't know what to think. I just can't figure out why that one guy was so quiet; he was hiding something. Holding back. It's so much, with the break-in, what we've had so many people hint at."

Jason's voice was uncertain, and his body language noncommittal. He didn't want to offer any theories. He wanted Blake to connect the dots he thought he saw. He couldn't trust his own perception anymore. Since the crash, he had felt ironically complete, thanks to his relationship, and he had already vowed to not jeopardize it with anymore *Beached*, RTN, or Billy talk. But, despite how hesitant he was, telling Blake his suspicions was fulfilling. Jason had to pull himself back from outright enthusiasm.

Blake looked up and, while she thought, Jason gripped the back of a dining room chair and leaned against it. He said nothing.

"I mean, I can see your logic. All the things you mentioned when you first got back that were already suspicious. Then you talk about it publicly, and your house gets broken into. The network ignored you at the finale and reunion. And you keep talking about it. And then you're nearly killed. Along with Will, who happens to be the only other person you know who is openly talking about Billy's potential murder."

"Yeah," Jason said and nodded.

"But, still, none of that is concrete. Windows get broken and people get into accidents all the time. Contestants get ignored at the finale every season. It can be explained. And the last time you talked like this the situation was consuming. Are you losing perspective again?"

Blake tapped her feet on the floor a few times. After Jason broke eye contact, she took a long drink from her coffee mug. After swallowing, she held the mug to her face for an extra few seconds of pause.

Jason felt triumphant, but as though no one else could understand the language he spoke. Yet, he was also hesitant. After all, he was happy and resolute. He paced around the table while Blake continued to talk.

"What did Will have, that you guys were going to work on?"

"He had information, names mostly, and suspicion about specific crew members and former crew members. But, again, none of it is, like, hard evidence or admissible in court. Just a lot of suspicious pieces that add up. And when so much adds up, from all fronts, even with nothing iron-clad, it seems undeniable that something's happening."

"And you believed him?"

Jason shrugged and shook his head. "I don't know. It was worth looking into."

"You were so close to being done with all this. Moving on, feeling okay. I'm so sorry this happened. And you might still be particularly right about what happened to Billy, but I don't think this is all that helpful for your own well-being. RTN may have covered up their own negligence, but don't you think this is extreme?"

"Yeah, I hear you. But there's a part of me that may never move on from this. Or maybe it'll take a long time. Every time I push, something horrible happens. And there's nothing to be gained. Billy's already dead. Will and I have already been attacked. Allegedly. And, since the accident, things have felt right again. Like it hasn't since I got back from the island. And it's not the drugs I'm prescribed." Jason laughed.

Blake smiled.

"Look, I'm pushing back the daily visit to Will's room until tomorrow," Jason said. "I'm glad to have your care and support, but I need to think about all this. I'm going to read in the solarium to get my mind off it for now. There's a small chance I may have been nearly murdered, which feels weird. Will's close to recovery. I may have been sort of right all along. It's a lot."

"That makes sense," Blake said. "And I'm so sorry I have to be so blunt about this. I can't fully understand what you're going through."

"No, don't sound so sad. I need your perspective," Jason said as he walked to Blake's side.

Blake faced him, and Jason put his hand on hers. "Seriously. I love you," she said. "Despite all this. Nothing is more important than you. And whatever you need to look into, I'm by your side whether or not it makes sense to me. I'll help you work through it all to process it. And I think you'll see how this is coincidental."

Blake stood and wrapped her arms around Jason's waist. He pulled her tight and draped one arm over her shoulder and put his other hand on the back of her head. After squeezing each other tight and wading out of the hug, they shared a kiss. A static kiss, lips pressed together.

Jason tilted his head back and spoke. "Do you want me to order food? Or I can pick something up later. I'm getting a little hungry, even though it's a weird time. Unless you want to head home or have errands to run."

"Hang on a sec, I need to finish my thought. I can't say I agree with you and your thoughts about Billy's death; actually I disagree strongly. But I'll help you look further into this. I get that you need closure and clarity. You need to know. I get it.

"I've been thinking about how I would handle a patient with similar needs, and I'd help them explore the truth until they see it for themselves. And RTN won't help you, and neither can anyone else, so I want to."

"So I need psychiatric counseling?"

"Who doesn't? Don't be defensive. I'm trying to help, but this is a struggle for me, too. Maybe you'll find something I buy into, but I'm not there yet. I'll play devil's advocate until that happens."

"Sorry. You're right. Whether you believe me or not, your input is helpful. But I need something to eat. Should I make something?"

Blake flashed a puffy smile. "I'm in the mood for shepherd's pie, if that sounds good, and there are plenty of potatoes in the pantry. Something comforting. I can help. And we can talk more later, whenever you're ready. Please let me know, so I can help."

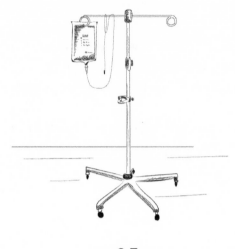

23.

"THERE HE IS." Jason's voice rang with affected, but not entirely false, enthusiasm.

The nurse beside Will's bed tensed, shocked at Jason's entrance.

"Hi, thanks for coming," Will said. The sound of his voice made Jason uncomfortably aware of his own throat and vocal cords.

"Hello, Mr. Debord. I'll be finished in a moment and out of your way. It's lucky that you caught Mr. Bradford awake today. He just woke up, actually," the nurse said.

"Excellent. Thank you."

"Yeah, Jason, have you been intentionally coming when I was asleep?"

"No, why?"

"Well, I keep hearing about getting visitors, but I haven't seen a single one. Well, that is apart from the exceptional hospital staff. Especially the lovely Miss Cromer, here."

The nurse, engaged in swapping out Will's IV bag, smiled politely. "Looks like the medicine is doing its job."

"Yeah, Will, I don't think I've ever heard you this talkative."

"Glad to be alive, my friend. Glad to be alive."

Jason and the nurse shared a glance.

"Excellent," Jason said. "I'm glad you're alive as well. I had my doubts about both of us."

The nurse grabbed a clipboard and headed for the door. "If you need anything, I'll be down the hall."

"Thanks."

Jason moved out of the entryway and sat on the firm brown chair next to Will's bed. He had become familiar with just how uncomfortable the chair was over the last week. Every time he sat he thought of how many nights Blake had spent trying to sleep, or at least rest, on an identical chair in a different room.

"So, again, I can't say how happy I am to see you. Well, anyone. But you're a good visitor," Will said.

"Glad to hear it. It's awesome to see you getting better. You might be out of here someday soon."

"Why would I want that? This is the life of luxury. I'm surrounded by fine artwork, I get my meals made by a chef and delivered to my room, and I get to lie around watching soap operas all day."

Will had gestured at the still-life print of a vase of flowers that hung next to his bed, the tray of half-eaten pizza and pudding, and the 32-inch TV on the opposite wall. The print looked like it was from an early 2000s overstock warehouse, faux gilded frame and all.

"True luxury. I didn't realize how much I missed my time here," Jason said.

"Speaking of, what have you been doing since you got out of here?"

Jason paused and contemplated what he wanted to tell Will. After too long he had no choice. Will might have been sick, high, and in a hospital, but he deserved the truth. Plus, he was almost recovered.

"Well, actually, I've been dealing with the police." As Jason spoke, Will's brow furrowed.

"I think," Jason continued, "the accident might have been intentional, and we only survived by a fluke. The other car had stolen plates and avoided traffic cams. I mean it's possible. The police are still trying to figure out what happened. It sounds serious. They'll definitely want to talk to you, now that you're awake."

Will nodded. "No shocker there. Hmm. And how have things been with Blake?"

"Well, you're taking that surprisingly well. And thanks for asking. We're good, but the accident was a shock."

"Yeah. I know she didn't believe you about Billy and the network."

"Well, I don't know that she had much reason to. But, with the accident, something clicked. And it did for me, too. Talking to the cops, I think. I had doubted everything myself. But she's helping investigate online and spin ideas with me. We're a lot more careful, though."

"So what have you found out?"

Jason held his hands up and shrugged. "Not much. But Desiree apparently has information, and I emailed her to see. I set up a secure account where she can upload whatever she has, but I'm still waiting. Might be banking related—she's a teller. Or it could be unrelated."

Will nodded and adjusted his bed to sit up more. "Yeah. She mentioned something on one of those cards over there."

Will gestured towards the cards stacked on his windowsill. Jason remembered the display Blake had set up for him, and he felt sorry that no one had visited Will consistently or helped make his room more comfortable.

"Did you get a lot of cards?" Jason asked.

"Yeah, stuff from the show. Actually, almost everyone from the show wrote me. A few co-workers. A group of college friends. Grim, but you get a good turnout when people think you're dying."

Will laughed.

Jason had taken to propping up the cards against the window. "Nice. No family though? I don't know much about your personal life."

Will's laugh stopped. He opened his mouth while considering how to respond.

"No. I don't have the best relationships. Haven't talked to my family in probably ten years. Since then my mom has died. I have two brothers. No clue if they're married, have kids. But, que sera sera. Don't look so serious. I've come to terms with it."

Jason offered a sympathetic smile before sliding into contemplation. Whenever the topic came up regarding his own family, everyone regarded him with pity. He couldn't recall someone who was so blasé about not having family.

"Seriously," Will said. "It's cool. Family can suck. They didn't like things about my life, and I didn't need them."

"No, I get it. How do people usually react when you mention you don't talk to any family?"

Will's eyes bulged. "I forgot you don't have any living family. My bad. But, you know what it's like. People give you pity and treat you like a leper. Like, it was my choice. Just because you're related to someone doesn't make them a good person."

"Yeah." Emily, Billy's sister, flooded Jason's mind.

"Not many people," Jason continued, "that I know are in a similar situation. Pretty strange that we both can relate."

"Mm-hmm."

"I can't help but think about Billy, too." The words came out with incredible weight. Jason and Blake had decided to be careful, each for very different reasons, but here he was, engaged in open discussion with a drugged conspiracy theorist. Something about Will elicited trust. Will was incorruptible.

"Yeah, that's right. You told me about trying to see Billy's family. His sister, Emily. Hard to believe those wounds can still be raw even after death."

"I agree. But what could lead to that? Billy's sister wouldn't tell me. And, I'm still thinking through this all, but Blake sent me a text right before I got here. She said she was watching reruns of a police procedural. One of the *Law and Orders* —I can't remember which one. Anyway, she said we should try to think about it as one of those cases. And, what if it had nothing to do with the game or show? What if it was about Billy's life at home? That could apply to either murder or suicide."

Towards the end of Jason's words, Will developed enthusiasm.

"Smart," Will said. "Like, maybe Billy was up to something shady, which is why his family is so violently opposed to having him around, and maybe that's what happened. Probably drugs, gambling. Something like that, huh? Maybe his family was involved in something shady, and he was the one who wanted out. He seemed so moral."

The two men sat in pregnant silence as they contemplated the possibilities. Jason knew what he had to do: speak to Emily Gerding for the third time and figure out why she cut Billy out of the family. He hoped that the envelope he'd left might have softened her anger. At least enough that she wouldn't immediately hang up on him.

Their reverie was pierced by the audible vibrating of Jason's phone from his jacket pocket. He reached in and extracted the phone. Will didn't even glance over.

After a moment, Jason spoke. "Will, you said *almost* everyone from the cast sent you a card. Who didn't?"

"Uh, just you and Hunter," Will said, and Jason's eyes narrowed. "But you're here in person, so no worries. I didn't send anything down the hall your way, either."

"That's too fucking obvious, right?"

"What do you mean?"

"I got a message from everyone except you and Hunter. Even Nick. And Blake just sent me a text. She's at my house, looking into some stuff I asked her to. She said 'May have something further on Hunter. Weird.' And he's the only one who's avoiding us after the car crash."

"That can't be," Will said. After another moment, he added, "I can't wait to hear what she has. And what Desiree found."

"Damn, I had suspicions about him a long time ago, but I trusted him. He was having weird conversations and meetings with RTN. Hunter definitely knew something and they were trying to keep him quiet. I could swear on that. I shouldn't have trusted him."

Jason's phone vibrated again. Blake had sent the link to an article. "I'm not sure if he's stupid, suspicious or a combination," the message read.

"STILL GOING HOG WILD, BUT HUNTER'S COURSE TAKES A SHARP TURN SINCE BEING BEACHED"

CAMERON FLYNN, NATIONAL ENTERTAINMENT REVIEW

LOS ANGELES— In case anyone out there thought that losing in the finals of *Beached* would get America's favorite self-proclaimed "hollerin' hillbilly" down for too long, we're happy to report that Hunter Brown hasn't slowed down. Hunter, in fact, has made his way back to the West Coast after traveling to Los Angeles for the finale and reunion, where it was announced that he had fallen two votes short of winning the one million dollar prize. That prize was awarded, instead, to Jason Debord, of Cincinnati, Ohio. While in L.A., Hunter was spotted touring homes in Santa Monica, apparently searching for a residence outside of his native Tennessee. After his property search, Hunter has spent the last few days frequenting some of the area's most exclusive clubs. Fans have interacted with Hunter and his entourage (who appear to be friends and family from his hometown) in VIP sections at Tarot, Gold, and Cabana, often posting pictures online and raving about how lavish his parties are. What's next for Hunter, you may wonder.

"You know, man, I'm getting a place out here," Hunter told an *Entertainment Review* reporter. "I just put the money down, for real. Tennessee'll always be home for me, but with my success and everything, being a public face, you know. L.A. is just more my speed right now. I love it. I think you'll be seeing me around here a lot more. And I'm going to try to fund some projects, get my face out there.

You know, what can I say? I loved being on TV, and I think America loved seeing me there. I'm going to make more of that happen. 'Aye?"

Hopefully, the *Beached* star is met with more success than most of the show's previous cast members when they tried to transition to acting. But, given the lavish spectacle that surrounds Hunter these days, it's hard to see anything slowing him down.

Make sure to check out the photos of our interaction below.

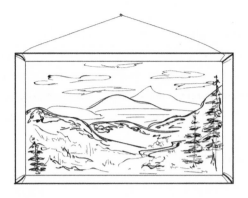

24.

AS SOON AS Blake hit send on the text message linking Jason to the article about Hunter, she slid the phone into her pocket. She was leaning against a metal pipe that shot out of the wall in her home office. It was spray-painted gold and held an overflow of books. While waiting for a response, she pushed away from the wall and paced.

One absentminded step after another, her mind mulled over her knowledge of Hunter, Billy, and RTN. She needed to help Jason find closure, and she planned to lead him to it. Her eyes scanned her books and rested on Margaret Atwood's name. She pulled the book out. The bookmark held a long forgotten stopping point. According to the dog-eared page, Blake had completed the fifth story in the collection, "Death by Landscape." She recalled an older woman consumed by the unsolved death of her friend when they were children, but couldn't think of many specifics. Only the struggle stood out.

Blake turned towards her desk, an eight-by-eight-foot table, and pulled the phone out of her pocket. She glanced at it but there was no alert. She had only imagined a vibration. She tapped the book and pressed it to the table, open to the story. The antique chair creaked when she sat. Her laptop was on the table but its screen had gone dark. She stared at the void and allowed her mind to wander into possibility.

Her momentary respite was interrupted only by the sound of the television she had left on in her living room. The house was large enough that this required extreme stillness and silence. Blake wasn't a fan of all the space and had considered whether she and Jason would, one day, inhabit her house or his. At first, she hadn't hoped to stay at hers, but, as she designed rooms and decorated, she couldn't imagine ever leaving.

She could hear gunshots from the TV. Three quick pops.

Finally, her phone vibrated, and she instinctively opened the message from Jason.

"Very interesting. Will and I think Hunter's being too obvious if he's involved. But, the money. I'm anxious to hear your thoughts."

Blake started to type those thoughts, but another message came through.

"Also, we got talking about something prescient you said. We need to look at Billy's personal life. I don't know much. I'm going to talk to his sister again, soon. Heading out now from the hospital, but I'll forward you an email with the only personal information I have on Billy. It's from Ronnie. I never looked closely at it, but it involves a psychiatric ward, so I thought you might be able to make more sense of it."

As Blake was still reading, she felt another vibration, and a third message filled the screen.

"Also, sorry for writing a novel. I love you!"

A few seconds after Blake smiled at Jason's message, she dragged her finger across the track pad. The screen illuminated. She clicked on her open Gmail account and saw that Jason had sent the file.

Blake double-clicked the pdf, scanned the first page and printed it. She ordinarily worked digitally, but when Blake needed to annotate, she preferred a hard copy.

After the printer fell silent, Blake picked up the document, along with a highlighter and green pen and walked towards the living room. As she approached, there was another round of gunfire. Without looking up from the document she was reading, Blake walked around her sectional couch to where she had been sitting earlier for her afternoon tea and picked up the remote. She turned off the television without looking. Out of habit, she also set the remote down in its usual place. Her eyes never left the file Ronnie had provided Jason months earlier, against his better judgment.

Blake's expression solidified as she opened the highlighter, set the stack of paper on her sofa, and circled a paragraph she had already read twice. She replaced the cap on the highlighter, and without hesitation walked back into her office to retrieve her cell phone. Jason needed to come over and see what she found. As she walked, she felt a light-headed sensation and remembered she hadn't eaten since breakfast.

As she approached her desk and leaned over to pick up the phone, she saw that her computer screen was still on. She went to close the lid, but as soon as her fingers closed around the aluminum screen, she saw another email had arrived from Jason. It was titled only "From Desiree."

When Blake double-clicked the email, she saw another attached pdf and a short note from Jason. "I haven't looked at this yet. Like, at all. But I wanted you to have a copy. I'm on my way to yours, and I'll pick up burritos on the way. See you soon."

Further down the message, Blake saw that Desiree's email had been blank. It only contained the attached three-page document Jason had referenced: "richard-brandtinfo." She included no signature, no body, and no subject.

"BREAKING NEWS: RTN BRINGS BEACHED BACK WITH FANS' HELP"

NATHAN HARDAWAY, ENTERTAINMENT NEWS NOW

SAN JOSE— It appears that fans who worried about the fate of *Beached*, the long-running reality competition, may instead be seeing the show return a few months sooner than expected. And it looks like they'll have a more active role than ever before. Reality Television Network, the network that produces the series issued the following statement late this afternoon:

> "Beached *returns, ready to strand another 14 people. And, for the first time ever, you get to decide who gets* Beached. *Vote online or on the RTN app until December 25th."*

As listed on their website, RTN has brought together a list of over seventy-five former contestants and fan favorites from the franchise, which has been on the air for fifty seasons. Fans will get to vote for their three favorites, and the top fourteen vote-getters will return to our TV screen next summer. Fans can vote once per day, up until Christmas Day, at which point RTN will announce the winners of the contest. We have sent messages to all the contestants who are eligible vote recipients but have yet to hear back from anyone. We will keep you updated as we are able to make contact and get further information.

The contestants on the list impressively cover the breadth of the franchise and include members who were on the show as far back as the third season. Many fans will be delighted to see reclusive favorites on the list, such as handyman Randall Evers, from season fifteen, and exotic dancer Lynne Saunders, from season thirty-six. The contestants listed also include former winners, as well as those who were eliminated early in the show.

Notably, however, the only seasons not represented are seasons one, five, five, and fifty (the most recent season to film and air). Most of the contestants from the earliest seasons are much older now, so that's not much of a surprise. The exclusion of season fifty cast members, however, seems strange, given the popularity and recency. In fact, many people credit season fifty and its dynamic personalities with reinvigorating the series, which was facing cancellation after the controversy surrounding the death of a contestant. RTN declined to comment on the exclusion of recent fan-favorites, such as Hunter Brown and Desiree Zimmerman.

Regardless, the next season promises to get fans excited and provide a fascinating new entry in the show's storied history.

TELEPHONE

7 DECEMBER 2025, 1:21 PM

JASON: Hello. This is Jason Debord.

OMID: Jason! It's Omid, from *Beached.* I got your call.

JASON: Oh, awesome. I was wondering if I'd ever hear from you. It's been since right after filming wrapped.

OMID: Yeah, I'm sorry about that. I talked to Seth once, on the phone, since you've been back. He said you were having a hard time.

JASON: Yeah.

OMID: But, since then I've been traveling, so I'm sorry I didn't get your messages sooner. I think you called way back in September or something.

JASON: Yeah, I did. It's no big deal though. I had a lot of questions at the time. But what have you been up to this whole time?

OMID: Well, yeah, traveling. I had saved up money and didn't have time while I was working for RTN because the show was always so time-consuming. I was in Turkey mostly, but I also got to Prague and Vienna. Actually, I took your recommendation and stayed in Sweden for a while. It was my first time in Europe for an extended period.

JASON: Great to hear. You'll have to tell me about it—especially Sweden. It's been too long for me, too. But, are you not working for RTN anymore? Seth didn't think so.

OMID: Nope. They didn't renew my contract after your season. Unfortunately, too. I liked working there. But I'll find something else.

JASON: Wow, that's shocking though. You were there forever. I talked to you about production, what, years before I ever went on the show.

OMID: Yeah, they hired me back in 2013. But, they cleared house this time around. Pretty much got rid of everyone I know.

JASON: What do you mean?

OMID: They fired basically the entire crew. Hiring all new people, I'm sure. I only know a few who stayed on. But, it's okay—I have some exciting opportunities lined up. Corporations, man. But what are you up to? Anything exciting to do with your winnings?

JASON: I haven't even considered that part of my experience. So lame. I'll be boring and pay off my house. My big splurge will probably be a trip with Blake—we haven't decided where, yet. Or when.

OMID: Well, that's good to hear. Are you two a couple then? I think I remember Seth mentioning that might be about to happen.

JASON: Yeah, yeah. Great to hear you guys gossip about me. But we are. Things are going well. She's at work now, but we're having dinner tonight. We've been together non-stop since I got back.

OMID: Awesome news. And how's teaching? Any good classes?

JASON: I'm actually taking the rest of this semester off. I'm recovering from a pretty brutal car accident. I was in the hospital for ages, and the other passenger is only now getting discharged from the hospital. It was weeks ago.

OMID: I heard about that, actually. I didn't want to bring it up unless you did. But I'm so glad you're doing better.

JASON: Yeah, I am.

OMID: So how are you keeping yourself busy?

JASON: Uh, well, I'm just doing some research now. I have my desk covered in documents at home. Trying to make sense of a lot of loose ends.

OMID: Always productive. Try to get a publication out, at least.

JASON: Yeah, we'll see. Something like that. But, tell me about this mass firing. You all did such a great job on the show. I'm still shocked. What reason did they give?

OMID: I was shocked, too. I think everyone was. But we probably should have expected something, though. After Billy. I'm not in contact with many people anymore. We were mostly only work friends. I didn't have much in common with a lot of the crew. But, all they told us was that they wanted fresh people working on the show and that they had decided to go in a different direction. Everyone there works on a yearly contract, so there's nothing we could do about it.

JASON: And they did this with everyone?

OMID: Well, like I said, most everyone I know. I think some upper-level people stayed on.

JASON: What about Curtis David?

OMID: Oh, I didn't know you knew him. Yeah, I'm pretty confident he's still there. I've only talked to him once or twice, though. I mean ever. He works mostly in props and is in L.A. for most of the production.

JASON: Interesting. How are they going to find an entirely new crew? I heard they're planning on starting the next season even earlier than ours.

OMID: Beats me. It might be self-centered, but I think the quality will suffer. Significantly suffer, if they're trying to turn it around so quickly. But I do know there might have been some kind of tax situation. They were saying they would only hire Americans to work on the show. No locals from the island. No foreigners.

JASON: That seems weird.

OMID: Well, it's rare, but not entirely unheard of. Actually, when I got hired RTN had just had a huge turnover. Back in 2012 or 13. And that was unrelated to an earlier guy—I think it was just one cameraman—who got fired because they were distributing cocaine. The rumor is that people floated it onto the *Beached* filming beach from a boat offshore and he retrieved it to smuggle it inside production equipment.

JASON: I can't believe I didn't know that. Isn't that when Seth worked for RTN?

OMID: No. He actually left the show a year earlier. On his own that was. They didn't fire him. And then I met him when he came for a set visit a few years after I started. He was friends with the producers, and they invited him to come whenever he wanted.

JASON: Yeah, okay. He's never mentioned the firing, or the smuggling. Well, I'm sorry about what happened to you. I'd be fascinated to know if you find anything else out about their plans, or reasoning.

OMID: Yeah, I'll let you know. Although, they never explain stuff like that publicly and I'm out of contact. But, speaking of, you said in your last message you had some questions for me. Something I could help with. What's up?

JASON: Right. I was going to ask if you knew someone. I'm trying to track this guy down for some research I'm doing. On the show. His name is Joel Markani.

OMID: Joel Markani. Hmm. No, I don't think I know him. Did he work with me? It was a big crew, but that's embarrassing.

JASON: I don't know. He worked for the show, and I'm doing some research on the production. The production of reality TV and whatnot. I need to keep all my names and roles straight.

OMID: Yeah, I don't think I've ever even heard that name. Maybe he was before my time. Perhaps in that 2013 purge, or whatever.

JASON: Okay, cool. I figured it was a long shot, but I came across the name and need to place it. Again, if that randomly comes up, just keep me posted. I'd appreciate it.

OMID: Of course, man.

JASON: Great. Well, it was awesome to talk and catch up. We need to do a more extended Skype session. I need to hear about Europe. And I'm sorry about the mass firing.

OMID: Yeah, great to hear your voice. And don't worry about me.

JASON: Nice. Well, let me know when we can set up that Skype session.

OMID: Definitely. Take care.

JASON: You, too. Bye.

OMID: See you.

TELEPHONE

8 DECEMBER 2025, 12:44 PM

EMILY: Hello?

JASON: Hey. Is this Emily?

EMILY: It is.

JASON: Did you open the envelope I left at your door? Back in October.

EMILY: So this is Jason?

JASON: It is.

EMILY: Huh. Well, that's a cryptic way to begin a conversation. But, I opened the envelope. And I understand you were unaware of the situation. Thanks for doing what you thought was the right thing. Now, I think we need to move on. Hopefully, you have some peace and can enjoy your winnings.

JASON: Wow. You watched the show?

EMILY: Well, not every episode. But I got caught up in it. Enough people in my life knew I was related to Billy, given what the show aired and how much attention he got. I'm relieved the media never brought us into it. But, yes, I watched the show because I couldn't help it.

JASON: Okay. Well, good. I guess I'm glad. And I hope it never impacted your family in any negative way. The kids, I mean.

EMILY: No. It didn't. We were pretty vigilant, plus they're young enough it was okay. They're with their father for the day, having some rare bonding time while he's off work, and they're happy.

JASON: Awesome. Great to hear. [Pause.] So, since you're free for a moment, could you maybe talk to me? Just give me a couple minutes to ask some questions? Seriously, only a couple minutes. And I'll leave you alone forever unless you want to talk more. And no one in your world will ever know we had this conversation.

EMILY: I will regret this, but yes, depending on what the questions are. Then we can close this chapter of our lives. And you can stop unintentionally harassing me and dragging up bad memories.

JASON: Thank you. So much.

EMILY: Mm.

JASON: Okay, well, unfortunately, what I want to ask about may involve some bad memories. But, anyway, I'm curious about the time Billy was hospitalized. Back in 2016.

EMILY: I didn't think anyone knew about that.

JASON: Only a few people do. RTN wouldn't have let him on the show if they knew. At least I hope not.

EMILY: Yeah. Look, this is the stuff that can mess with my kids' lives. So, you need to keep everything private. Whatever you have.

JASON: I promise. I will be responsible with this knowledge. But, could you tell me what happened? I have the files that document his stay, but they don't give a detailed picture.

EMILY: Well, Billy was forced into a hospital for mental illness. And it didn't go well. It was a rough period. The day he went in was the last day I had a relation-ship with him. That was, what, nine years ago. I had just gotten engaged to Tony, and we were planning on having a family. Tony had just passed the bar. Billy was getting in the way. I've always felt a little sad about it. But he had too many chances.

JASON: Okay. I'm sure that was hard. But, what do you mean by too many chances? From what I can see, he had a mental condition and needed treatment and therapy. What caused the fractured relationship?

EMILY: Yeah, sorry. I don't know what those files are, but it wasn't just the depression. The depression was a long time coming. Brought on by his addiction to heroin, or whatever he was doing at that time. I'm not heartless. I'd help a family member I love through depression. But I can't have a perpetually relapsing junkie hanging around as I try to make my own life. Always wanting something. Lying. There just had to be a point, you know?

JASON: I had no idea. [Pause.] Sorry. I'm kind of shocked. Yeah, that sounds stressful. And paints a different picture.

EMILY: Yeah, I'm sure I sounded like a real bitch. Probably still do, but, whatever. Now you know.

JASON: No. I can understand to a degree. I've never been in a similar situation. And it seems like, however things worked out, it was enough of a wake-up for Billy because he got better.

EMILY: Maybe. I never trusted it.

JASON: Yeah. Well, that might help explain why he was forcibly admitted to the hospital. Court-ordered is what the paperwork notes.

EMILY: Right. Yeah, he got arrested for getting into dealing. I don't know whether he ever actually sold anything. But he hung around with all these shitty, small-time drug dealers. Just involved enough for it to be dangerous. And then one day they got busted. That's probably the most significant part, not even his endless addiction. It was how ingrained in a violent sub-culture he was. That's not who my family was. Well, any family's complicated. At the time we hadn't been speaking to our foster family in years. And our real parents were long dead. So, by 'family,' I guess I mean me and the concept of family I always had in my head. Anyway, they couldn't charge him with much, but while he was in holding he started withdrawal, and had these insane anxiety fits, followed by scary depression. I still have an occasional nightmare about visiting him. I'd seen him like that so many times. But the lawyer got him put in treatment rather than a prison sentence since there was no evidence of him dealing or anything, and he testified.

JASON: Billy never shared that with me. I mean, I knew you both were in foster care together, but he never mentioned depression, drugs, jail. Nothing. At all.

EMILY: I would imagine, from my experience growing up with him, there's a lot you don't know. Anyway, I never talk about this. I probably shouldn't have told you all that. But now I have. Is that all? I don't have too much more time.

JASON: Well, I appreciate you opening up a bit. This means a lot. One more question—I know you didn't have much contact with him, but how convinced are you that Billy was still involved in drugs?

EMILY: It's hard to know. Once an addict, always an addict. But, actively, with the show and everything? Maybe thirty percent sure. Ah, more like twenty. I just can't rule anything out with him.

JASON: Okay, thank you. I appreciate your story. I know that's hard to talk about.

EMILY: Yeah. It is. Do we have a deal?

JASON: Of course. Have a great life, Emily. I wish you and your family the best. Goodbye.

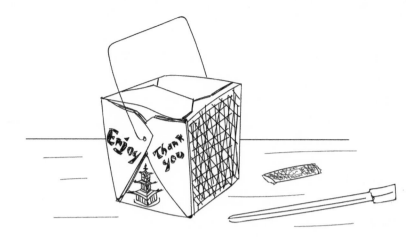

25.

WILL PRESSED THE FADED, plastic doorbell. He held his finger there, palm resting on brick, until the chimes stopped. The sun was beginning to set. He pressed again and stepped back. When he did, the rear of his boot caught on his suitcase. He had set the dented hard shell on its side, behind him, after walking the seventeen steps up to the porch.

Without slipping, Will pivoted and had to extend an arm to stable himself, doubled over. When Jason opened the door Will looked ready to collapse.

"Oh, god, man, let me get that," Jason said. He rushed forward and put a hand on Will's back.

Will leaned away from Jason's hand.

"No, no. Come on, I'm fine. I almost slipped because I forgot this damned thing was back here."

"Okay. Whatever you need. I wasn't expecting you. We didn't know who it could be when the bell rang."

"I told you I was coming," Will grumbled as he hoisted the suitcase.

"Right, but I thought you got out tomorrow."

Jason, facing Will, felt for the door handle behind him and opened the door wider for his reluctant friend. And, he assumed, temporary housemate.

"I had to get out of there. I was ready. Left against the doctors' advice. I had to sign some papers and whatever. But I'm good. And here. Well, I have an appointment in a couple days, but I'm here for now, I mean."

"Hey, Will," Blake called as the two crossed the threshold into the living room. Jason latched the door, but Will walked straight into the living room and dropped his suitcase with a thump on the wooden floor.

"So, this is the place I almost died trying to get to. Well, it's nice, Jason. But I wouldn't die for it."

Jason entered the room and Will nodded at Blake.

"Nice to see you, Blake. Outside the hospital, especially."

"Agreed, I'm so glad you're doing better."

"Yeah, me, too," Jason said. He resumed his place, sitting next to Blake on the sofa. "But, we could have gotten you today."

"Nah. There's Uber. I didn't need help and didn't want to inconvenience you. Plus, your time is better spent working."

Will's eyes scanned the room. It was illuminated by two floor-lamps behind the sofa, the glow from a small fire in the fireplace, and the bright LED of a television screen. Jason had a laptop in front of him on the coffee table, but it was closed. Not exactly a busy time. Jason and Blake had a glass of wine in front of them, each at vastly different levels of fullness. Scanning in the other direction, Will saw the bottle, only a few ounces remaining, on the dining room table. He also noted their outfits. Pajamas. So, this was intentional relaxation. And on the paused TV screen, an actor whom Will didn't recognize, adorned in furs and leathers, wielded a sword over his head in the midst of battle, while a dragon flew overhead. Hardly the beginning of a film.

Jason and Blake exchanged a troubled glance as they watched Will study the room.

"So, how much work, exactly, have you accomplished? I mean, other than the obvious." Will's eyes mulled the wine glasses and then the television screen.

"Hey, man. Calm down. We're taking a break. It's consuming and exhausting. We need a little life balance."

"Yeah," added Blake, "we just stopped after researching former crew members for, like, twelve hours. We can catch you up on everything we've found."

"Go for it." Will made no motion to indicate he would join them in sitting.

"Right," Jason said. "Where to start. Well, there's Richard Brandt. You remember the guy we each met with in L.A.?

Will nodded. "Fucking prick."

"Yeah, well, Desiree found some information on his past. She tried to send it ages ago when RTN first hired him, but I was trying to get away from all this. Anyway, it appears he has a past of being hired, short-term, by different companies. Desiree got ahold of his financials because she happens to be a bank teller in L.A., and was looking up RTN producers to see if they had accounts. She wanted to see how much they were worth, out of curiosity.

"She eventually got into RTN's payroll accounts and found a large, lump-sum payout to an individual. That individual turned out to be Richard Brandt. So, she looked at his account, which also happened to be through Seventh Financial. The man has had no stable employment, but gets a large deposit, every six months or so, from various corporations. Most we've never heard of. It looks suspicious."

Without hesitation, Will nodded. "So you're saying he's a fixer or something?"

"We don't know," Blake said, "but we're guessing he's brought on at high-intensity points, compensated well for whatever work he does, and then he never deals with the company again. He's well-connected and has a law degree."

"And," Jason added, "his name is non-existent on the internet. So, if he is some kind of fixer or deal-maker or whatever, he must be good. He doesn't ever seem to be a fall guy."

"Right."

"You're taking this pretty smoothly. I mean, when I first saw this, I thought it was crazy. It supports what we're saying," Jason said with a half-laugh.

"No, I'm not shocked." Will shrugged. His demeanor grew more relaxed.

"O-kay," Jason said. "So, beyond that, we also found out that Billy struggled with drug addiction for most of his life. He was familiar with dealers, may have dealt himself, and was entered into court-mandated psychiatric treatment for depression and anxiety which resulted from heroin abuse and addiction. That's why his sister no longer spoke to him."

"Hmm. Well, that might be a little shocking," Will said.

Jason exchanged a sideways glance with Blake. "Yeah," he said. "And there's something weird going on with the crew which I mentioned to you earlier in the hospital. So, when I talked to my buddy Omid, and he told me they fired him, he also said that nearly the entire crew was, too. Now they're hiring all new people, but no locals are allowed. He was adamant that the same thing happened before. About twelve years ago."

"You said 'nearly' the entire crew?"

"Yeah, some longer-term employees and L.A.-based crew are staying put."

"Well, huh." Will held his jaw open for a moment and stared into space. "And, I'm assuming this Omid had never heard of Curtis David? Or Markani?"

Jason studied Will's face before giving any further information. Will had a way to rekindle unease. Gone was Jason's manic pursuit from before the accident. Will awaited an answer. He was motionless, but restless to get moving.

Jason tapped his foot.

"Omid did nothing. Trust me. He's a friend."

"Of course not." Will's tone was different. Lighter.

"And he did have information about those two. He knows of Curtis David, but only in passing. He knew, for a fact, that David works in L.A. and was also immune from the mass firing in 2012. As for Markani, he didn't know the name. But, he assumed that this guy, if he even exists, was fired during the earlier purge."

After a moment, Jason continued, "I tried to verify any of that with my friend Seth, who used to work with the network a long time ago. He was a cameraman. But he didn't know anything. He keeps to himself a lot, so he doesn't have much intel. But, he at least got me in contact with Omid. Omid told me about the drug scandal in the past, where people were smuggling cocaine and RTN covered that up. And he provided the names of people working on the crew."

Blake twisted her shoulders, trying to get comfortable.

Will again shrugged. "And what about Hunter? I know you reacted when you found out he hadn't sent me a get-well-soon card or flowers. Plus all the weird contact he had with RTN. Is he involved here?"

Jason grimaced. "I don't know. What do you think?"

Jason grabbed the computer off the coffee table. He rotated it to face Will, whose eyes scanned the headline and first few sentences of the article Jason had pulled up.

"'Still going hog wild,' huh? And he didn't win. So, where did the money come from is what you guys are thinking?"

"Right," Blake said.

"So," said Jason, "someone must pay him for something, and he isn't working. But I do know RTN was very interested in what he saw and thought of the crew and show while on the island. So could this be evidence of some kind of payoff? At least, that's where our heads went, but it's sloppy of him." He closed the laptop and placed it back down.

"Wow," Will said. His pained expression hadn't shifted, but his tone relaxed. "It wouldn't be unprecedented from the network. I know there have been payouts before when they screw up competitions for certain players. This is a lot more than I expected. Awesome work, guys. And, I know you had most of that done a couple days ago based on what you hinted at while I was laid up. So, what are we up to now? Next steps?"

Blake again leaned forward in her seat. "Well, we've spent most of our time trying to track down crew members and rule them out. This Curtis guy seems suspicious, but so does most of the crew that was fired. We're hoping that if we can establish contacts with former employees, someone might know something."

Jason took a deep breath, and Will's eyes darted between the pair.

"I'm guessing that isn't going so well?"

Blake shook her head. "No. Most people are working elsewhere. Well, the ones we can find online at all, through IMDB pages or Facebook accounts. They're mostly working in foreign markets, from what we can tell. Lots in China."

Will pulled his attention away and slid his phone out of his pocket.

"And it's not like they have contact info posted anywhere," Blake finished.

Will hadn't looked back up. Instead, he typed rapidly on his phone.

Jason touched Blake's arm and nodded at Will. She shrugged, and the pair waited a few moments until Jason stood and Will looked up.

"What?" Jason asked. "Do you think you'll find something we missed, right now, on the spot? I mean, this has been a ton of work."

Will's head tilted. "No. I was ordering takeout. Chinese. Blake said China, and I realized how hungry I was. I assume you two are as well. I don't see any dishes."

Will waited for a response, but Jason and Blake only stared, dumbfounded.

"Great. It'll be here in twenty-two minutes. My treat."

With a grin and nod, Will walked over to the couch and sat next to Jason, who was forced to follow.

"So," Jason said, "what do you think about the information we've gathered? You don't seem fazed. What do you think we should do?"

Will frowned at Jason. "No. I think you guys have found plenty to prove something is going on. Plus, everything else we already knew. A man died. We were nearly killed. What's the saying: if there's this much smoke, there has to be a fire? I think it's time to take this and return to where our investigation began."

"Which is?"

"Come on, Jason. It started with reference to one Joel Markani, which appeared on Reddit."

"Oh, shit," Blake said. "We forgot to mention, but that one post has since been deleted. So that's a dead end. I'm unsure how much to buy into any of this, but I've tried to be supportive and helpful, thinking that working through all the information would help with processing and acceptance. You know, find the truth on your own and you'll come to better terms with it. Closure-wise. But, honestly, this piece is ominous. I mean, as soon as we look at it, the obscure information self-destructs? That's hard to explain away—someone doesn't want that name getting around."

Will's mouth opened, and he stared at a spot a few inches above Blake's head. Again, Jason and Blake awaited his response.

"Then it's time. Time to go public. If things are being deleted, then people know. Let's begin crowd-sourcing our search. Take to social media. Reddit, again, where this began."

"Are you sure?" Jason asked.

"Yeah. Plus, if everyone knows exactly what we're alleging, we'll be safe. It'll be printed and documented somewhere. We'll be way more untouchable. No more car attacks."

Blake took a long drink of her wine. She set the glass back down on the table with an audible clink.

"But, that Reddit post was easily deleted, and no one noticed. Things fall out of attention so quickly. I don't know that just appearing anywhere on the internet would count as published. And I don't know about going to a newspaper. You'll sound crazy."

Will tilted his head. "Are you sure? What about blogs? A newspaper would take this. At least for an online edition."

Without moving, Jason spoke. "Maybe. But I might have something. The podcast, *Beached* Bums. They've been trying to get me back on for ages after I couldn't bring myself to do it right after the season. Even if they think I'm crazy, they'd post it. Thousands of people would hear it. And they'd want it archived. Plus, the people who would hear my interview are exactly our target audience: people who know everything about *Beached* and its history."

Still, no one looked at each other. Each was deep in a separate thought on the shared topic. Everyone's eyes had unconsciously settled on the image of the man with raised sword on the television, ready to strike his foes down, completely unaware, or at least ignoring, the dragon flying overhead. They all nodded, peripherally agreeing to the plan.

"I'll call the podcast, try to go on in the next couple days, and I'll present our case. Just what we have and suspect. And I'll ask for others' input. We'll see what the fans and media make of it."

Will shifted his eyes to Jason and gave him a smile. Blake continued to stare, foot tapping like a metronome. Her eyes glazed over, looking at the suspended image on the TV.

"RTN: NO IDEA WHAT JASON DEBORD IS TALKING ABOUT"

ROSS KUSCHNER, TV UPDATE

FOLLOWING A SURPRISE PRESS CONFERENCE, RTN has issued the statement below. This comes just days after the network announced the details of their next, much-anticipated, season.

> "RTN completely refutes Jason Debord's allegations. Our lawyers will be in touch with him about the defamation that he is committing. We at the network find this turn of events most unfortunate. Debord had previously been offered psychological treatment from RTN following his season and its tragic events. Debord declined. There is no evidence for any of his claims.

> "We repeat: these claims are completely unsubstantiated, and the network is one hundred percent confident that there will never be evidence because nothing he has claimed is true. Additionally, Debord has no affiliation with the network and was only a filming subject. He has had no inside contact with the organization and has never had access to any privileged company information. He does not speak as a network

*representative or employee. RTN has always been a network
that respects its players, their safety, and the laws of the
United States, as well as the laws of the locations where we
film. We will continue to function as such."*

Arthur Cagney, who issued the statement, did not take any questions. The network has declined to comment further or be interviewed about the topic. This comes the day after Jason Debord, winner of the controversial fiftieth season of RTN's hit franchise *Beached*, went on a fan podcast and alleged corruption in the network, a cover-up of Billy Gerding's murder, and conspiracy within the crew members. Debord offered details, but no specific evidence. He looked to encourage anyone with information to contact him. Debord was unavailable for further comment. To date, *TV Update* is unaware of the veracity of any of his claims.

See below for a link to the full *Beached* Bums interview, as well as video of the RTN press conference.

MEANWHILE

HE THREW the door open and recomposed himself when the handle thudded against the wall. Pausing, he made sure no one was coming, alerted by the sound.

He crossed the threshold and closed the door. The handle had left a depression against the cheap drywall. Flailing his left arm to the side, he let out an unintelligible sound.

As he walked the three paces around his desk, the animated movements and haste caused him to trip against the right, rear desk leg. "Goddamn, bullshit."

Finally sitting, he threw the screen open on his computer and hunched over to write. With his hands suspended inches above the keyboard, he paused. Then, he gripped the bottom of his desktop and twisted his torso, trying to crack his back to no avail. Instead, he grabbed at the few books that populated his office's bookshelf. He slid three of the thinner paperback underneath his laptop, and readjusted. He let out a sigh and returned his focus.

"Didn't think I'd have to be so worried about this anymore. But, it'll still be my story. My hero and villain. I own this narrative and have control. No one can take this from me now."

His eyes scanned the screen, and he scrolled twice on the trackpad. "Going to have to rush. It can't be this hard."

The cursor blinked at him, and he pulled on his earlobes. Staring and thinking.

A muffled buzzing broke his concentration, but he tried to ignore it.

Until it happened again.

He bent toward the messenger bag resting at his feet and pulled out the cell phone concealed within its front pocket. Turning it over in his right hand, he only read the first word on the screen before slamming it back into his bag. "Jason."

"RTN MOVING ON, AND FAN BACKLASH FOR BEACHED WINNER"

MAURICE OVERBAY, ENTERTAINMENT NEWS NOW

THE LAST FEW days have been busy for the Reality Television Network and fans of their hit series, *Beached.* The Network announced earlier this month that they would be allowing the fans to vote and select the cast of their upcoming season. That announcement was greeted with enthusiasm, and millions of daily votes were cast. Today, we have learned that the leading vote recipients are en route to Miami, where they will be sequestered and leave for filming within the next few days. RTN representatives have said that filming will begin before the end of the year and that they are currently running contestants through both physical and psychiatric evaluations, which have been redesigned, before beginning. For details on the selected cast, see our article from yesterday which profiles each of the fourteen returning contestants—that link is below.

However, no matter how determined RTN and *Beached* are about moving on to this new, exciting season, the scandal from their much-discussed season fifty still hangs over them. Of course, this is the season when tragedy befell the show, and cast member Billy Gerding died while filming. Since the show has aired, winner Jason Debord has publicly accused the network of corruption, as well as covering up what he claims may have been a murder. Debord made these suspicions public while appearing on the fan-favorite podcast *Beached* Bums. RTN has contended that Gerding's death was a suicide and that they did everything in their power to prevent such an occurrence.

Debord's claims were short on detail and precision, but he stated that he believes Gerding was murdered. The network used the death to boost ratings, he claims, and they have worked to cover up the truth to protect their reputation. For evidence, Debord cited the recent large-scale firing of crew members, suspicious payouts by the network, and the lack of a public investigation. While not much motive was given, Debord did name specific individuals and made a call for information. Those Debord claimed to be suspicious of were Curtis David, Joel Markani, and Richard Brandt (all individuals who work, or have worked, for RTN), along with two of his own cast mates, Nick Santino and Hunter Brown.

Ultimately, Debord claimed that his appearance on the podcast was an effort to crowdsource his investigation into the matter. He asked for anyone, involved with the show or not, who had information to contact him via email (justicefor-billy@jdebord.com) with anything that might prove useful.

Thus far, however, the response has not been what Debord presumably hoped. Fans have been outraged, and many have taken to social media to vent their frustration with the recent winner who, many claim, is doing this for attention.

"He's dragging people through the mud just so he can have fifteen more seconds of fame. Honestly, I think he's probably never been able to handle the fact that fans didn't like him that much. Everyone I know wanted Hunter to win. Jason is a lunatic," Sophia Martin, a 29-year-old fan of *Beached*, claims. Her sentiment seems to be echoed on every corner of the internet.

RTN has not responded any further than denying Debord's claims. It's clear at this point that they want the controversy to blow over. If it doesn't, the recent winner of the show may be facing more than fan backlash, as the network has already threatened to sue for defamation. Debord and RTN were not able to be reached for comment.

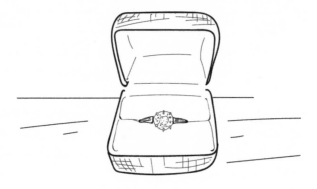

26.

JASON BROUGHT his hands together again and again. He and Blake followed the row-in-front's lead and stood.

She looked at him, and they smiled. Jason's hands were irritated from the repetitive motion, so his clapping got slower. He wished everyone would agree to stop. The cast took another bow. After they had again receded to the back of the stage, he stopped his applause altogether and hung his hands at his side while maintaining a smile. His mind was elsewhere, but he was always trying to be socially aware.

While he waited for the actors to leave the stage and the standing ovation to end—which it mercifully did moments later—he eyed his coat resting on his seat. The inside breast-pocket bulged ever so slightly, and he reassured himself that it was unnoticeable.

"What did you think?" Blake asked.

They had just watched a performance of *I Am a Camera*, based upon Christopher Isherwood's *Berlin Stories*. One of their shared favorites.

"Excellent performance," Jason said. He wanted to offer something more impressive or insightful, but no analysis came to mind, only emotion. "I mean, I've always been fascinated by Isherwood's character. But, seeing himself as a writer, meant only for observation? I don't know if that works anymore. Like, is he off the hook for doing nothing as he watched friends become Nazis? I think he has more responsibility to intervene. We have such a higher social responsibility than that allows for. I couldn't live with myself to only watch and write instead of doing something."

"Yeah." Blake nodded. "But, he's a journalist. Only instead of covering current events or anything involving the government, he's covering the personal side. The side that history and reporting can't touch."

Jason picked up his coat and folded it over his arm. They followed the rest of their row and filed down the aisle.

"You're right. That's probably more important, isn't it? Plus, there wasn't much he could do, up against that force. And he turned it into something impactful."

"I think so."

Jason nodded and smiled at the usher who held the door open as they passed into the lobby. Once space opened, Jason walked alongside Blake. Christmas decorations still hung in the marble, domed entryway. A few abandoned plastic cups with remnants of wine littered the high-top tables scattered throughout. The crowd was dispersing into the evening. A merciful draft flooded the room and Jason threw his coat back on, relieved that there was now no further chance of the ring-box in his pocket falling out if mishandled.

"Do you need to use the restroom?" Blake asked.

"Yeah, may as well."

"I'll meet you back here."

Jason relished the chance to rinse his clammy hands for the moments ahead.

———

"I'M NOT SAYING A DEFINITIVE 'NO.' Seriously. I am so sorry, and I don't know exactly how to say this and get it right. I would love to get married, one day. But, like I said, the timing isn't right. There's so much going on, and there has been for months.

"Speaking of, we've only been dating for a few months. We've been friends for so long, and we're amazing in that relationship, but shouldn't we let this dynamic settle before we rush into something? We might put too much pressure and ruin it." She took in his expression and kept nervously explaining. "Sometimes things can seem certain, definite. But then, time has a way to reveal the truth. How often do you feel like you definitely know something, only to find out you were wrong? I don't want us to be wrong together because we rushed. Please don't look so sad."

Jason felt blood rising to his ears and throat. He was dizzy, and had to consciously make sense of her words. "No. It's fine; I get it. Seriously. No worries." He smiled, but his wide, unblinking eyes didn't follow his mouth.

Looking at Blake was too awkward, so he turned to look out at the city. They were atop one of the highest hills and had a view of the city's lights for miles. Cars flowed throughout, and the abyss of the river reflected it all. The theater had a long driveway, with this wooded hill and view alongside, not to mention numerous benches and lookouts. A winter night, with the trees having already shed their leaves, provided one of the best views of the city. It hadn't been the perfect night.

Jason exhaled deeply, trying to control his breathing. The fog it created drifted up the hill towards where Blake stood, a few paces away. His right pant leg was bunched up over the top of his boots from when he had knelt on the damp, chilling concrete only minutes ago. He didn't bother fixing his pants.

"I love you, Jason. Are we okay? Can we just take it slow for a bit until our lives are more settled? I don't want this to be the end. Or an end at all."

Jason looked at her, more at eye-level than usual because of the hill. Small tears had welled in the corners of her eyes, and she was turning flushed, accentuated by her maroon knit hat. He couldn't recall ever seeing this expression. Distress?

He laughed despite himself. A deep laugh, coming from somewhere he couldn't identify.

"I don't know why I'm laughing," he said. "As for us,"—he shrugged with forced composure—"we're fine. I mean, this is one of the more mortifying moments of my life, and not what I expected, but I don't want this to be the end of us either. It doesn't change the way I feel about you. I love you."

Blake half-smiled and took the last step to Jason. She wrapped her arms around him and gave a soft hug.

"I'm not going to break," Jason said. He squeezed her until she gave a laughing groan, and he lifted her off the ground.

As they slid out of the hug, her smile was full.

"We'll get everything figured out. The stuff with Billy. Get Will out of your house. Slow things down. And revisit this conversation. I still want to spend the rest of my life with you. And I'm impressed with your proposal. Romantic, but not too much. Exactly what I want, just not when."

She kissed him, and they hugged again.

At the bottom of the hill, the last car beside theirs rolled out of the lot. The driver had gotten in his car just as Jason produced the ring. He sat in the driver's seat the entire time, appreciating the holiday romance, and he wasn't entirely sure if it had been successful.

27.

THE LAPTOP SAT in the center of the table with Jason perched before it. Blake and Will were opposite him so they'd be out of view once their awaited Skype session began.

Jason's arms stretched out in what began as an earnest pose of awareness but had faded into a slump. He tapped his index, middle, and ring fingers.

Will cleared his throat. He was tapping a blue ballpoint pen on a blank notebook page. His rhythm was out of touch with Jason's. "Nothing yet?"

Jason shook his head. "No. But, trust me. I'll let you know."

"I don't want to say it, but what are the odds we're being messed with?" Blake asked.

"Ninety-five percent? Nothing we got from the podcast has turned out. No one else took it seriously. This guy seemed like he might actually know something."

"You're wrong," Will said. "It was ninety-five percent before the call was twenty-eight minutes late. Now, it's ninety-nine percent that this is a joke. But I have no faith."

Jason shrugged, smiled at Blake, and ran his finger over the trackpad to re-illuminate the now dark screen.

After another silent moment, Blake stood and walked around the end of the table, passing Will, and stood to face the wall of her home office. Jason couldn't tell precisely what she was reading, but she was in the section of wall dedicated to 2008–2009.

They had taped documents and notes all over the room, which was usually a chic, designed space. Now, they had turned the walls into cluttered investigation boards, modeled after their favorite crime procedurals. They had stopped short of the yarn connecting various pins in a labyrinthine web of theory and conclusion.

"Think of something, Blake?"

She held her hand up for silence, and Jason thought of the ring that wasn't there.

His phone vibrated in his pocket. A message came through from an unknown number with what his phone told him was a Florida area code. "Okay, guys. Just got a message. It says 'bow.'"

"Bow?"

"Yeah. Oh, wait." Jason's phone vibrated again, this time in his hand. "Another one came through. 'Now.'"

Will rolled his eyes. "This is definitely going to be some teenager."

Jason again swiped the laptop's trackpad, and the screen returned to normal brightness. Will and Blake both watched.

"Indeed. But, the username we were given is online, so I guess I'll send the call. Why not?"

Blake sighed, but Jason ignored them both and hit the camera button to engage a video call, and within moments was looking at a man far older than he expected to see. He was sitting an uncomfortable distance away from the screen. His white sneakers were visible.

"Hello? Hello?" the man yelled.

Jason's eyes widened at the volume while Blake's and Will's brows furrowed, unable to see anything other than Jason's reactions.

"Yes. Hello, Mr. Markani. It's Jason. Jason Debord."

"Yeah, I'm the one who texted you. Now, what do you need to ask me? Unbelievable. One message left up on a message board from a decade ago, and here we are. You've been industrious."

The volume of his voice clipped on the speaker inside Jason's laptop.

Jason opened his mouth to speak but froze. Will, meanwhile, scribbled on his notepad.

"Yeah, can you hear me?"

"Oh, yeah, sorry," Jason said. "I guess I'm wondering why you went to such great lengths to hide from *Beached*. As you heard, we're trying to figure out who would have had the ability to commit murder. And cover it up."

Markani leaned as far back as he could in his chair. "And, presumably, you're trying to figure out who broke into your house and then tried to run you off the road?"

"Yeah. Exactly that."

Will held up a sheet of paper, on which he had written, in large capital letters, "ask about firing."

Jason looked away from the sign and again focused on Markani, but Will only held the sign closer and waved it at Jason. Blake, who had been aloof since the Skype call began, walked to Will, placed a hand on his, and forced the note back to the table before resuming her seat at the table.

"Well. Listen, there's a reason I don't talk about any of it. Why I tried to delete every trace of myself from the internet. See, I knew this day would come. I hoped it was all over, but I pay attention, and I saw the signs. I was idealistic. And here you are, asking the questions I always feared. After all, I was one of the few who escaped so it's probably my turn."

Markani held up a finger and stood. "Actually, hang on. Let me grab something."

The man walked behind the computer, giving Jason an up-close look. As he leaned behind his camera, his lower legs took over the screen thanks to the curiously angled camera setup. Both legs were covered in plain black tattoos. Central in both designs was an eight-pointed star on each kneecap, while the more intricate designs were too hard to recognize through the pixelated connection. Otherwise, the man looked like a standard Midwestern father. Golf shirt, khaki shorts, receding hairline.

After a moment's pause, Will again thrust his sign behind the laptop screen, instructing Jason to ask about RTN's firing practices. Blake forced Will's arm down, and the two glowered at each other. Jason only tilted his head at them, grasping for silence.

Before the commotion was resolved, Markani was back on the screen, also thrusting a document at Jason. It was a photograph, printed on paper, worn with folds. The image depicted a group of men, all presumably in their early twenties, holding camera gear and sound equipment on a beach.

"This was my first day," Markani said. "And these guys would end up being some of my best friends."

He sighed and continued, "I haven't seen or heard from them in over a decade."

"Right. Well, I'm sorry about that. And I don't want to sound dismissive, but maybe we could discuss this kind of stuff another time. The early days of the show's filming are fascinating, but I need to know what you wanted to tell me."

"What I'm trying to say is, this is you right now. Innocent. Safe." Markani tapped his index finger against the picture, which was still close enough to the camera lens that Jason could scarcely see around the blurry edges. "I mean, you've seen the darkness, but this is mostly you. Drop it all. Live your life so you don't become what these guys became. Myself included. Hiding away in a forgettable life within a forgettable part of the world."

Jason nodded, ignoring the new sign that Will was holding, which now read "ask about Curtis David."

"Mr. Markani, I appreciate the warning. But, as you said, I've seen whatever this darkness you're alluding to is. My friend is dead. Not to mention my house and the car attack, which you mentioned yourself. I'm kind of stuck in this now, and I've been discussing it publicly. For months, I've considered whether I imagined this all. It's been ruining my life and fracturing my mind.

"Now, I'm sitting before you, and you're the closest I've gotten to having actual proof I'm not insane. Proof there is something going on here. I need you to be more direct with me. What is this darkness? Who is involved? And why are you in self-imposed hiding?"

Jason gripped either side of his laptop screen. Will put his sign back on the table without Blake forcing him to. They all waited.

Markani removed the photo from the screen and returned to his seat, six feet away from the computer.

"You want facts. Alright, fair enough. Well, as you know, this has happened before. That was when I was involved and why I hoped it had all stopped. Why am I in hiding? I'm keeping in the shadows to avoid my old life, and prison. The reason I haven't talked to those guys in the photo is that I'm pretty positive they're still in jail somewhere in Central America. You think RTN covered something up? Of course they did. Again, this has happened before. But, I don't know how much blame RTN gets.

"Well, I honestly don't know who's to blame for any of it. But, trust me. It's safe to stay quiet and keep your head down. It's worked for me. That's why I agreed to talk to you; to help prevent another person from falling victim. I played my part in the past, so this is atonement, I guess."

Jason's grip on the screen loosened. "So, you're saying people were arrested the first time they cleared the crew out?"

Markani nodded with a frown.

"And you think this is connected to Billy? What were they arrested for?"

"There are a lot of things Central America is known for, beyond the beauty. Stuff that gets people arrested. And stuff that can make a struggling cameraman rich if he plays his cards right. Things that should only be said over a secure line."

Will held up another sign as soon as Markani finished: "deaths?"

"Okay," Jason said, "I think I follow. Has anyone else ever died?"

Markani repeated his nod.

"Come on. I need names. Something to go on. Give me something."

"You miss my point, Mr. Debord. Do you think I got in touch with you to help you expose someone or something? That's the opposite of what I want. Anything further—anything specific—that I give you will only do you harm. You need to drop this. I'm serious. As I told you, this is real, and you're an amateur. I mean, do you think you're in some paperback novel or serialized procedural? You're going to take on these unspeakable crimes and a major corporation covering its ass? All in some misguided quest to get justice for a guy you knew for a few weeks? Trust me and my experience; whatever happened was done for a reason."

Jason couldn't react.

"Jason Debord, I hope to never hear from you, or about you, ever again."

The call ended as the video feed cut out and Jason was again staring at his Skype contacts list. After he closed the laptop, he stared at the space the screen had occupied only moments ago.

Will slammed his hand against the table. While Blake and Jason continued to stare, he threw his pad of paper into the air. It hit the wall, making the taped documents sway, before slapping against the ground. Jason still didn't flinch. Blake, however, rose and walked to where the notepad had landed. She picked it up and laid it on the table. Her attention didn't come with it. She was resuming her earlier study of the documents on the wall.

"Whatever," Will said. He swiped his arm along the table, again flinging the pad. Neither of his companions reacted this time. "Are you guys not pissed?"

Jason was deep in thought.

"What a dickhead," Will continued. "As if he's going to give us all this cryptic bullshit without telling us anything. He has all the answers to stop whatever this 'darkness' is, but he'd rather hide. And discourage anyone else. Whatever. I guess I never had any hope that would pan out, and it sounds like he helped smuggle drugs."

"I mean, we didn't even really expect it to be him," Jason said. "We thought it'd be a prank. But it was him so that's a win. Right?"

"No. It's another fucking set of questions without answers. So now there are drugs involved, but we don't know any specifics. So, thanks a lot, Joel Markani. I mean, do we even believe this guy is legit? We might still be right, and he could be a fraud. He couldn't give us one goddamn name or specific detail. Nothing to prove he was connected in any believable way."

"I mean, he did," Jason said.

Will threw his arms up and shook his head. He looked to Blake, who remained aloof from the conversation, and turned back to Jason. "What details, then?"

Jason finally looked up. "We know people got arrested. That there are drugs or gangs involved. That RTN likely knows about it. And that there is, without a doubt, someone capable of and willing to do the things we suspected."

Will stood sharply. "So, I guess we should go to the police now. We have the whole thing sorted out for them. And I guess we're safe to go back to normal again."

"Also, my friend Seth was in that photo he showed. And he has tattoos that match Markani's after swearing he didn't know who he was. Maybe we should just let the police handle it. Step back, I mean."

Blake turned and looked at Jason while Will studied the floor.

"Do you think he knows something then?" Will asked. "Was he one of the guys Markani said was in jail?"

Jason shrugged, frowning similarly to when he'd botched the proposal. The cold wind against their faces. The swipe of their coats touching.

"It could be a coincidence," Will said. "I mean, has this old man on Skype got you spooked? We're going to go about our lives now? Do you remember that Billy was killed, and they tried to smash our heads against a highway divider at eighty miles per hour?"

"Those are exactly the kinds of reasons we should step back. Maybe Markani is right. We don't know what we're doing, we have no resources, and we're sloppy. We're a joke. And this is exactly what they train real police for. And I think we have enough for a detective to take us seriously."

Will gritted his teeth and locked Jason's gaze. The sound of tape being torn from the wall broke the standoff, and the feud was halted. Blake pulled down one of the documents she had been fixating on.

"You guys. We might have been wrong this whole time. About Billy I mean. I'm thinking about his life and trying to fit it into a narrative. His whole life was ruined because of his drug addiction, right? So, he's out on the island, reduced to his weakest self. Starved. No sleep. Without shelter, safety, trust. Would you guys agree?"

Jason nodded while Will folded his arms.

"So," Blake continued, "if these people were involved in the drug trade, what are the odds Billy could get his hands on some? Whatever he wanted would have been there, and he had nothing but time, opportunity, and desire. This isn't the first time drug smuggling has come up. Wasn't someone floating drugs to shore from a boat?

"With what you all went through, it's not out of the question. And after dedicating so much time to getting and staying clean? How do you think that relapse, coupled with the stress of the island, might have affected Billy? The most straightforward explanation, which is usually correct, is that Billy relapsed and took his own life out of guilt and shame. Maybe RTN isn't lying.

"And, why would the presence of drugs lead to them murdering Billy? This makes more sense. And, Jason, you've known this all along. Didn't drugs lead him to grief and paranoia? Like in the psych report from Ronnie. You wrote about him experiencing that. In your journal from the island."

The three stood, each on their respective sides of the table, and no one moved.

———

"HE WON'T COME OUT," Jason said, hours later as he ran his hand down Blake's back and pulled her into an embrace. She was leaning against Jason's kitchen counter while reading the news on her phone. His entrance broke her gaze.

"Seriously?"

"Yeah. No matter what I said all I got was, 'Leave me be for the night.'"

Blake set her phone on the counter and rotated to face Jason. He leaned against her, and they wrapped their arms around each other.

"I'm going to the police," Jason said. He hung his head and kissed her hair.

"We've—you've—done everything you can now. If something is going on, they're best equipped to handle it." Jason's hoodie muffled her voice. She cleared her throat and slid a step back. "And what about Seth?"

Jason followed Blake's lead and stepped back before opening the fridge. "You want anything to drink?"

"I'm okay."

Jason nodded and pulled a single beer off the fridge's bottom shelf. He set the bottle, an Old Rasputin, next to the sink. His eyes jumped to the drawer—past Blake—that housed the bottle opener.

"I think I have to tell him about everything," Jason said. "He might have been involved at some point and I don't want him to find out from anyone else."

"Do you think he had anything to do with something criminal? You sound worried."

"No. Maybe. I guess if he was I wouldn't have any idea. But Seth definitely knows about a lot of this, and I don't understand why he hasn't told me. At least about the firings. He's definitely culpable in something he doesn't like. And it's felt like we keep getting close to homing in on something or someone before something bad happens. Cars get crashed, homes get broken into, someone dies, and posts get deleted. Someone knows what we're up to. They're nearby. If he was involved before, in 2012, he might have some answers.

"But it's a damn awkward conversation to have with a friend. How do I say 'I think you might have been in a drug smuggling ring and know something about the death of my friend Billy'? But I have to because his name might come up. He'll be one of the first people the cops will talk to because he's one of the few concrete connections I can give them. And, I suppose, he might still be a part of it—who knows anymore?"

"Does it seem safe?" Blake asked. "I mean, it sounds like you can't rule him out of involvement. I don't know him, really, at all. If he is involved, or is some kind of criminal, should you be confronting him about it? And saying you'll go to the police? Not to mention, if you're wrong, that could devastate your friendship, not to mention career."

Jason grabbed the beer again and rolled it between his palms. The label felt mushy and ready to fall off.

"I think I trust him, but I'm growing more suspicious of everyone. I'm suspicious of everyone except you. And Will, I guess, after the accident. But Seth, if I think about it, has been weird. He's asked me all these prying questions but pretended not to care. Almost like he's keeping track of what we knew and suspected. Kept claiming he didn't know anyone even though he worked there for years. Damn..."

Jason trailed off. Blake attempted to hide her mixed look of pity and fear, but Jason saw it lurking at the corners of her mouth.

"I'll do it in public," Jason said finally. He set the bottle down on the counter again.

"Hopefully that's a good idea. Either way, you'll get some answers. But, what about your old thoughts about Nick and Hunter? How do you see them fitting into your theory?"

"They must have been helping. It makes sense that you'd want to plant some cast to help them with the rest of the show. Direct attention elsewhere. That explains why Nick was so confrontational about people asking questions. And how Hunter has such a cash flow."

Blake approached and hugged him in a mirror image of their earlier embrace, only instead of comfort this moment felt different. As though they were both trying to overcompensate for the fear or tension they felt.

After a moment they exited the kitchen, and a few moments later the turntable of the record player in the living room spun. Distorted, fuzzy guitar. Jason's beer remained on the counter, warming and sweating.

28.

THE FIRST THING Jason noticed was that there was no one else on the courts. Privacy for the upcoming conversation was a relief no matter what he'd said to Blake about being in public. Only Seth was there, bouncing a fresh green ball on his racket. The other four courts were empty.

After a few more bounces, Jason was at the back gate. He lifted the latch and crossed through. His tennis bag got caught on the handle, making it slam shut and jerk Jason backward after a few steps. While he pulled the bag loose, Seth noticed him, but still kept bouncing the ball in the air. He had it going nearly twenty feet high, approaching the rafters.

"Hey, hey. It's so good to see you. Welcome back to campus, man," Seth said without looking.

"Yeah, good to be back. I need some fresh air and exercise. Badly."

Jason placed his bag on the ground next to the court's mesh bench, where he flung himself. Seth let the ball hit the ground and caught it on a bounce before walking over to Jason and taking a seat next to him.

When he had first spoken of his suspicions, Seth had dismissed Jason. Later, he had grown quite interested and routinely asked for details about the various cast members' opinions. The vacillating interest made his stance hard to read.

Jason could concentrate on nothing but the tension that Seth was entirely unaware of.

"I'll bet," Seth said. "What have you been up to lately? You seem a bit despondent."

Jason took his shoes out of his bag and pulled off his boots, which left wet footprints on the clay court as the remnants of snow melted. He was determined to not mention his proposal or anything about his and Blake's relationship. Maintain advantage.

"You know, not that much. A lot of research. It'll be good to get into more of an exercise routine. After the island, and then the accident, my weight has been fluctuating wildly, and I've been so sedentary."

"Yeah, I bet. But what kind of research have you been doing? I saw what happened with the podcast you appeared on and everything. Are you doing okay?"

Jason was bent over, tying his shoes, but he looked up to see the earnest expression of concern on Seth's face. It stirred an annoyance in Jason. He felt like an impostor. Without acknowledging Seth's question, Jason returned to his shoes and kept his gaze turned downwards, at their legs and feet.

"Actually," Jason said, "I was doing more research on *Beached*, and I found a photo of some other crew members who had those same eight-pointed star tattoos. I thought I recognized it at the time but couldn't place it."

"Interesting. Yeah, I guess we rarely hang out in shorts. But, where did you find this photo?"

Seth stood again and bounced the tennis ball between the ground and his racket, focusing on the ball's trajectory. Jason finished tying his shoes.

"I found it digging around online. It was from an old Reddit post. You might have been in the photo. Hard to tell because it was such poor quality," he lied.

"Huh. Any idea who the others were? Or who posted it?" Seth misjudged the ball, and it bounced away onto the next court. He turned to Jason.

Jason shook his head. "I don't know. I didn't recognize anyone, and there weren't any posted details. I was hoping you could help identify them since you have a matching tattoo."

"Weird. I don't think I've ever seen this photo online. Yeah, a number of us got these together."

Jason stood, grabbed his racket from his bag, and took a few cursory practice swings in the air.

"Cool, what was the meaning behind it?"

Jason walked onto the court, still stretching out his arms. A couple of days hadn't shaken the chills that coursed through him. Seth grabbed a ball to replace the other and followed Jason, taking his place on the opposite side of the net.

"It was pretty stupid, actually. First tattoos I got. Everyone thought it would make us look like badasses. A Russian guy was working on the crew, and it was his idea. They're inspired by a traditional Russian tattoo. It means something like 'I bow to no one.'"

"Okay. Do you keep in touch with any of those guys?"

"Not at all. So the stars are a weird reminder. I don't know. Memories of the past." He shrugged. "Do you want to get playing?"

Jason backed up to the rear of the court. "Sure thing. Let's get my beating over with. Your serve, man."

Seth threw the ball up and swung his racket overhead. The ball collided with the rim of his racket and shot straight into the ground before bouncing into the adjacent court. Jason was glad it hadn't made it over the net. He wasn't focused on the racket.

"Rough start. You want me to grab another ball?" Jason called.

"No. I'll get it. It's my own damn fault."

Racket in hand, Seth flashed Jason a smile and jogged after the still-bouncing ball. With every one of Seth's steps, Jason's urge to run grew. He needed to get out of there. Something was off, and this wasn't the right time to broach the situation with Seth. Could Seth have been involved? Or was his change in behavior merely social awkwardness? Watch, Jason decided, patience. Like a camera.

After retrieving the ball, Seth served again. This time, it made it onto the court, and Jason returned it with ease, putting it to Seth's backhand. Seth transitioned smoothly and struck the ball five feet past Jason, outside the baseline.

This wasn't right for a confrontation. Their interactions were vaguely off, while Seth's behavior felt specifically wrong. He was no longer as sure as he'd been. About anything.

"Uh, love-fifteen," Jason said. "I thought you were supposed to be good."

"Yeah. I did, too."

TEXTS

31 DECEMBER 2025, 9:02 PM

JASON: I'm going to bring it up tonight. Tennis last week wasn't the right time. Our conversations are going well so far, and there's no other option at this point. I love you. I'll let you know what happens.

BLAKE: I love you, too! I'm really pleased you're talking about it—I hope Seth can clear everything up. Are you enjoying your party? It's stuffy here.

JASON: Work parties are the worst—but, at least professors drink a lot. I'm planning on being home early, though, given the talk with Seth. And you're right, he deserves a chance to tell me what's going on. But he's definitely involved— I'll text you right after.

BLAKE: And I'll see you shortly after that! I should be over to yours around midnight to debrief what he says. I'm so sorry I can't be with you.

JASON: Seriously, don't even think about it. Like I said, I can handle Seth. Nothing to worry about!

BLAKE: Still, just be gentle about everything, and back down if he gets too aggravated or angry. I know you can get worked up about this (which is understandable). Plus, remember, he's not the enemy, and he may have information that can help you understand what happened.

JASON: Thanks for the advice, but Seth's not about to have some kind of scene in front of the whole faculty. That's part of why tonight's ideal. Plus, if he's involved in some criminal conspiracy then he deserves it. We can notify the police on Monday. Let them handle it. I'm comfortable with our plan.

29.

GLASS SHARDS CRUNCHED under Jason's feet as he paced in front of the fireplace.

"What the hell, man?" Seth stared at Jason, deep breaths audible through the indignation.

"No, you're not going to act like I'm crazy. Not anymore. You've been a part of this all along. You know what happened, and you're going to fucking tell me right now. Everything."

A woman in a silver-sequined evening gown rushed into the room holding a flute of champagne. Her heels clicked with steady efficiency. She stopped alongside Seth. "Christ, what happened? I heard a crash."

"Nothing," Jason said. He didn't bother looking in her direction.

"I think Jason might be having a rough night. Maybe a bit too much to drink, but I'll clean this up and get him home," Seth said. "Sorry, Holly."

"No. It's fine, really. But, what happened?"

"Well, he kind of smashed that bottle against the fireplace bricks. He's convinced I've wronged him in some fashion. Haven't the foggiest what that might be about, but I guess I'm the villain here. Nothing else is broken though, just the beer bottle."

Jason paced away from them and threw his arms in the air.

"Again, no. I am not drunk, I've had like four beers over as many hours, and you know that. We came here together. And you need to answer me, Seth. What is your role in this? And why have you kept it from me?"

Holly shot Seth a frown tinged with pity and he placed a hand on her bare shoulder. "I've got this. You can get back to the party."

Holly walked, again, through an archway of ornate molding. This time, however, the sound of her shoes was obscured by Seth's voice.

"Jason, seriously. What the fuck. She might be the wrong person's house for this. And everyone from work's here. Why don't we head out?"

Jason lifted his head. His shoulder-length hair hung in a tangled mess. Despite the New Year's Eve glamour, his tie was half-undone and crooked, while his shirt was untucked on the left. His ordinarily immaculate suit was disheveled from his gesticulating, but his eyes were firm and piercing.

"I'm not going anywhere with you. And you're not leaving until you give me the truth. The matching tattoos; that's too much of a coincidence. I talked to Joel Markani. He was involved the first time, and he thought it had ended, but it hadn't. You had to know, and that's why you're always asking what people are saying and thinking. It's why you're so curious about my suspicions even though you pretend like I'm delusional. You're worried for yourself.

"So tell me, now. Richard Brandt, Joel Markani, Curtis David, Hunter, Nick. I know who's involved here. I know there are drugs involved, too. And why don't you try to explain the two cell phones? Come on. It's not like I think you killed Billy yourself—I just need the truth."

Seth broke eye contact and measured the situation.

"Come on." Jason thrust the sole of his dress shoe hard against the wooden floor and Seth looked up.

"Okay, you have some questions. I get it." He returned Jason's gaze, and this time smiled, before laughing a few times, inaudibly. "I mean, I kind of figured this would happen after our game of tennis the other day, but not in such dramatic fashion. There have been ongoing rumors about the show, but I can assure you there's no substance to them anymore. A few guys were arrested with cocaine, but that was isolated. And I don't personally know Joel Markani or these other people."

He paused. "Jason, I'm so sorry. I didn't realize this is what you were going through and I probably made it worse."

Jason felt his face redden, but couldn't give an intelligent reply. He only looked on, trying to rebound from whatever he was feeling, but couldn't pin down. Deflation? Confusion? He needed his focus.

"You're sorry? Tell me what you have to do with this, and keep in mind I already know a lot. How did you make it worse?"

"Well, I know you lived a lot of it. And so did these other people. But I took a lot of liberties, and most of it was reacting to what you were doing. Or the other members of the cast. I guess it was inspired by a lot of others, but it's still my original work. Planned and composed it all myself."

"Specifics, now."

"Okay, okay. Man, I'll even let you read it. I've been worried to tell you, but knew I'd have to. I've been afraid to show it to anyone, and just sent it out for the first time this week. How do you even know? Does RTN know?"

"Sent it out? I don't know what you're talking about. I don't know if RTN knows; that's something I thought you could answer. But, I figured this out on my own. I mean, I had some help, but no one told me."

Seth took another pace closer to the fireplace. "What are you accusing me of exactly? I thought you were messing with me because you knew about the screenplay."

"Screenplay?"

"You don't know then? Well, either way I should have told you. Been more up front, I mean. Because, like I said, you were a big part of the inspiration. And you helped so much, but I was afraid to tell you about my writing. I didn't have much of a choice though. I think I told you how badly I was searching for creative inspiration. This seems like just what I needed. My moment. I tried to listen and ask questions and be a supportive friend, but I guess that wasn't working."

"I don't buy this at all. Some screenplay? I have too much evidence," Jason said. "Don't try to lie to me now. That's over."

"Oh, right. Evidence of what?" Seth's eyebrows furrowed.

"So much. I'm sure you all think this is covered up and you'll throw me off now, but you left too much to find. That picture I mentioned, with the matching tattoos, the other information Markani gave me. All the suspicious behaviors. The car attack, the break-ins. RTN's corrupt behavior."

Jason's eyes hunted for weapons and exits. He had expected Seth to break down, to tell him everything, and to ask for forgiveness. To show remorse for his involvement. Not this. Then again, what should he have expected from someone involved in drug smuggling and murder? This was a missed calculation.

He identified the back door, past the dining room. It was far, but Seth was blocking the front door. Plus, there were plenty of witnesses if he went through the rest of the party. There was a decorative nutcracker, left over from the Christmas decorations. It would break but could be swung once or twice.

Seth only stared out the floor-length windows that faced the dark, imposing woods behind their host's home.

After a moment, he again opened his mouth to speak, but laughter penetrated the room and a door was closed. Once again, the clacking of heels was coming their way.

"It's best if you keep quiet just now, yeah?"

Jason nodded, but he wasn't sure why he had agreed. Impulse took over. Or maybe something else. He was no longer sure how to stand naturally so he rolled his shoulders, trying to adjust to casual posture. Jason looked into the eyes of the friendship he'd decided to end days ago and didn't know what he now clung to.

"Well, here they are." Holly entered through the room's arched doorway.

Jason smiled and waved. Along with Holly was Grace Everill, another member of the English department.

"Everything alright, guys?" Grace asked.

She grinned, but slipped Jason a sideways glance.

"We're just getting into the kind of deep conversation you can only have when you're good and drunk," Seth said. He patted Jason on the back.

Grace shook her head. "Fools," she declared and downed the remainder of her wine. Pondering the empty glass, she tilted it towards Jason. "Not quite on that level, but I suppose I'll get more. Need a drink for when the ball drops. I mean, that only seems proper."

Grace turned and left the room.

"About time to find someone to kiss?" Seth's voice was calm. Jason flashed to every conversation they'd ever had. The moments muddled his mind. Tennis.

Lunches. Drinks. Soccer matches. Hanging out at the office. Texting back and forth. Watching *Beached*.

"Genuinely, we are getting close to the midnight hour," Holly said. "Leave the broken glass for now and come join us outside. We should all be together, no matter how much fun we've had. After all, that's why we're here."

Jason nodded, trying to appear as though considering the option.

"Of course, Holly. We'll be out in a second," Seth said.

"Okay, then. Let me know if either of you needs anything. Loads of snacks in the kitchen. Drinks on the counter and beer in the fridge."

Holly exited stage left from Jason's delusion.

Seth turned on Jason, who was surprised to see his smile had not faded with Holly's presence.

"So," Seth said, "are you calmer? I didn't consider how you'd take it until I was too far in and already in love with the concept. How can I make it up to you? I'm happy to show you my writing. Actually, I'd love your feedback. You guys lived it. Hell, I'd love for you to be a part of this. Depending on the deal I get, I'm sure I can get you on the writing team."

"What? No. Stop this. You killed him. And smuggled drugs. And the crash and break-in. You knew about this. And RTN knows. They've covered it up. You were in jail, and the others."

Seth only waited.

"Come on, Seth. Don't do this. Just tell me. Stop trying to confuse me."

"I'm getting concerned, man. Are you messing with me now? I said I'm sorry. I didn't know how to act. I felt guilty for helping you get on the show when it was such a traumatizing experience. I probably should have brought up these past controversies, but I didn't want to make your struggle worse. I don't know what else to do. Are you feeling okay? You look sweaty."

Jason struggled to feel his legs or feet. "So,"—he stumbled as he sat, knees bent, against the brick surrounding the fireplace—"you weren't involved in murdering Billy? Or smuggling drugs? Or trying to silence me and Will? Okay. So, I guess Joel Markani made all that stuff up. And this is all just a coincidence. You're right —I'm insane. Silly me, you were curious and trying to be supportive, which explains your gang tattoos and the second cell phone. I'm sure you're telling the truth."

"Listen to yourself." Seth sat across from Jason, at a slight angle. "Do you really think I'm capable of murdering someone? Or smuggling drugs? Or putting a hit, or something, on one of my friends?

"I understand being irritated with me, but all I've been doing is writing to try to save my career and do something successful. You jumped to so many conclusions, like you wanted to see this all along. You made so many assumptions from circumstance. Jason, I was just writing."

While the words hung in the air and Jason only held a snarled expression, Seth continued, "So, you're trusting some random guy you don't know from the internet? Some conspiracy theorist. More than me, the network, half the cast and crew? This is hard to understand. I know you were working through stuff, but what is this? Now I'm offended.

"I have questionable tattoos because I liked the design and had a misplaced sense of rebellion in my twenties. It was like a group initiation with the crew back then. It had been going on for years before I started working. The second cell phone doesn't exist anymore; I was having trouble migrating from my old phone, so I carried around two for a while. Texts were going to one while most of my apps only worked on the other. I need to learn to back-up my phone more often.

"But, I mean, really? You got to live your dream on the show. You got what you thought you always wanted, and it didn't live up. I get it; that happens. But this isn't the solution. There isn't always an answer that you want to hear, and I don't have a role in whatever grand confrontation you think is happening. I don't fit very well into whatever story you're trying to tell. Think about it. I just explained everything in a minute."

Jason couldn't move his arms or legs, and he couldn't look Seth in the eyes. There were too many emotions that Jason had placed there. He'd found the truth. Unless he hadn't.

"So you wrote a screenplay? Based on the show?"

Seth nodded solemnly. "I got the idea once you started voicing all of your suspicions and fears about Billy's death. I incorporated what you told me, but added my own ideas, too. Like I've said, I needed something beyond my experience in reality television, or else there was no way I was going to advance my career. I have an agent I already heard back from. I would show you the email, but Christ."

Jason felt his breathing increase involuntarily. His vision clouded. Finally, with much effort, he was able to wipe his eyes and shield his face with his hands.

"I'm not wrong.

"I can't be.

"I did know all along. I needed to say something. I should have seen it coming.

"I don't know…I don't know…I…"

"Jason, I had no idea it was this bad," Seth said. "I'm so sorry. What can I do to help? It's going to be okay."

———

TREMORS COULD BE FELT through the floor. Police rushed into the room. Jason wanted them to take the problem off his hands. That was all he had wanted for months. Let someone else take this. Or were they paramedics?

Seth watched on, fading away as the three white-shirts rushed to Jason. Jason tried to stand, to protest, but nothing happened. He didn't move. Everyone else moved through his stillness.

After an uncertain amount of time, the only voice that could pierce the deafening silence broke the stasis. Someone pressed a cell phone to Jason's ear. Blake's voice muffled its way through the fog. "I'm going to be there soon. I love you. Everything's going to be okay."

"Yes," Jason mumbled. His voice shook and trailed off. So much more to say. He knew, finally. He should have, needed to have, said something. Anything.

———

THE RINGING DIDN'T LEAVE his ears until minutes later, outside, when he was being loaded into an ambulance. Motion swarmed around him, but Jason lay in slightly conscious silence, staring into the dark trees. They looked like they had been painted with an expressionist's brush.

He wanted to ask the EMT to his right if he'd had a heart attack, but the words wouldn't form.

The man noticed Jason's glance and pulled a thin fleece blanket from the back of the ambulance. He draped it over Jason's body, which had formed a layer of sweat despite the winter cold.

Jason wanted to thank him, but he couldn't suspend his focus on breathing. After he stopped twice inside the house, to the point of choking gasps, he had regained momentary focus and clarity. Enough to see a woman he didn't recognize grasping the sides of his face saying, "You're hyperventilating. You need to breathe. Deep breaths."

That was the one thing he understood: breathe.

So, Jason had continued to count off his breaths and focus on rhythm. He hated being fussed over and wanted to get up from the stretcher, but he was frozen and unsure what was happening to his body.

Someone approached—Jason could sense them—but he didn't look at them.

"Jason, it's Holly. I'm right here. You're okay, and Blake is on her way. She should be here any minute, and she's going to ride down to the hospital with you. Just so they can check you out."

He tried to contort his head to look in her direction and was forced to blink to clear tears from his eyes. At no point had he realized he was crying. It was unclear why he was crying, or when it had started.

He wanted to describe to her his past panic attacks, in graduate school. How they were nothing like this but somehow similar. All he managed was opening his mouth, then involuntary convulsing.

AGAIN, Jason stared through foggy vision and gasped for breath. He was unsure whether he had passed out or had a heart attack. A second heart attack? Why was he not seeing the doctors more quickly? Breathe, he told himself.

He felt his body sway to the left. Gone was the darkness of the forest and night sky. Instead, there were bright LEDs. He was in an ambulance. One, two, three, breathe.

He had the urge to wipe off his sweaty palms, but he was still strapped down. Strapped in, he tried to correct his mind. Calm down. Nothing to worry about. Breathe.

While he focused on taking in his surroundings, a blurry proposition, his hand felt something. Another. Blake's hair in his face. She kissed his left cheek and pulled back, but not before whispering in his ear. "Happy New Year. I love you, and I'm so sorry. But I'm here for you and not going anywhere. I've got you."

Jason wanted the pressure on his body to lift, for restoration. But there was no cinematic recovery. Nevertheless, he felt hope, for the first time that night, that he would be okay.

Blake had done more than she probably expected, and he wanted to tell her. When he tried, Jason's eyes bulged as he was again reduced to gasping for breath, struggling to filter air through the last six months, and feeling all 180 days of pressure on his lungs.

TEXTS

14 AUGUST 2026

8:19 am

JASON: Hey. I know it's been months, but I wanted to reach out to tell you I'm going to Boston to attend a service for Billy. I'm in a better spot. Things are going well. I'm sorry for what happened and how I confronted you. If I can make up for it, let me know.

11:48 am

SETH: It's good to hear from you—I wasn't sure if we were still talking, so I was giving you some space. I didn't know about the service, but I hope that goes well. I'm so glad you're doing alright—that was scary. And, again, I'm sorry for not being more forthcoming or playing a role in what happened.

JASON: Thanks for saying that. And no worries. If I wasn't consumed with what you were up to, I would have latched on to something else. How is the screenplay coming?

11:52 pm

JASON: I hope you didn't take that the wrong way. Seriously. Ha. I'm in support of the idea and would be free to talk with you about it. Your process or the details. Whatever. But, I hope I gave you a good enough ending.

BLAKE'S OFFICE

"THANKS AGAIN, really. I mean for, like, everything. I don't know what I would have done, and I hope there's someone else in Arizona that's anywhere close to as great as you."

Blake smiled and stood up from her desk. Her teenage client, Natalie, followed her lead. She picked up her purse and slung it over her shoulder before facing Blake.

"It's been so great getting to know you. If you ever need anything, make sure you get in contact."

Natalie extended her arms and gave Blake a hug. Unprecipitated contact always made Blake uncomfortable, but it was not atypical for a final appointment. Something about finality and goodbye allowed people to break conventions.

The embrace didn't last long, and Natalie broke away before heading to the door. She turned back as she twisted the handle and gave Blake one last smile before walking across the threshold and disappearing from her life forever. The tear-tinged smile brought out Blake's guilt. These moments usually moved her. Rarely did she feel a sense of accomplishment or have time to reflect on her profession, and right here was such a moment, presenting itself, but she couldn't quite seize onto it.

Blake abandoned the unfulfilling moment and went back to her desk. Before she could sit, however, Sydney was tapping, ever so slightly, on her door frame.

"Yeah, hey. Come on in."

Sydney nodded and took Natalie's place in the seat before Blake. As she sat, she kept her gaze averted to the floor and affected an unthreatening, closed posture.

"So, how are you?" Sydney asked.

Blake took a dramatic breath and stole a look at her clock. Quarter past three.

"I'm okay, you know. Ready for a break; everything's been a lot lately. Natalie's in a strong place, though."

"Good. And, I thought I'd let you know, Jason is here in the lobby."

Blake looked through the open door, but only saw the hallway.

"Well, that's early. How long has he been here?"

Sydney shrugged. "I don't know, not too long. But he seems okay. He looks really good." Her voice had a forced enthusiasm when she spoke of Jason.

"Well, yeah," Blake said, "he's fine when he's not in the middle of a panic attack. They've been happening a lot more lately than they had earlier in his life. But he's working through it responsibly now that he knows what's wrong with him. What he's dealing with. It's nothing to worry about on a daily basis. I mean, I know it had a big impact on me personally, and I appreciate your concern. But we're good."

Blake had been adjusting her hair but her hand worked its way down the collar of her shirt out of habit. She stopped and jerked her arm away. The movement caught Sydney's eye, and her gaze lingered on the necklace hanging around Blake's neck. The one she had almost grasped. Blake noticed and couldn't help but comment.

"It'll happen," Blake said, "but we need to wait for the right time. It's my decision, and what I eventually want."

Sydney nodded. "I only just noticed it. Have you been wearing that for a while?"

"A couple weeks."

Blake smiled and regretted that it was defensive. She was genuinely happy, but not in the mood to put on the public display. Her looming travels were weighing on her. She allowed her hand to continue what she had stopped in an attempt to support her smile.

The necklace was a thin white-gold chain that hung six inches below Blake's collarbone.

"It's stunning. Do you think you two will be engaged soon then?"

"It's hard to say. Blake stood and pushed her chair in. "I mean, it's been months, but we want to get it right. That's the only reason we didn't the first time, timing. We definitely will, and it's getting closer, but Jason is still going through…" She trailed off for a thought. "I should have noticed what was going on. I was trying to be supportive, and it backfired. So we both need to be able to move forward. But it's what we both want."

Sydney moved toward the door. "From my perspective, you two are great together. And don't punish yourself. Think what it would have been like if you weren't there."

Blake nodded.

As Sydney left, her wilting smile couldn't mask pity. It left Blake standing alone in the middle of her office, wondering how many of these rhythmic inter-actions it would take before she was confident nothing would unexpectedly collapse around her.

Her shoulders slumped, and she turned toward her desk. Her purse was packed. She had also heard her phone vibrate minutes ago and not yet checked it.

When she finally did, as one final delay before leaving the room, she saw Jason's message. "I'm in the lobby, but take as much time as you need. I love you and can't wait to spend the weekend together. Thanks again for coming with me. This should be a big step. For everyone. I need you there, and I appreciate it so much."

―――

JASON WAS PERCHED on the edge of his waiting-room chair with one leg crossed over the other. He sat in the chair farthest from the door, against the back corner's wall and window. Sydney was back at her desk, but the room was other-wise empty. As Blake walked into the room, he didn't notice. The television in the lobby played ESPN, which drowned out her footsteps, and Jason was absorbed in the most recent issue of the *Atlantic*. He'd folded the magazine so only a corner of the cover was visible. Something yellow. He tapped his foot on the floor as he read.

By the time she was within three paces, he shifted legs, and the transition was enough to force him to look up. He closed the magazine at once, tossed it on the seat next to him, and hopped out of his chair. As he straightened, he ruffled the beard he'd grown out. It was trimmed and shaped to his face, though, in contrast to the wild, unkempt island look.

Blake smiled at him, this time genuinely, and he kissed her. It felt relaxed and comforting. Some unknown tension released.

"Thanks again for meeting me here. I had to finish up."

"No problem. Your office is much closer to the airport. Are you ready?"

Jason's eyes searched hers.

"My bag's in the car, and I have my purse. Let's go."

"Great." Jason stood.

Blake turned back to Sydney reading something on the computer. "Thanks, Syd. Have a nice weekend."

"Yeah, you too. Both of you. Have fun in Boston. Or, you know, as much fun as you can, given the circumstances, anyway. Good luck."

"Thanks, we'll try," Jason said. With a slight nod, the pair headed through the office door, the building's exterior door, Blake's car doors twice, and the sliding airport terminal doors. Then, they were through the Boeing 737's hatch.

30.

JASON SAT in the back seat of a newish Volkswagen GTI, gripping his phone, screen down, between his legs. He watched Boston's winding streets turn suburban through rain-streaked windows and pulled out his phone. The screen illuminated. Blake sat next to him, pretending to gaze out the window but preoccupied with his every movement.

He typed out a quick message to Phoebe: "We're running about twenty minutes late, but don't wait on us. We'll get to see everyone later. I'd like some alone time there anyway."

Jason hit send and looked back out the window as they passed an abandoned row of warehouses.

"Is it up here on the left?" the driver asked.

"Not sure. I've never been here, so I only have the address. I can pull up the map on my phone though."

"Nah, it's cool, man. That's what I'm using, too." The driver tapped on the side of his phone, attached to the dashboard.

"Oh, right. Sorry, I'm out of it."

"Well, where you guys are headed, I think anyone could expect that."

"Yeah." Jason nodded. He looked at Blake and smiled. He was fine, he hoped to say.

After another turn, the entrance to the cemetery opened up before them and Jason sat up from his slump.

"Actually, you can let us out here. I'm not sure where the grave we're looking for is, so we'll have to stop by the front gate and ask for help. Hopefully they can point us in the right direction."

"No problem. Good luck."

The car made an abrupt stop, with the front hood crossing through the gates. Jason exited, thanked their Uber driver, and Blake slid out behind him. He closed the door.

"Check in?" Blake asked.

Jason nodded.

Without watching the car have to back up twice and adjust, they walked towards the worn but substantial neoclassical building at the cemetery's entrance gate. There was illumination from the building's rear right window, which Jason presumed was from a reading lamp or TV. He rang the doorbell while Blake stood a step behind him. After only a moment, the door slid open.

"Hello, we need help finding a friend's grave site. His name was Billy Gerding. It might be under William. People should already be gathering there for a small service. But, I know the place is large, and there may be multiple groups here. I figured it'd be better to check with you rather than try to search on our own."

The man nodded wordlessly and held the door open for them to follow him inside while he checked. The man's mouth moved, rhythmically chewing the last remnants of some unseen meal.

⊏▭⊐

THEY HADN'T ACCOUNTED for the long walk. Well, Jason hadn't, and Blake was allowing him to call the shots today with no questioning. He needed to relearn decisiveness and trust himself again. Mistakes and all.

By the time they'd walked to the sixth intersection and gone three rows of tombstones to the left, as instructed by the caretaker, they saw the crowd they intended to join. Jason tried to count them, but the distance was too vast and he gave up. Roughly twelve, he guessed. And it looked like someone had brought young children with them.

Three cars were parked behind the figures. A black sedan and two silver SUVs. The individuals stood silently around a grave marker.

Jason pulled up short of being able to make out faces. They knew he was coming, but he hadn't seen anyone from the cast in months after keeping himself in near isolation.

"Are you ready? We've come all this way. This'll be good," Blake said.

Jason nodded. "Here we go. Thanks again for coming."

"Of course, J."

When they got within a few feet, nearly everyone looked up, but no one spoke. Jason saw Phoebe, Will, Anna, Maddy, Desiree, and Ronnie. Along with them was a surprise: Emily, Billy's sister, and presumably her kids whom Jason had never seen. He gave a solemn nod of recognition and followed their lead of head-bowed reflection.

At the ground, only inches from their feet, was a humble stone rectangle that had been laser etched with "William Gerding," along with the dates 1989–2025. It was a slate-gray stone, polished, with no mention of meaningful quotes or descriptors. Yet, despite the brief text, Jason read it, over and over again. Blake leaned against him at his side.

The wind crept through both of their rain jackets a welcome relief from the summer humidity.

Someone had placed a wreath of flowers—peonies with green leaves and grapevines.

"I still don't understand what happened," Jason said, breaking the silence.

"That's why everyone's here. To understand, together," Blake said. The others could barely hear her words across the grave.

"It's good to see you, Jason. How are you?" Phoebe asked.

Jason shrugged. "I guess as good as I can be. Given everything. How are you all?"

Phoebe looked around at each member of the group and nodded encouragingly. "Yeah, same. For those of us here."

"Ya know, it was a lot we had to deal with, so it's good to keep in touch and support each other. It's been rougher on some'a us,"—Ronnie nodded at Jason —"but we're gettin' through it in our own ways."

Will had yet to make eye-contact with Jason or Blake. His hands were shoved into his jean pockets. He shuffled.

"I thought Hunter would be here," Jason said.

Desiree and Ronnie both opened their mouths to speak but said nothing.

Anna looked at the cars behind them and tilted her head in their direction. "He's sleeping it off. He stayed up all night and wasn't making too much sense. Maybe went too hard."

"Every time I've seen him for the last six months," Phoebe added at a much lower volume.

"Damn." Ronnie kicked at the ground.

Jason's eyebrows raised and he looked around the circle of people. "We have to get him help. This has been going on for so long. We should talk to him, at least. I can—"

"Yeah," Phoebe interrupted. Her tone softened as she spoke. "We do. We need to do all of that, but not here and not right now. We should have for a while, honestly. But today's about Billy."

"Mm-hmm," Jason said. "I've just been doing a lot of reflecting. You're right. What about the others?"

"Well, Nick hasn't spoken to anyone in months," Desiree said. "Dimitri's going to meet us later. He had a meeting he couldn't get out of and hit traffic leaving the city. All things considered, an impressive turnout."

"It is," Jason said. "And Emily, I'm pleasantly surprised to see you here."

"Yeah, I am, too. To see myself here, I mean. I should have been around a year ago, but now I've had time to process and grieve. Didn't want to miss the one-year mark. And it seemed past due to introduce the girls to their uncle." Emily glanced at her daughters, standing just to the left of the group.

Jason smiled at the girls, impressed with how well-behaved and solemn they were.

"Oh, and I'm sorry, I've been rude. This is Blake, who I'm sure you've heard me talk about. But Ronnie, Maddy, I don't think you've met."

Jason had nodded at Blake, who stepped towards Ronnie and Maddy and shook their hands in turn.

"It's weird. I feel like I know you both, but it's great to meet you," Blake said.

"Likewise," said Maddy. "Despite the circumstances. Other casts have gone to

Vegas together. Or taken a cruise to celebrate the anniversary of their season. And here we are."

"Well, I think it's great you put this together. It should be cathartic. Cope with this, talk about it, and reflect together. To be there for each other. Exactly what some of you need."

At Blake's words, Jason felt eyes on him, despite his gaze focusing on the earth at his feet. He felt the pressure to look up, but he didn't want to see their looks of pity or concern.

"Emily invited everyone back over to her house for dinner—pizza or something. Rather than going out. We can swap stories."

Phoebe stopped talking when Will moved forward without warning. He ambled around the gravestone and straight up to Jason without raising his head or saying anything. When he reached Jason, Will threw his arms around his chest. Jason froze for a second but returned the hug. No one spoke but watched the two until they broke off seconds later.

"I'm glad you're better," Will said. "And I want you to know I feel horrific about the role I played in everything."

"Stop." Jason shook his head and frowned. "You have nothing to apologize for. We were both a part of it. No one's to blame. It was fine to look into everything to come to terms, but we pushed it."

"Yeah, we jumped to some wild conclusions. Trusted circumstances. But I was so sure."

Jason shrugged, but no one dared move or speak until he gave some sort of okay. "We treated—I treated—life like it was following a script. Like it needed to be a story to make sense, and someone was editing it down. And Blake tried to tell us there at the end. She told me all along."

Will nodded. "Me, too. But we pushed her away instead."

Will then turned his focus to Blake, who stood a few feet away.

"He's right. I am so sorry. You went through so much because of us. And I got to walk away while you and Jason had so much to put back together. Thank you for being such a quality friend and I'm sorry I didn't return that."

Blake took a deep breath. "Seriously, like Jason said, stop. There's no playbook for dealing with any of this. I tried to help and didn't do an effective job, honestly.

And I'm sorry for that. But, I think it's best for everyone here if we accept apologies and move on. A lot of stuff happened, and we did what we could."

Will smiled, as did Jason behind him. Blake's ability to turn a room always impressed Jason. She could shift the atmosphere with a few words.

"I like the necklace. When did you start wearing it?" Will asked Blake.

Blake lifted her necklace up so that others could see. They looked at the white-gold ring that housed a dense, dark oblong sapphire in the center surrounded by tiny glistening diamonds. "Around my neck for a few months now. Since back in May. I love it."

Will smiled and nodded. "Should we go get that pizza, then? It looks like it's about to start up again." The sky overhead had indeed returned to a menacing gray, clouds obscuring the sun, and the air was dampening.

"See everyone back there. Phoebe texted the address," Emily said.

After a few additional pleasantries, Desiree and Phoebe hopped in the car. Emily and her kids were in one SUV while the others shared a second.

"You coming?" Phoebe called from the open driver's door. "Where did you park? We can give you two a lift."

Jason and Blake shared a quick glance before Jason called back. "Thanks, but we'll stay here for a moment. I appreciate it. We'll meet you there."

"Cool," Phoebe yelled before closing the door. Hunter was sleeping in the passenger seat across from her.

They stood for a few quiet moments, still taking in the scenery, while the three cars left. Out of sight.

Jason pulled Blake close, closed his eyes and kissed her on the top of her head. He held his face against her hair and kept his eyes open to the sprawling cemetery.

"They noticed the ring," he said.

"Yeah. Are you worried about what they're thinking?"

"No. I'm actually not."

AUTHOR'S NOTE

Thank you for checking out *Cut Reality*. It's a real honor that you made it this far. If you enjoyed this book or have thoughts to share, I would really appreciate if you posted a brief review with your retailer of choice. Those reviews are critical in helping other readers find my work, and I'd also love to hear your thoughts.

ACKNOWLEDGMENTS

In the time it has taken me to complete this work, I've accumulated some huge debts of thanks. First and foremost, thank you to Maria Tedesco for the perpetual, yet always essential, encouragement, support, and advice. This wouldn't exist without you.

I also had excellent friendship and support, beginning in the planning phases, from my partners in writing, Billy Garrett and Paige Hater, who helped with plotting and developmental editing.

Thanks to my editor, Sam Kates, who really worked to bring out my strongest, snappiest prose. A number of friends also helped read at various stages and provided me with crucial feedback and advice: thanks to Will Bradford, Adam Wanter, and Joe Tedesco. Others provided much needed encouragement and support in specific ways (whether they know it at the time or not)—thanks Chris "Queequeg" Moran, Michael Schenk, and Bobby Burgess.

Many of the ideas in Cut Reality were also bolstered by some excellent, generous people who helped provide me perspective on the reality TV experience. Thank you Tanya Vance, Jonny Fairplay, Matt Bischoff, Mario Lanza, and Avi Duckor-Jones for answering the my random questions or supporting/inspiring my novel.

All of my writing owes everything to the creative people I find myself regularly surrounded by. Thanks to all of my dear friends, but especially Wesley Thompson, Mary Rose Leisring, Maxie Flynn, Andy Finke, Alyssa Finke, and Harriet Bree. Further thanks to my friends from We Want a Podcast (WWAP) and the band moonweather, who supported the novel's release. Also, Drew Shannon, who always brings out my best. You lot keep my life interesting and weird enough that I'll never run out of inspiration.

My family has been instrumental. Suzy, you taught me a love of books, and Lenny, you taught me a love of stories. Thank you both for that. To the rest of my family—Zoey, Grandma, G-paw, Gary, Tuesday, Jake, Christie, Nick, Mama, Papa, Brooke, Grant, Diane, Chris, and the entire Zentmeyer and Tedesco clans, I couldn't be who I am without you. And of course I can't forget the three kitties in my life.

To my department and school community, thank you for contributing to a culture that allows me energy and motivation to be creative.

Finally, a special shout-out to all my students, past and present, who have taught me more about writing and resilience than they could know.

CPSIA information can be obtained
at www.ICGtesting.com
Printed in the USA
LVHW112337140519
617895LV00004B/27/P